BROKEN SHADOWS

SHADOWS LANDING #5

KATHLEEN BROOKS

All Rights Reserved. No part of this book may be used or reproduced in any manner whatsoever without written permission, except in the case of brief quotations embodied in critical articles and reviews.

This book is a work of fiction. The names, characters, places, and incidents are products of the writer's imagination or have been used fictitiously and are not to be construed as real. Any resemblance to persons living or dead, actual events, locale, or organizations is entirely coincidental.

An original work of Kathleen Brooks. *Broken Shadows* copyright @ 2020 by Kathleen Brooks.

Kathleen Brooks® is a registered Trademark of Laurens Publishing, LLC

❀ Created with Vellum

Bluegrass Series

Bluegrass State of Mind

Risky Shot

Dead Heat

Bluegrass Brothers

Bluegrass Undercover

Rising Storm

Secret Santa: A Bluegrass Series Novella

Acquiring Trouble

Relentless Pursuit

Secrets Collide

Final Vow

Bluegrass Singles

All Hung Up

Bluegrass Dawn

The Perfect Gift

The Keeneston Roses

Forever Bluegrass Series

Forever Entangled

Forever Hidden

Forever Betrayed

Forever Driven

Forever Secret

Forever Surprised

Forever Concealed

Forever Devoted

Forever Hunted

Forever Guarded

Forever Notorious

Forever Ventured

Forever Freed

Forever Saved

Forever Bold (coming Jan/Feb 2021)

Shadows Landing Series

Saving Shadows

Sunken Shadows

Lasting Shadows

Fierce Shadows

Broken Shadows

Framed Shadows (coming Apr/May 2021)

Women of Power Series

Chosen for Power

Built for Power

Fashioned for Power

Destined for Power

Web of Lies Series

Whispered Lies

Rogue Lies

Shattered Lies

Moonshine Hollow Series

Moonshine & Murder
Moonshine & Malice
Moonshine & Mayhem
Moonshine & Mischief

PROLOGUE

Months ago in California...

Trent Faulkner drove his rented pickup truck up to the large iron gate and stopped. A security guard stepped from a booth made to look like a miniature Spanish-style house similar to the gargantuan mansions behind the gates. He wasn't in Shadows Landing anymore, that was for sure. Trent looked in his rearview mirror and saw the large box truck come to a stop behind him.

"Good afternoon," the middle-aged security guard said as he stopped by Trent's open window. He had a tablet in one hand and rested his other hand on what looked to be a can of mace.

"Good afternoon," Trent greeted him with the Southern manners born and bred into him from generations of Southern mommas. "I'm Trent Faulkner, and the truck behind me and I are due at Miss Jessamine's house for a three o'clock appointment."

"Company name?" the man said as he scrolled through the tablet.

"TAF Designs."

Trent looked around at the tall gates and fences. It felt caged-in here, right down to the gated entrance and guard on duty. Give him wide-open lawns and views of the river or ocean any time. But, being from the small town of Shadows Landing, South Carolina, just outside Charleston had made him biased. He loved his hometown and couldn't imagine living anywhere else.

"Ah, there you are. Miss Jessamine's house is down the fifth road on your right. It's in the back on the left."

"Thank you. Have a good day," Trent told the guard. He put his truck in gear as the gate slowly rolled open.

Skye Jessamine, Trent thought as he followed the directions to her house. He still couldn't believe the top-grossing Hollywood actress had commissioned him to build a dining room set. Trent had seen a couple of her movies, but he was more of a book guy than a movie guy. It didn't mean he didn't know who she was, though. It would be hard not to. Skye Jessamine's face was on the cover of practically every magazine on the newsstand. Then when you did turn on the television or go to the movies, you were sure to see her on the screen.

Trent turned into the mansion's driveway and stopped at yet another gate. He pressed the call button and a woman answered it. "Yes?"

"This is Trent Faulkner. I'm here to install the dining room furniture."

"Oh, yes. I'll open the gate and meet you out front."

The gate opened and Trent and the box truck drove slowly down the long driveway and into the circular drive by the front door. Front door didn't quite describe the twelve-foot double doors that looked to be from hand-carved mahogany with large brass handles.

One of the doors opened before Trent even had the truck in park. While he might not be up to date on pop culture, he knew the woman waving at him wasn't Skye Jessamine. In pictures, Skye had shining brunette hair and blue eyes that were so bright they looked turquoise. This woman's hair was a glossy dark brown on the verge of being black and her eyes were a soft and welcoming walnut color.

Trent smiled at her and stepped from the truck. "Hello, ma'am. I'm Trent Faulkner."

The woman smiled widely up at him. She was taller than Trent's female cousins. He'd put her at five feet nine inches and from what he could see of her exposed arms in the flowy tank top she wore and her legs on display in colorful shorts, she was definitely an athlete.

"I'm Karri Hill. I'm Skye's friend. May I have everyone's cell phones, please?" Trent shook her hand as his mind worked.

"You're the assistant who emailed me," he said as he remembered the message that got this project rolling.

He handed over his phone as Karri rolled her eyes but kept the smile on her face. "Assistant and chef. However, I'm her friend first and foremost. We saw your furniture in that architectural magazine and both fell in love with your style. Skye's finishing up a call and will be here to help us install the piece. Do you want to see where it'll go?"

"That will help, thank you." Trent had always felt that his furniture was both art and meant for everyday life. It could be shown in exceptional light to look its best, but it was also meant to be part of the household. It wasn't just a showpiece. The various pieces were where you ate dinner every day, slept every night, or relaxed on when you needed a moment to yourself.

"Right this way. We've been talking about this day since we ordered it six months ago."

Trent motioned for his movers to follow him into the mansion. The four men kept quiet behind him as they walked into the large marble-floored entrance with a modern light fixture hanging down from the three-story high entrance hall. Skye's house didn't quite feel like a home. It was more of a showpiece. At least this entrance was.

"Skye loves architecture and design. She helped create every room in the house."

"She'd get along great with my cousin Ridge. He's an architect and builder. In fact, the way she uses original historic pieces mixed with modern touches is very much his style."

Karri nodded. "Oh yes. After she looked you up, she found several references to Ridge and just loves his work."

Trent was surprised at that. Skye had taken the time to look into him and his family just because she liked some of his work? That was more hands-on than he thought she'd be.

"I reached out to you first, but after you agreed to build the set, Skye researched everything. I might have sent the email, but ideas were all hers."

They turned down a hall that was lined on one side with nothing but old Spanish-styled glass doors that were all propped open to let in the warm California breeze. "This is the private wing of the house. The first room we come to is the dining room. It'll be the only room in the private wing to be photographed next week for Skye's article in the same architectural magazine that you were featured in," Karri explained.

"Private wing?" Trent asked as the hallway ended and the private wing began to sprawl outward.

Karri stopped at the arched opening to a large and mostly empty room. However, the far wall was the only decoration needed. It was a view of the Los Angeles cityscape off in the distance. The floor-to-ceiling glass doors could be opened to let in the breeze or to make a party flow effortlessly between indoors and outdoors.

"Yes. Skye has the main wing decorated for parties, media interviews, and at-home shoots for magazines. However, she doesn't live there. She lives here in the private wing. It's just the two of us here. And I'm in the pool house, so it's not like she needs the space," Karri laughed as if it was a big joke. "Sorry, if you knew where we met you'd get it. Anyway, this is the private wing and where she actually lives."

Trent stepped into the room and looked around. By all accounts the room appeared to be self-contained and only open to the hallway. The right wall was filled with a glassed-in wine rack that went from the floor to the top of the eighteen-foot ceiling. To the left was where he'd put the large credenza he'd built.

"Where does this door go?" he asked about the door built to look like part of the wall to the left.

"To the kitchens."

"Multiple kitchens?" Trent asked, not really expecting an answer but more just wondering why.

"Yes, one is personal and one is for catering."

"Of course," Trent said. Anyone who had a public and private wing would have both public and private kitchens.

Trent walked into the center of the room and made a

slow circle of the space. He took in the glass doors, the direction they faced, the walls, the electrical outlets, the lighting, and even the floor patterns.

"Is there going to be a rug?"

"Yes." The voice he heard wasn't Karri's. It was smooth and sexy and with that one word Trent knew when he looked up he'd find Skye Jessamine.

Trent thought he'd be prepared to meet a celebrity. After all, he knew many rich and powerful people. His cousin Ryker didn't talk about it but probably had more money than even the A-List actress could ever dream of. When he raised his eyes, though, he wasn't ready for the woman in pink athletic shorts and a white tank top. Her famous luxurious hair was in the same kind of sloppy bun his female cousins favored. There wasn't a bit of makeup on her and she was barefoot. She was breathtakingly beautiful in her natural look.

Karri moved to stand next to her and was just an inch or so taller than the actress. However, they had the same build. Both appeared to be athletes with curves that could kill and kind smiles.

"Trent Faulkner, I presume. I'm Skye," she said, holding out a hand that was bare of jewelry.

"Trent. It's nice to meet you, ma'am." Trent was worried he'd break her hand when his covered hers. Her skin was like silk, but her grip would make Harper smile with appreciation. His cousin was a fan of women capable of kicking ass.

"I cannot thank you enough for coming to install the pieces yourself. I am such a huge fan of your work. I have two rugs laid out in the living room and I just can't decide which one to put in here. Can I see the pieces and then can we decide? I'd like to have your opinion."

Trent smiled at her as he relaxed. Honest praise for his work was hotter than any skimpy outfit. He hadn't expected America's Sweetheart to even be here, never mind wanting to participate.

"Sure. Gentlemen, can you open the back of the truck?"

Karri hurried out with them as Skye fell into step with him. "What did you think of the lights I selected? I can change them if you think they're not a good fit. I was going for subtle since I want the furniture to be the center of attention."

"I think they're perfect. Miss Hill was telling me you're going to use it in a photo shoot next week."

Skye nodded. She looked up to him with such joy that Trent instantly felt comfortable. He'd expected aloofness and elitism, but Skye wasn't any of that. "I have a dining room in the other wing. But if I have a chance to show off a custom made TAF Design, then I'm doing it. You are an artist with wood."

They walked out the front door as Karri clapped her hand to her chest. "Oh, Skye. You're going to freak."

Skye gave up all pretense of calm and ran barefoot down to the driveway to look into the back of the truck. "Oh my gosh. It's better than I imagined. Trent, you're a genius. Karri, look!"

Trent held his breath as one of the movers brought out one of the pieces and set it down. He didn't tell her about this design and was nervous that it might have been too personal.

"How did you know?" Karri asked even as her hand still covered her mouth with surprise.

"I did my research, too. I couldn't find much information on it, but I kept finding references to how much the Onondaga Nation meant to you. I read that you regularly go back there to speak with the kids on the reservation. I took a chance that it was special to you."

"I grew up on the reservation. I'm part of the Wolf Clan," Karri told him with tears in her eyes. "Skye and I met freshman year at Syracuse University. And since Skye's family is from Iowa, she spent a lot of time at my home and has done a lot to help our reservation. She was made an honorary member of our clan a couple of years ago."

Trent looked down at the carved pattern on the piece of wood. It was the pattern from the Hiawatha Belt.

"The two squares at each end and then the two rectangles on the inside symbolize each of the five nations —the Seneca, Cayuga, Oneida, and Mohawk—with the Tree of Peace in the center representing the Onondaga. Then the line that connects them all represents that each nation is connected in peace," Karri told him as her fingers traced the carving.

"This is beautiful, Trent." Skye had her arm wrapped around Karri as they both wiped tears from their eyes.

Skye turned and suddenly she was in his arms. Her arms were around his waist and her head on his chest as she hugged him tightly. "I can't tell you how much this means to us." Skye let go of him and then turned to Karri. "Your parents are so going to cry when they come to visit next month. Now, let's take a look at the rugs and then we can start moving things inside."

THE PRIVATE WING was nothing like the public wing. The living room was still large, but it was soft and welcoming. Skye had turned this wing into a real home. There were pictures everywhere and not a single one had another celebrity in them.

"Who's this?" Trent asked as he looked at a large picture of a little girl sitting on a huge tractor in the middle of a cornfield. She had freckles across the bridge of her nose and her hair was in braided pigtails.

Skye looked up from where she was deciding which rug to put in the dining room to see which picture he was referring to. The movers were with Karri in the dining room waiting to be called in. "Oh, that's me. My parents live in Grundy County, Iowa. I grew up on a small farm."

"You're a small-town girl?" Trent asked, feeling bad when his disbelief was clear for all to hear.

Skye smiled and nodded. "My high school class had eighty-three kids in it."

"Ugh," Trent groaned. "You beat me. Ours had eighty-nine."

"City slicker," Skye teased, and they both laughed. Trent was man enough to admit he'd been completely wrong about Skye. Well, he was right about her being drop-dead gorgeous, but the small-town girl manners had his heart and his libido in overdrive.

"Ouch, no need to insult a man," Trent joked back.

"I can't tell you how nice it is to spend the day with you. People around here forget where they came from. Jim and Lenny, they're my agent and manager, both try to get rid of any small town girl left in me. What they don't know is that you can take the girl out of her small town, but you can't take the small town out of the girl. Now, I think I like this rug. What do you think?"

It took over an hour to get everything in place. They'd ended up moving the furniture until it was just right, but the result was something Trent was beyond proud of. The movers left and Karri headed into the private kitchen to make dinner.

"It's been a real pleasure, ma'am," Trent said, holding out his hand.

Skye's smile fell. "You can't leave yet." Trent looked around to see if something was out of place and Skye laughed. "No, everything is perfect. It's just that this has been really nice. And maybe I'm overstepping. I don't even know if you have a girlfriend, but I was hoping you'd stay for dinner. I have to thank you for your hard work."

Trent didn't know how to respond. Was she flirting?

"No girlfriend and I'd love to stay for dinner."

"I'll tell Karri to make an extra," she said as she grabbed his hand and led him to the living room. "I'll be right back. Make yourself at home."

A minute later she was back and sat down on the couch next to him. Trent couldn't believe how fast time flew and before he knew it, Karri was telling them dinner was ready.

"It's been a pleasure meeting you, Trent."

"Are you leaving?" he asked Karri, who nodded.

"I help coach a local lacrosse team. Skye and I played in college and we have practice tonight.

They said their goodbyes and he followed Skye into the kitchen. "How about we eat outside?"

"Sure." Trent picked up the bottle of wine and his plate of food. He then followed Skye through an opened glass door to a pool patio that overlooked the cityscape.

Trent had been nervous, but he and Skye got along as if they'd known each other for years. She told him stories of growing up on a farm and he told her about the pirates of Shadows Landing. Hours went by. The sun had long since set yet they were still talking and laughing.

"When do you leave?" Skye asked as they reclined by the pool.

"Tomorrow afternoon."

"So soon? Then we better make the most of tonight." Skye bit her bottom lip and suddenly looked nervous. "I thought I was brave, but I'm not. I was going to kiss you." Trent's breath stopped and he forgot how to breathe. "But I chickened out. I've never been the type to make the first move. Am I crazy thinking that there's something between us?"

"I thought I was crazy for thinking there was," Trent admitted as he lifted his hand and brushed his fingers against her cheek before sliding his hand to cup the nape of her neck.

"Then let's be crazy together," Skye whispered. She tilted her face up and offered her lips to him. Trent didn't hesitate to accept her gift.

In fact, he took everything she offered. She'd been right: there *was* something between them. Something that made her feel like home to him. Something that when she stood up and held out her hand, he knew he'd take it and never look back. Something that left them both calling out each other's names multiple times that night. Something that was so strong that his heart had been irrevocably taken by Skye.

∽

IT WASN'T the morning sun that woke Trent. It was the feeling of not being alone in the giant house. Trent opened his eyes to see Skye sound asleep next to him. There was another sound and then footsteps coming toward them. Trent pulled the sheet over Skye's nude body and jumped into his clothes as the door opened.

"Who the hell are you?" Trent asked as he put himself between the man and Skye.

"Lenny Daniels, Skye's manager." He was a little past middle-aged and had gotten a lot of Botox and probably some other work done over the years. He was fighting a losing battle against age, but he wasn't waving the flag of defeat yet. "I think the better question is, where did she find you?"

Trent looked back at Skye. He didn't like that Lenny had just walked into her room. Manager or not, he was still a man and she was still naked. Trent gestured with his chin to take it outside. Lenny made a face but moved out into the hall as Trent grabbed his shoes and met him.

"I'm Trent Faulkner, the furniture maker."

"Figures. Skye loves her blue-collar men. Come with me."

Trent followed the man who was in excellent shape, but even so, probably in clothes thirty years too young for him. Not that Trent was a fashionista, but the skinny jeans with loafers and no socks just wasn't a good look.

They entered an office and Trent kept his eyes on Lenny as he pulled open a drawer and handed Trent a piece of paper. "Our standard NDA. I need your phone to make sure you didn't take any pictures."

Insulted wasn't even touching what Trent felt. "I wouldn't do that."

"Yeah, right," Lenny said sarcastically. "And all the men before you wouldn't ever do that because, what? You're in love with Skye? Get real. She's a celebrity and you're a nobody. She doesn't love you. She enjoys the worship your kind gives her. Now, sign the nondisclosure and you can be on your way."

Trent shook his head. This wasn't right. He wasn't just a number. They'd connected. "I want to talk to Skye."

Lenny looked at his watch and then back up at Trent. "Your time is up. It's sad you don't see that. Sign it and leave before things get awkward. Enjoy the night you had with America's Sweetheart and know I'll sue you for every penny you have if you ever tell anyone about this night." Lenny paused and let out a sigh. "I'm sorry. You probably think what happened was real. You think you had a connection. You didn't. This is just Skye's way. You are just the next in a long line of normal guys who have fallen for the glitz and glamour of it all."

"Then why should I sign it? Why shouldn't I go out and tell everyone she pretends to be this small town girl to get laid?" Trent asked, his heart hardening with every word Lenny spoke.

Lenny looked at him sympathetically and pushed forward the paper with a pen lying on top of it. "Because deep down you care for her and don't want her hurt. I'm sorry."

Trent looked down at the paper. Had it all been fake?

"Did she tell you she grew up on a farm? That she sought solace at the reservation in college because there was just something about family that gave her peace? That she never does this? That she never feels this way about a man after just meeting him?"

Trent listened to Lenny's words and his heart broke in two. He silently picked up the pen, signed the paper, and walked out. He never wanted to hear from Skye Jessamine ever again. He was a fool for falling for her. Even more a fool for thinking someone like her actually saw him for who he was and adored him for it. Trent hardened his heart. He was a fool no more.

1

THE SMELL of fall was heavy in the air. Even in Shadows Landing, South Carolina, Trent could smell the season's arrival. The leaves were changing, the air was less humid, and grills were fired up for tailgating before football games. He'd spent last night in his workshop, building a new piece of furniture for his new line that was about to be picked up for national production. It had been months . . . shoot, almost a year at this point, but Skye Jessamine still haunted every minute of his life.

She had a movie coming out in a month and her face was on every magazine cover, her voice on every radio talk show, and her picture on every billboard. Then there were the TV talk shows, the interviews, and the ads running for the movie. Trent felt as if he literally couldn't escape her.

And there were her texts. Still, even after all this time. Trent received a text from Skye once or twice a week. *Thinking of you. What are you up to?* He'd never responded, yet she'd kept texting. Sometimes she'd tell him about her day or send a funny selfie. He hated to admit it, but he looked forward to each text she sent. He'd eagerly look at his phone only to feel the betrayal of being just one of many.

Karri had even come a couple of weeks after he'd left California without so much as a "see ya." She'd brought a gift basket full of all the things he'd told Skye he loved. Bourbon, books, even a tool he'd been thinking about getting. Trent had looked at Karri and shoved it back at her.

"I don't understand," Karri had said to him.

"You don't need to buy my silence. I won't sell my story," Trent had said back to her as if he wasn't in pain.

Karri had looked at him questioningly then. "Look, just talk to her. Please. She's my best friend and I've never seen her like this."

"Like what?" Trent had asked.

"In love."

Karri had spun around and left. The gift basket was at his feet as she drove away. Had he been wrong? Was Skye in love with him? He'd pulled up her text and stared at it. All he'd need to do is type and send two letters— "hi" and he knew she would reply.

Instead of texting her, Trent googled her. She'd released a new interview and desperate to hear her voice, he'd watched it. Then he'd heard her say she was leaving to film in Europe.

"What kind of impact does all this travel have on your personal life?" the interviewer had asked.

"What personal life?" Skye laughed and memories of their night together flashed before him. "No, but seriously, I don't have time to date. Right now my career comes first."

So Trent had put down the phone and never picked it up again . . . except to look at the news alerts. He still couldn't stop wanting to know how Skye was doing. Now, even months later, Trent picked up his phone when it sounded with a news alert. He clicked on the article and there was a picture of Skye smiling as Hollywood's leading man hugged her tightly to him. *Love on the set of Skye Jessamine and Mason Hemming's new movie!*

Trent turned off the phone and set it down, vowing to be done with Skye Jessamine.

"Still pining away?"

Trent rolled his eyes as his cousin Ryker's voice came from the door of his woodshop. Trent had opened the bay doors to allow the fall air in as he worked. Unfortunately, that also allowed nosy cousins to sneak up on him.

"I am working with pine. How did you know?" Trent asked innocently as he looked down at the wood he was shaping into a rustic headboard.

"I meant for the actress."

Trent turned around and saw his cousin standing with his hands in the pockets of what had to be a handmade suit. To say Ryker, business tycoon extraordinaire, was out of place in his wood shop was an understatement. "Did you need something?" Trent asked, ignoring the question about Skye.

"Yeah, you're late for dinner."

Trent's head fell back as he groaned. "I forgot. I was so wrapped up in this piece."

"Piece of something." Ryker was determined to push, but Trent wasn't going to give him the satisfaction. "We all ate, but we're hanging out at Harper's. Come on, let's go."

Trent took off his safety goggles and stripped the gloves from his hands. "I need to shower."

Ryker shook his head. "Gator and Turtle just got back from the swamp, so no need to worry about showering. You can't possibly smell worse than they do."

"Okay, but please no Skye talk."

Ryker shrugged his shoulders and walked out, leaving Trent to shut down his shop and hurry after him.

"Did you see that article about Skye dating her co-star?" Trent's cousin Tinsley asked the second he entered the bar owned by his cousin Harper.

The Faulkner cousins wasn't an especially large group. There were seven of them, but the seven were quickly expanding as they married. There was Trent and his brother, Wade, who was in the Coast Guard. Wade was married to Darcy, an oceanic-treasure hunter. Then there was his doctor cousin, Gavin Faulkner, and his wife, Ellery, who ran an art gallery. Gavin's little sister, Harper, owned the bar and her husband, Dare, was with the ATF. Tinsley was an artist and her older brother, Ridge, an architect and builder, had married Savannah not too long ago. Ryker was an only child and it showed. He liked things his way so it was good that he ran who knew how many companies. Trent knew about the shipping company but also knew there were many other companies and "business interests" that Ryker either owned a part of or ran outright. That expanding family now meant way more people to butt into his private life.

"I heard it was that Mason fella. He's been in the news saying all these great things about her," Gator said from the bar as he hooked a thumb into his overalls. Gator was aptly named since the mountain of a man in overalls and a worn ball cap did actually wrestle alligators.

"That's a right good-lookin' man if I can say so," Turtle, Gator's little-in-every-way cousin, said back. Women sighed in agreement. Even the men nodded their heads.

Gator took a swig of beer and set the mug on the bar. "I don't think any man can compete with that."

"Did you see Mason in *Spring's Redeeming Bloom*?" Turtle asked, and the women all blushed and began to fan themselves. "They showed him bathing in a creek. And I mean they *showed* him . . . his little turtle and all."

"It was wicked hot and not little in the slightest," Georgina, the bartender, said, waving her hand in front of her face.

Gator groaned. "Miss Georgie, I know you're from up there in the north somewhere, but you've been here long enough to start makin' sense."

"I said, 'wicked' again, didn't I?" Georgie bit her lip and looked up at the ceiling as if she were thinking. Georgina Grey was from Martha's Vineyard, Massachusetts, and Gator thought she was speaking another language. "Let's see, Mason Hemming is finer than frog hair split four ways?"

Gator saluted her with his beer. "Now I know what you're talking about."

Georgina beamed with approval and Trent was ready to leave.

"Now, I'll grant you that Mason Hemming is someone you'd write home about," Tinsley said to them all before turning to Trent. "However, just because the paper says they're together doesn't mean they are. Is she still texting you?"

"I don't want to talk about Skye Jessamine," Trent said between clenched teeth. He loved his family and town, really, but this was too much. "G, I'll take a bourbon. Straight up. Make it a double."

"That'll wet your whistle," Georgina said and then winked at Gator and Turtle who golf-clapped for her use of an expression they understood.

Trent took a seat with his family. Everyone stared at him. Trent let out a suffering sigh. "Yes, she texted me a picture of her on set this morning. She said it was her last day of filming. Then next month starts her press tour for her movie coming out then. She told me she'll be in Atlanta doing press and wondered how far it was from Shadows Landing."

"See!" Tinsley shouted joyfully.

"See what?" Trent asked as Georgina set the bourbon down in front of him.

"She still likes you," Harper said without hesitation.

"Strange way to show it," Trent muttered.

"It's probably a fake relationship. I've read about those," Savannah told them.

Darcy and Tinsley nodded in agreement.

"You need to talk to her. Find out what's going on. I know God gave you some common sense. Use it," Ellery told him and again everyone nodded in agreement.

Trent glared at her and then suddenly her face crumpled up and she burst into tears. "Sweet magnolia! I'm so sorry. These pregnancy hormones make me say the darnedest things."

Gavin looked concerned as he pulled his pregnant wife against his side and promised Trent wasn't mad. Now he couldn't even be irritated with Ellery since she sat there crying buckets as she held her slightly rounded belly. What made him smile though was the look of abject fear on Ryker's face.

"I have a call I need to make," Ryker said as he was out of his chair and out the door before anyone could tell him he'd left his phone on the table.

"She's right," Harper said to Trent as everyone tried to cheer Ellery up. Harper and Trent had always been close. They both had the same no-nonsense, tell-it-like-it-is personalities. Then Harper met Dare and she'd changed. Not in a bad way, but the protective shell around her heart had melted. Trent didn't like to think about it, but most of his cousins had changed as they found love. They were happier, lighter, and more comfortable with who they were. Trent was envious because as they talked about love, he knew he'd felt it once and then lost it all in one night.

"Trent," Harper said, getting his attention again. "You've never backed down from anything. You were the first one to enter a fight to protect any one of us. You never quit chasing your dreams even when every roadblock possible was thrown at you. So why are you backing down now? Let me guess, because I have some experience—it's scary as hell. When I started the bar, it was scary to invest everything I had in it. What did you tell me?"

Dammit. Harper did know him well. "The bigger the risk, the bigger the reward."

Harper grinned. "That's putting it nicely. I remember something along the lines of 'grow a pair'"

"I'll think about talking to her, okay?" Trent finally relented.

"You know you taught me that trick."

"What trick?"

"The one where you promise to think about it but not do it."

Trent winked at her and shot the rest of his bourbon. He could promise to think about it since thinking of Skye was all he'd been doing since California.

"Here, Ellery. Will this help?" Georgina asked as she put a Shirley Temple in front of her with extra cherries. Ellery promptly burst into a new round of tears over the nice gesture.

The door opened and Skeeter walked in wearing

oversized jeans and a sweatshirt two sizes too big for his frame. He looked around, shuddered, and narrowed his eyes at Ellery. "Miss Ellery, you've done scared the ghosts out of here with your caterwauling."

Everyone sucked in a breath and stared in horror as Ellery froze. Then her lips parted and a laugh burst out. "Y'all, I am so sorry. Gavin said it'd get better the farther along I get."

Gavin leaned back and tried to look innocent. That caused the rest of them to laugh. Tinsley asked about the baby, the married couples looked at each other as if having a silent discussion about babies, and Ryker poked his head back in. He returned to the table when he saw the tears were gone.

His family and friends talked all around him, but Trent didn't hear them. They'd given him his space when he'd gotten back from California, never expecting what had happened there. It was another matter when Karri arrived. Then the questions had started, though only his brother, Wade, knew the full truth. That probably meant that Darcy did, too. For that matter, they all probably did but had the good manners not to mention it.

"The women have a point," Wade said as Darcy joined in talking about baby things. "You know that the media can take an innocent picture and flash a fake headline on it. The only way you'll know for sure is to talk to Skye."

"I agree," Ryker said on Trent's other side.

Trent's eyebrow rose in surprise. "You do? The man who has shut himself off from every personal attachment since that night—"

"I told you never to bring that up," Ryker snapped.

"Exactly my point. It's a 'do as I say, not as I do' situation. I don't see you moving on and taking a risk with your heart."

Wade clamped his mouth shut and sat back as if Ryker just might explode.

"What do I care if she's the love of your life and you're too scared to go after her?" Ryker tossed back his drink and stood up to leave.

"I'll remind you of that someday," Trent said as he looked up at Ryker.

"There's a difference. I'll never have that opportunity. But you do and you're too chicken to go after it."

Ryker strode angrily from the bar and Trent was left with Wade's *he has a good point* shrug. So what if he had a good point? It's right there in black and white—Skye had moved on. *But what if she hadn't?* The voice in his head grew louder the more he tried to ignore it. He'd been hurt and he'd been angry. He'd been betrayed. Could he even afford to recognize the little glimmer of hope that began to take root in his heart?

2

"Has he responded?" Karri asked as she and Skye sat by the pool.

Skye shook her head. Tears threatened to spill in frustration. "I thought he would this time. I saw the three dots hovering. He's seen it, he'd thought about writing something. Then he didn't."

Karri shifted uncomfortably. "I might know why."

Skye's heart plummeted and then sprang to life. There was a reason? Not just the complete silence she'd been receiving? She'd woken up from the best night of her life to find an empty house. Well, that wasn't true. Lenny was there getting her ready for some meeting. But Trent was gone. Lenny said he hadn't seen him and Karri hadn't either. She'd immediately texted him and . . . nothing. She wasn't going to give up, though. Her parents never gave up and fought for every harvest and she was going to follow their example.

So, Skye had texted—over and over. First she'd asked where he went. Then she told him how much that night meant to her. Then she'd flown Karri there to make sure he was still alive while Skye was stuck getting ready to film a movie. When Karri returned, she'd been quiet but said this life might be too hard for him. Celebrity had its upside but also it had a colossal downside. Right now the downside was all she was experiencing. Sure, her career had never been better, but her personal life had never been worse. She'd found love and lost it in less than twenty-four hours.

"Why?" Skye asked and held her breath as Karri turned her phone around. There was a picture of her co-star and friend Mason Hemming, hugging her from behind. Then she read the headline. Crap. Crap. Crap. It was worse when she read the article about how much Mason gushed about working with her. It was nice and professional, but the news twisted it to make it sound like they were dating. "Assholes! Don't they bother to fact-check anything?"

"Either they did or they pretended to. It says a source from the set with inside information gave them the scoop and then they pulled quotes from Mason's past interviews to make it seem as if you two are an item instead of him just being supportive of your career like the good friend he is."

"You mean they want to make money off me and this will run traffic to their site?" Skye was bitter. She'd come to Hollywood because she loved acting. She loved the craft, the writing, the stories, and the magic of it all. Now she hated it. At some point, her life had stopped being hers. Her agent told her what movie roles to take. Her manager told her how to live. Even Karri told her what to eat to maintain a camera-ready figure. Her PR team told her what to say. Her stylist told her what to wear. It went on and on, but the common factor was Skye didn't have a say in anything. She felt that she'd become nothing more than a dress-up doll with everyone else pulling her strings.

"What am I doing, Karri?" Skye sighed before taking a long sip of her wine. She looked over the cityscape that used to bring her so much happiness and wondered why it didn't anymore.

Karri frowned and reached over to wrap her arm around Skye's shoulder. "You're putting your career first."

"Is it really my career, though? I've made enough money to retire and I'm not even thirty yet. I used to love this. I loved the hours spent getting ready for big events. I loved the camaraderie on set, and I loved talking to people about the movies I was passionate about. Now? Now all I want is to have my own life away from the spotlight."

"Don't tell Lenny and Jim that." Karri rolled her eyes and Skye smiled into her wine glass. "Speak of the devil," Karri groaned as they both heard Lenny calling out to them from somewhere inside.

"Out here!" Skye yelled as she didn't even bother to look at the man who was something like a stern father figure to her. Her own parents were still on the farm, but she missed them more and more every day. She'd offered to give them enough to retire, but they'd insisted it wasn't work when you love what you do. She'd understood that at the time. Now she wasn't so sure. Instead, she'd paid off their mortgage and every Christmas and birthday she surprised them with something for the farm. A tractor, a CropBot, or any new agricultural toy they'd secretly wanted but never would buy for themselves. Maybe it was time to go home for a visit.

"Ah, there you are." Lenny bent down and placed a kiss on the top of her head. "I brought someone with me. We have great news."

Skye forced a smile for Lenny. He might be a stern father figure, but he was still a good one even if she felt like rebelling against him right now. She looked over her shoulder and saw Jim in his ever-present casual suit that practically screamed that it cost a fortune. Basically, it was a full suit minus the tie. He thought that showed he was relaxed and casual.

"Hi, Jim. I guess it's something big if you're at my house tonight. Did I get nominated for an Oscar or something?" Skye asked with a bit of sarcasm to her voice, which she instantly felt guilty about. This man got her to where she was with the best movie parts she could ask for. They just weren't the kind to win awards. He was the reason she had this house and the ability to make sure neither she nor her parents ever had to worry about money.

"It's big, Skye. Huge! The role that will get you the Oscar for sure," Jim Hexter of Hexter and Stein Agency said with a grin. He and Lenny were both in their early fifties and similarly built, but Jim looked completely different. He exuded power from his shaved head down to his bright blue eyes, the bespoke suit, and the fifty thousand dollar watch on his wrist. Lenny, meanwhile, went for a surgically-enhanced death grip on youth and clothes that tried to show how hip he was. In Lenny's mind, he was still twenty-five years old.

"Did I get the lead in the Marie Lockend drama?" Skye pulled her legs from the warm pool water and jumped up to face Jim.

"Better. I got you the lead in the Tony Ketron film everyone is talking about."

Skye heard Karri gasp as her own mouth fell open. However, it wasn't from good news. "I told you I would *never* do a Tony Ketron film. Not. Ever. What part of that did you not understand?"

Jim's smile fell into a scowl. "I lobbied hard to get you this role. You should be grateful. Every A-list name is being floated around and you got it."

Skye's anger fueled her as she fisted her hands and

placed them on her hips. "Tony Ketron is a sexist pig. Every one of his movies has left the actresses feeling sexually violated after being naked on set for twenty hours a day. You know I'm friends with Gina Toussaint. You know Tony tried to force her to have *un*simulated sex during his last movie. There was no reason for it, but he claims all the nudity and horrific things the actresses go through is for art. Bullshit! It's so he can get off on having actresses humiliated. His movies have no plot other than how to degrade women."

Jim's jaw tightened. "This is *the* talked-about movie, Skye."

"I know that. You sent me the screenplay and I rejected it. A woman whose powerful husband finds her ugly after she's given birth so she sends the baby to live with her mother as she finds a way to win her husband back through sexual acts of escalating humiliation where consent is a *big* issue. No way, or have you forgotten my contract has a no-nudity clause in it?"

"When you posed nude on top of a dining room table for a magazine, your nudity clause went out the window." Jim stepped forward as he shoved his hands into his pockets and stared down at her.

"I was covered, Jim, and you know that. You were there. There isn't even a hint of the curve of my ass in that picture since I had on flesh-colored underwear. That's beside the point. I won't do it. Period. Tell Tony to shove it. I'd rather never win an Oscar than prostitute myself to him for his so-called movie. End of discussion."

"Listen here, missy. I made you and I can unmake you. You don't get to make decisions. That's for the big boys to do. You do what I tell you, smile, and say thank you for the money I make you."

Skye felt Karri come to stand slightly behind her in support.

"Are you threatening me? I can have any agent in Hollywood take me on if you think you can tell me what to do."

Jim smiled, but it wasn't kindly and Skye felt herself shiver. "Don't you remember our contract? The one you signed when I discovered you in New York City?"

"I do, and I remember the no-nudity clause in it," Skye shot back.

"Then you also must remember the lifetime agency rights you granted me. *Lifetime*. I own you, Skye. Forever. So pull up your big girl panties, or should I say pull them down?"

Anger and fear coursed through her, but she wouldn't back down. "No. I refuse and I'll challenge you in court to break the contract. You taught me that, Jim. That every contract can be renegotiated."

"Not this one, so you better get used to it. I'm done with your princess attitude. You're twenty-nine years old. You're aging out of these roles and into motherly ones. I'm going to milk you for every penny until you're all used up and there isn't anything you can do about it. I *own* you, Skye Jessamine. Down to the trademark I have on your name for merchandising. You're taking that role and I don't want to hear a single word about it or I will blacklist you faster than you can blink."

"Don't you threaten me," Skye shot back at him.

Lenny held up his hands and stepped toward them. "Okay, okay. Let's take a deep breath, everyone. No more threats. We'll table this conversation until later, but the reason I'm here is just that. Threats."

Skye's stomach plummeted even further to the point she

was nauseous. There was nothing that scared her more than what she feared Lenny was about to tell her.

"Another one?" she asked and Karri wrapped her arm around her.

Lenny nodded. "And this one wasn't mailed to me like the others."

Skye had layers of security to protect her privacy. To get to her, someone had to get through Jim's secretary, Jim, Lenny, and then Karri. Only then would the phone get handed over to Skye or the email sent to her private account. Jim and Lenny had her private information, but for the general public to reach her, that was the protocol.

She'd gotten her first threat three days after Trent left. It had been mailed to Lenny's home. Someone had tracked him down and he was shaken. They all were. The message itself wasn't ominous, just the fact that it had been mailed directly to Lenny. The message was from a diehard fan. He wanted to meet her. They'd gotten tens of thousands of these kinds of letters sent to her PR firm. After they were all read by agency staff, the threats were taken out and the rest were sent to Lenny. He'd read them and filter out any that worried him. Then he gave the rest to Karri to review before they finally made their way to Skye. She loved her fans and wrote back to as many as she could.

However, this one was a little different. It was a fan letter, but it had given them all a bad feeling. Then, once a month a new one arrived.

"How did you get it?" Karri asked as she squeezed Skye's hand.

Lenny looked to Jim who nodded. "It was attached to your gate."

Skye gasped and leaned into Karri. The unknown fan had been too close to her. "I need to hire private security."

Lenny nodded. "I'm on it. I'll have candidates here tomorrow morning for us to interview, but everyone who is anyone here uses Star Power."

Skye reached out and took Lenny's hand. "Thank you, Lenny."

"That's what I'm here for. Let's get this threat taken care of and get you safe. Then we can all sit down and read through this Tony Ketron script and see what we can do. Everything is negotiable. Right, Jim?" Lenny stared him down and Skye felt some relief at having someone on her side, even though she was not going to take this role whether hell froze over or not.

"I'm sorry, Skye. I got carried away. This puts everything in perspective. Your safety is paramount. We will discuss it later this week. Do you want us to stay with you tonight?" Jim asked and while Skye knew he would push this movie, here was the Jim she'd known for the past eight years.

"We're okay, thank you. I think I just want to lock everything up tight and go to bed."

Lenny hugged her and promised to let the neighborhood security know. Jim even hugged her. "I'm sorry. I'm just trying to do my job."

Skye nodded and watched as they walked out of her house. She and Karri followed them and immediately locked the doors behind them and began to check every door and window in the entire house. As they closed the sliding doors to the patio, they finally took a breath and Karri turned to her with concern on her face.

"You know what Jim did was bullshit, right? That was not okay."

"I know. Let's get the contract and look over it. I don't remember that section about lifetime rights, but I wasn't going to argue that until I'd seen it with my own two eyes. Then I'll talk to my lawyer about it."

Karri shook her head as they walked to Skye's private office. "You can't."

"Why not?"

"Bernie Ganoti might be your lawyer, but he was hired by Jim. The agency is his main client," Karri pointed out and Skye stopped at her desk.

She looked up at Karri with surprise. "You're right."

"Haven't you realized I'm the only person in your life not put here by Jim? He even hired Lenny"

Skye had thought all these others controlled her life, but it wasn't them. It was all Jim. "He hired my PR people because they represent all his clients. Lenny hired my stylist and makeup person because they worked with Jim's biggest stars. You're right. You're the only person in my inner circle not put there by Jim."

Skye leaned down and pulled out the thick contract she'd signed eight years ago.

"I'll stay in the guest room tonight."

"Thank you." Skye looked down at thick binder. "And I have some reading to do."

3

"Skye!"

Skye's eyes popped open as Karri flung her bedroom door open at six in the morning.

"What is it?" Skye was instantly awake. She might be a Hollywood actress, but it would take a lifetime to quash the up-with-the-rooster farm life she'd lived for the first eighteen years of her life. When she was in college, she and Karri were up at dawn to get their lacrosse workouts in before their first class.

Karri didn't say anything as she grabbed the remote and turned on the local news. "Skye Jessamine's sexy photo shoot was even hotter than the cover photo published by the architecture magazine," the celebrity reporter said into the camera as a photo of Skye nude on Trent's table flashed on the screen.

"What's going on? This is the magazine cover and I'm not really naked." Skye was confused until the next image snapped onto the screen. "Oh my God. That's not me!" A woman wearing the same robe Skye had been wearing was snapped with her robe wide open. Hair covered her face, but it was made to look as if it were in Skye's dining room. Skye couldn't stop watching as image after image appeared. They showed her crawling naked on the table and jumping around as if she were dancing. They were blurred out but she knew they'd not be blurred online. "I never did that! You were there, you know that!"

Karri's phone began to ring and she answered it. "Yeah, Lenny. I'm with her now. Yes, we know it's not her. No, she's not all right. Yes, we'll see you soon."

Her phone rang the second she hung up with Lenny. She snapped her fingers to get Skye's attention, showed her the photographer's name on the screen, and put the phone on speaker. "Please tell her we had nothing to do with this. I'm an artist, a professional. I would never leak film from my set and these aren't even real."

"You need to come out with a statement right now and tell the world these are fake," Karri said sternly.

"I will. I'll have my publicist send out my response immediately. Please tell Skye I'm so sorry. She's too nice a person to have this happen to."

"I'll tell her. Thank you." Karri hung up the phone and held open her arms. Skye collapsed into them and let the tears flow as both of their phones blew up. She didn't even answer when Mason texted to see if there was anything he could do to help.

∼

"The poor girl," Tinsley said to Trent as if he had any idea what his cousin was talking about.

The morning air was invigorating and Trent was inspired. He was hard at work in his shop when Tinsley had walked in a couple of minutes ago carrying two coffees.

Ryker lived in an enormous house on the river. Ridge lived in a neighborhood across the street from Ryker. Gavin and Harper were down the street from them, but in town. Wade was just a couple of blocks from downtown while Trent and Tinsley lived out in the country. Being the creative types they were, they found the quiet and beauty of nature inspiring.

"What poor girl?" Trent asked, taking the coffee and thanking Tinsley.

"Skye Jessamine. Someone just leaked all these fully nude pictures of her. They're everywhere. I can't imagine how violated she must feel right now."

Trent broke the pencil he held in his left hand. The one he marked the wood with before he cut it. He didn't like being used by Skye, but she didn't deserve this. He picked up his phone almost expecting a text from her.

"You're not going to look, are you?" Tinsley gasped.

"Of course not. I wouldn't violate a woman like that. I was just wondering if she'd texted."

Tinsley looked at him sympathetically. "Maybe now is the time to let her know you're here for her. Well, I'm off to paint now that I've ruined your morning."

"You didn't ruin it. It's Skye's morning that is ruined."

"Text her!" Tinsley called out over her shoulder as she left his shop.

Trent picked up his phone, then put it back down. She wouldn't want to hear from a one-night stand. Not with everything she was going through right now. He'd text her in a couple of days. Trent went back to work and ignored the little voice in his head that was calling him a coward.

∾

Skye sat curled up on the couch in her living room as Karri hovered around her. Her entire team had immediately descended on the house before the sun was even up. She'd heard them when she'd been on the phone with her parents and then she'd conferenced Karri's parents in when they'd called. They all were worried about her and told her to come to either house or they'd fly out and rally around her.

At first, her parents had been taken aback by Skye's closeness to Karri, her family, and the entire Onondaga Nation that blossomed quickly during their freshman year at Syracuse. That had dissipated after meeting the Hills at parents' weekend that fall. Karri's family would live-text the girls' lacrosse games to her parents and basically wrapped the entire Jessamine family in love.

The truth was, Skye wanted to go home more than anything, but she'd told them she'd let them know after her meeting. So now she sat as everyone around her talked. Lenny was on the phone pushing back the bodyguard appointments until tomorrow. Jim was on the phone with the studio. Her lawyer, Bernie, was threatening to sue every outlet that was publishing the pictures. Rebecca Collins, her publicist, was spinning the hell out of the story.

Skye sat there for hours nursing hot tea and listening as her world collapsed and noticing that not a single person in the room, with the exception of Karri, had even asked how she was. That was until the deep sexy voice asking if she was okay drew her attention.

Skye looked up and almost cried with relief when Mason sat down next to her and pulled her into a tight hug. "I am so sorry. This double standard is such bullshit. If it were me naked, I'd be praised."

"Thanks, Mason. You're the only one besides Karri who understands. It's real nice of you to come over."

Her friend smiled down at her and reached over to the bag on the table. "I got your favorites. Has Trent called to check on you?"

Skye looked into the bag and pulled out all her favorite chocolates and junk foods. "You're so sweet. Thank you." Everyone thought Mason was Hollywood's tough guy, but he really was just a good friend. They spent hours talking in each other's trailers. And while he came off as arrogant in the press, he was far from it. The press liked to link them together, but the truth was that Skye was the only one in Hollywood who didn't want him. She wanted Trent, and Mason knew and supported that. He'd never asked her for a date and their relationship had always been platonic.

"No," Skye said sadly. "I haven't heard from Trent since he left. After this and that article that made it seem like you and I are together . . . I'm afraid it's time to give him up for good."

"He doesn't deserve you. I'm always here if you need me. Well, except for right this moment," he laughed. "I have a meeting."

He leaned over and kissed her cheek before walking out like the action hero he was. Skye sat in the silence for she didn't know how long until a scream jolted her from her mind.

"Dammit!" Rebecca yelled, drawing a momentary silence before her team rushed to finish up their calls.

"What is it?" Skye asked as Karri perched herself on the couch above her and placed her hand on her shoulder to calm her.

"There've been more leaked photos and this time they're really of you. They're not fakes," Rebecca told her.

"Where are they?" Bernie asked as all their phones pinged.

"I sent them to you."

Skye clicked the gossip site link and felt exposed. It was her. She knew because the birthmark on her ass was on full display.

"Is this all of them?" Jim asked.

Rebecca shook her head. "The site says they have full frontal but they wanted to make sure it was really her before they ran with them."

"I'm on it," Bernie said as he yelled at his secretary through the phone to patch him through to the owner of the gossip site.

Jim looked to Rebecca for guidance but then his phone rang. "It's Tony Ketron."

Rebecca took a deep breath. "Okay, we can spin this. We can tell the public they're test shots for Tony's new film and Skye's not some drug-induced, out-of-control actress like the press is reporting."

"No!" Skye almost threw her tea at Rebecca. "Don't you dare! I will not take that part. Is no one concerned that someone doctored photos of me and then someone obviously had a view into my bedroom to take these photos?"

"It doesn't matter what actually happened," Rebecca said gently. "The narrative is already out there. Now we just have to make it work for us."

"No. I refuse to allow you to attach my name to Tony's for any reason. These meetings are over. Everyone out!"

Skye leaned over to Karri and whispered her instructions. "Okay, ladies and gentlemen. Right this way," Karri said as she picked up all her personal items. "Skye needs some time to think. Let's give it to her."

"You're leaving too?" Jim asked Karri with surprise.

Karri nodded. "She said she needed space. So, we'll give it to her. Let's move everything to text, okay?"

Skye watched as Karri ushered everyone out the front door and waited. Ten minutes later, Karri was knocking on the back patio door. "What's your plan?" Karri asked, plopping back down on the couch.

"I want to contact the FBI. This has to be illegal," Skye told her. She wasn't going to take this sitting down. She was going to fight it.

"Let's do it."

Skye Jessamine drew a deep breath and took the first step toward taking control of her life.

4

SKYE KEPT it together as she gave her testimony. The FBI agent nodded as he took notes, all the while his phone recorded the entire conversation.

"Could your phone have been hacked?"

"Agent Shaw, I know you're the head of the L.A. office and have dealt with people much more famous than me, but I'm not your typical gossip rag celebrity. There are no hidden sex tapes, there are no indecent texts, and no nude photos on my phone or anyone else's."

"Tell him about the film role," Karri hedged and Skye launched into the fight she had with her team regarding Tony's upcoming movie.

Agent Shaw had been appointed to clean up the L.A. office after he helped bust a major case some years ago when some agents had been killed or hurt. That's what he'd told her when he said he was really a guy from a small town in Idaho who could understand her mindset as a small town woman. Skye had liked him and trusted him when he told her he'd be the only one looking into this to avoid any leaks. If he needed help, he'd ask her first. Skye appreciated feeling as if she had some control over her life once again.

"Do you think they're connected?"

"I don't know, but that's how my people want to spin it. But then there's these letters I've been getting. The last one was put on my gate."

"Can I see them?" Agent Shaw asked.

Skye sighed, "Lenny has them. I'm sure Jim has some copies too."

"I'm going to have to talk to them if you want me to fully investigate this."

Skye looked to Karri who nodded. "Okay, but only talk to them. I don't want to tip anyone off that I'm looking into this. They're going to be mad. They wanted to handle this internally."

Shaw stopped the recorder and put his notes away. "Miss Jessamine, with all due respect, you're the victim here. I only care about your feelings and keeping you safe. Your agent and your manager don't scare me. Frankly, I would worry if they don't want my help. I'll talk to them tomorrow and let you know how it goes. In the meantime, is there somewhere safe you can go?"

Skye thought about it. Karri was the only one she trusted. "I could go home to Iowa or I could go to Karri's parents in New York."

"Let me have your cell phone number and I'll keep you up to date personally instead of going through your entire team to get to you."

Skye unlocked her phone and handed it to him. "I'd appreciate that. Will you put your info in there?"

She waited as Agent Shaw entered the information and then paused. "Do you mind if I look at your phone?" Skye sat up and regarded him with concern. Privacy was everything to her and she already felt violated. "I don't want to look at your photos. I want to look at your apps and your settings. I want to see if any are vulnerable to hacking."

Skye exhaled as that sunk in and nodded. "I'd like that." She waited as Agent Shaw went to work. She didn't think there was anything on there that would be worrisome, but then she saw his mouth turn down into a frown as his brow creased. "What is it?"

"Who put this calendar app on here?"

Skye and Karri both leaned forward. "It was on the phone when I got it."

"Did you take it out of the box yourself and set it up?" Agent Shaw asked and a pit of dread opened up in her stomach.

"Lenny got us both our phones to keep my name out of any records. He handed us both these phones in their boxes, but he'd charged them so they were ready to use. Why?"

"Because this calendar app doubles as a tracking app."

"It's a shared calendar among the three of us. Is that what you mean?" Karri asked exactly what Skye was thinking.

"No. It's a GPS tracking app hidden in a regular app. Parents use them to track their kids without them knowing it."

"Get it off!" Skye almost screamed as her heart started to race. Why was Lenny tracking her when he already knew where she was? The thought made her shiver as she thought about what she and Karri had talked about. She had nothing in her life that was just hers. Not even her phone.

"I'll screenshot the calendar and then would you check my phone too?" Karri asked Agent Shaw.

"Of course." It took him twenty minutes but then they

were both handed back their phones with guarantees that they couldn't be traced.

"I'm not saying that your manager even put it on them. It could have been where he got them from and he might not have known about the GPS tracking in it. The fact is, we don't know anything yet. Or maybe he knew, but it was for your safety. I put an encryption app on both phones that will run in the background." He held up his own phone and showed them the app. "This helps close any loopholes left by any apps. Your email will be safe, your call history, your cloud storage, and your social media. It's disabled all GPS tracking so even the retailer won't be able to track it. It will be very difficult for any hacker to get into that now. Tomorrow I'll come back and look at the angles of the photo taken in your room to try to determine where it was taken. That will be our starting point."

Agent Shaw stood, and when he did, Skye stood with him. She held out her hand and thanked him. They walked him to the front door and he paused. "Have you thought about hiring personal security?"

"I'm meeting with them tomorrow. I was supposed to do it today, but the last thing I wanted was a man around I didn't know. Karri, do you have the list of candidates?" Skye asked as Karri bent her head and went to work on her phone.

"Here they are," she said, showing Agent Shaw her phone. He looked over them with a quick glance.

"They're the norm for bodyguards to celebrities, but not if you're high risk. I'll shoot you an email when I get home with the names of a couple of people I've worked with in high profile cases. Most of them are retired U.S. Marshals."

Finally. Skye felt some relief. "I'll hire whoever you recommend. Thank you so much, Agent Shaw, for coming out to my house in the middle of the night. I feel a lot better now."

"Good. I'll touch base with you tomorrow."

Karri closed the door and they both visibly relaxed. "I'm going to sleep here again tonight."

Skye reached for her friend and squeezed her hand. "Thank you. I'd appreciate it. Why don't we sleep in the guest rooms tonight? I don't feel safe in my room after those photos were taken, even though I have shades."

Exhaustion was taking over Skye's body. It felt heavy as she climbed the stairs with Karri right behind her. Instead of turning toward her master bedroom, Skye and Karri walked to the other end of the hall and turned toward the guest suites.

"You were brave tonight, calling the FBI," Karri told her when they stopped at the guest rooms.

"I don't feel brave, but I feel more in control. And I'm ready to fight for that control tomorrow. I'll find a lawyer to look over my contract and Agent Shaw will, hopefully, get a lead on how and where the person took the photo of my bedroom." Skye reached for her best friend and hugged her tightly. "Thank you. Thank you for uprooting your life to come out here with me. Thank you for being the sister of my heart."

With a heavy heart and heavy eyelids, Skye crawled into bed fully dressed and passed out.

Skye was dreaming of Trent and never wanted to wake up. He was reaching for her with a smile on his face and Skye was running toward him. Then his hand grabbed her arm hard. Skye gasped, but no air came into her lungs as Trent's face loomed over hers and morphed into sneering lips and evil in his eyes.

Skye's eyes popped open as a hand pressed against her mouth and covered her nose. It didn't matter that Skye opened her eyes as the blackout shades were drawn and the room was completely dark.

Skye felt her nostrils flare as she clawed at the hand over her mouth. She felt more than saw a head moving closer to her face. She felt his warm breath heavy on her face. Skye tried to scream as she kicked and clawed with all her strength.

"Shhhh."

Screw that. Skye reached for the bedside table and swept her hand in a blind panic. Her fingers connected with the lamp and she shoved it, causing it to crash to the ground. A second later her door was kicked open. The man paused to look over his shoulder, but he was too slow. Skye's college lacrosse stick swung through the air and smashed into his face.

Karri hollered and raised it swing again as the man stumbled back. Not waiting to see what happened, Skye leapt from the bed and charged. The man was running for the balcony as Karri swung. She knocked the man in the back as Skye reached for him. She grabbed his shoulder, spun him around, and jammed her knee as hard as she could into his cowardly balls.

The man cried out and bent over as he stumbled backward and into the blackout curtains, which parted where the balcony door was. As she and Karri charged him again, he pedaled backward through the curtains and out the now open balcony door. His butt hit the railing and his arms pinwheeled in the air as he tried to catch his balance. Skye and Karri grabbed for him. He looked at them, seemed to come to a decision and threw himself over the railing with a grunt.

Skye and Karri rushed to the railing to find the man sunken into the eight-foot tall hedgerow. He groaned, crawled out of the hedge, and limped off into the night.

"Still got it," Karri said with a smirk as she spun the lacrosse stick in her hand. "But now we're getting the hell out of here."

Karri and Skye packed as much as they could in two giant suitcases then Skye woke Agent Shaw up to tell him what happened.

"I can get you into a safe house if you'd like."

"No thank you. I know exactly where I want to go. I'm going off the grid. It's best that way, isn't it?" Skye asked as Karri wrinkled her brow at her. She hadn't discussed it with Karri yet, but the fact was there was only one person she trusted right now.

"Are you going to your parents?" Agent Shaw asked.

"No. I'm going to South Carolina."

Karri's eyes went wide, but she didn't comment.

"Where's that and why are you going there?"

"A town called Shadows Landing, it's near Charleston, and I'm going there because there's someone there that I trust that no one can connect me to."

"Name?" Agent Shaw asked all business.

"Trent Faulkner."

"Okay, let me see what I can find. I'll call you back in ten minutes."

Skye zipped her suitcase and then looked over to Karri. "Let's get your stuff. I'm not leaving you here alone."

"No complaints from me. The barbeque in Shadows Landing is to die for. If we're doing this, we can't tell anyone besides Shaw where we are. That means no flying and no credit card use at all."

"No problem," Skye set the bags down at the top of the stairs and headed to the spare room she'd been sleeping in. Karri followed her, asking what she was up to. Skye didn't answer as she went into the bathroom and opened the cabinet under the sink. There were some extra towels, a hairdryer, and an open package of maxi pads. Skye pulled them all out and then reached into the back near the water pipes. She placed a finger in the hole the pipes went down and pulled up. The cabinet floor came sliding up as she angled it out. The space underneath was filled with ziptop plastic bags of cash. "Mom told me to hide money away in case of an emergency."

"Way to go, Mom," Karri said in wonder right before she hurried into the bedroom and came back with a pillowcase. "I can't believe we're doing this."

"Me either, but everything here feels wrong. I don't know who to trust in this town, so the only option is to get out of Hollywood."

"I agree completely." Karri held open the pillowcase as Skye filled it. Then they were on the move again.

They were halfway through packing Karri's things when her phone rang. It was Agent Shaw. "Does Trent pass your test?"

Agent Shaw chuckled. "More than you know. The reason I got this job is because of Agent Ryan Parker who is now in Lexington, Kentucky. I called him after I ran my search on Trent. Turns out he and your friend Trent are cousins. Not only that, but Ryan is friends with the Charleston Agent in Charge, Peter Castle. I'll notify him of our situation and he'll be your in-person contact. With your approval, that is."

"You trust these agents?" Skye asked, not really liking

more people knowing about her. But she remembered Trent's author aunt whose books were all being picked up for movies. She lived near Lexington, so the cousin thing was likely true.

"I trust Ryan Parker with my life. If Ryan says Agent Castle is trustworthy, then I trust him. I'll talk to him first and let you know what I think. I assume you know better than to fly, right?"

"I'm going to drive my car," Karri told him.

"No, I'll get you a car that has no connection to you or any of your friends. If this is serious, they'll know to look for not only your car, but Miss Hill's too. Meet me at the FBI office in thirty minutes."

"Thank you for everything, Agent Shaw. You're a good man."

"See you soon, Miss Jessamine."

5

SKYE YAWNED as her eyes fluttered open behind her large sunglasses. The tinted windows of the borrowed SUV Shaw had signed out of the FBI for *training purposes* did a good job at cutting the glare of the sun beating down on them.

Skye stretched and Karri glanced at her. "Morning, or should I say afternoon? Agent Shaw called while you were asleep and told me that Jim and Lenny are *pissed*. He also figured out where the photos were taken from and is working on seeing if he can get more information before he passes it along to us. Mason texted me after he tried to reach you. He wanted you to know we could stay with him if we didn't feel safe. I thanked him. He's a sweet guy. Kinda like the real-life version of the superhero he plays."

"Agreed. I missed a lot while I was sleeping," Skye said even as she yawned. It was four in the afternoon and they'd been driving since four in the morning. She had taken the first shift, but by eleven in the morning, Karri was ready to drive. "Where are we?" Skye asked as another Interstate 40 sign went by. They'd be on this interstate all the way to Memphis, Tennessee, before they dipped down into

Alabama and drove through Atlanta on their way to South Carolina.

"Halfway through New Mexico. I figured we'd stop in Amarillo, Texas, for the night. Also, Agent Shaw said he talked to this Agent Castle guy in Charleston and really liked him. With your approval, he'll fill him in."

"What do you think?" Skye asked as she looked around.

"I looked him up when I stopped for gas. He's a hottie."

Skye saw Karri wiggle her eyebrows and shook her head. This was why she loved her friend. She could make her laugh under any circumstances. "But was he a trustworthy hottie or a bad boy hottie that you give a fake name to and sneak out in the morning?"

"Definitely a trustworthy hottie. The kind you take home and introduce to your mama and use to piss off your snooty cousin."

Skye might have snorted as they broke out into belly laughs. "That says a lot since you haven't brought a man home since our junior year of college."

"Don't remind me. I should have known better than to bring a track athlete home. He could run away too fast."

Skye shook her head as they remembered the day news got out that Karri brought home a boyfriend. Every person on the reservation within three miles had come to check him out. Which was really just a kind way of saying they'd tried to determine if he was good enough for Karri. They believed the right man wouldn't run. This one had run —fast.

This was how the next four hours passed. They talked, told stories, and Skye listened to Karri lust after Agent Hottie.

Broken Shadows

IT HAD BEEN a couple of days since Skye's photos leaked, so Trent thought it would be safe to go out this morning without hearing about them. He was wrong. Trent's face was buried in his sketchbook as he listened to the knitting club at the table next to him at the Stomping Grounds Diner. He'd thought he'd slipped in late enough to miss the morning rush, but early enough to still grab breakfast. Apparently everyone in town had the same idea.

The knitting club was to his right. Gator and his crew were to his left. Behind him were Maggie and Gage Bell, having been run out of their house as it was fully occupied for some fall festival in Charleston. Their parents ran a bed and breakfast in their old family estate.

"Did you see those pictures of Skye Jessamine?" one of the knitters clucked with disapproval.

Edie Green Wecker, a childhood friend of the family who had moved back to Shadows Landing a couple of years ago after her Navy Seal husband had been killed, shook her head. "It's horrible. Someone invaded that poor woman's privacy and then probably sold the photos to every news source they could. How would you like it if someone took a picture of you in the shower and then spread it across the world?"

Edie cast him a quick glance, knowing Trent was so over this discussion. He couldn't look on social media. He couldn't turn on the television. He couldn't go anywhere without talk of Skye, and each time his heart broke for her. He might be mad she'd had her lackey cast him off, but that didn't mean she deserved this.

Skeeter leaned over to see around Trent and talk to the knitting club. "I swear I see her everywhere."

The knitting club agreed and broke out into a debate

with Skeeter, Turtle, and Gator about Skye and her relationship with Mason Hemming.

Edie stood up and quietly left the table to join Trent. "I assume you know everything?" Trent asked as he dropped his voice. People in town knew he'd built Skye's table, but they didn't know about her assistant flying out here and about the night they shared. Nondisclosure be damned, his family knew something personal had happened, he'd had to sign the NDA, and now Skye was texting him.

"I know what it's like to lose someone you love. Now mine was taken from me, but yours is right there—"

"Right there if I just reach out and talk to her," Trent said with a sigh. How many times did he have to hear it? Maybe it was finally time to suck it up and talk to her.

Edie shot from her chair and pointed out the window. "No, *right there!*"

"I'm exhausted," Karri groaned as she parked the car a block from Main Street in Shadows Landing. "There's this great diner up here. Let's get something to eat, clean up a little, and then find Trent."

Skye shoved the door open and grabbed her purse. "Great idea. I can't see him like this. We've been in the car thirty-seven hours out of the past forty-eight. He'd run screaming for the hills." Skye laced her hands above her head and stretched as they began walking toward Main Street. At least no one would recognize her looking like a travel weary hot mess.

"I told you the town was cute," Karri said with a smile and suddenly looking even more relaxed than Skye had seen her recently. That was when reality hit Skye hard. Karri was her sister. Her *ride and die, help you bury the body and give you an alibi* bestie. It was her fault that Karri wasn't relaxed and happy. She would do something about it. Skye didn't know what, but she'd figure it out. Karri stopped walking and cocked her head. "Do you hear that chirping sound?"

Skye paused and listened. "It's coming from up ahead. Is it a baby bird?"

Karri listened again. "Not one I've ever heard. It also isn't coming from a tree. Maybe it fell out of the nest."

Skye and Karri stepped forward as they scanned the palmetto-lined street. They'd just passed a nature area and were approaching the back of what looked like a government building when they heard something else.

"Now I hear something like that T-Rex in *Jurassic Park*."

"Lots of guttural vibrato." Skye paused and listened. "I still hear the chirping and now this rumbling." Skye turned slowly as she scanned the area and froze. A giant alligator was moving toward them. It was clear it had come from the swamp area behind the town and was now sprinting across the grass behind Main Street buildings.

"Karri, do you run when an alligator is chasing you or play dead?" Skye asked in growing horror as she watched the gator advance steadily toward them.

"I know you're not supposed to run with bears, right? Why?" Skye didn't have to tell her as Karri turned as saw the gator.

"Screw it, we're running!" Skye screamed as she grabbed Karri's hand and sprinted for the diner.

"Help!" Karri yelled over and over as Skye kept her eyes on the large windows of the diner. She saw faces in them as they turned at the commotion. Someone could open the door, and then they'd fly through it and be safe.

An even larger and even louder alligator hissed as it

clambered into the middle of Main Street between them and the diner, which changed everything.

"We're surrounded," Karri gasped as they slid to a stop and grabbed onto each other.

"G‍ATOR!" Trent yelled as he ran out of the diner door so fast Bubba snapped at him in surprise.

Gator, Turtle, and Skeeter were by his side in a second.

"This isn't good," Gator muttered. "That chirping is Big Bertha's baby, and you can see her coming to the rescue. In fact, every gator around here will come at that sound, just like Bubba did. "Skeeter, you grab the ladies. Turtle, I need you to help me tackle Bertha. Trent, do you think you can get Bubba?"

"Yup," Trent said with his heart in his throat. He could catch a gator with the best of them. What worried him was how close Bertha was to Skye and Karri.

"Go!" Gator yelled.

Skeeter took off like a shot. The distraction of him racing by Bubba made Bubba take his eyes off Trent just long enough and that's when he jumped. Karri and Skye screamed but Trent couldn't take his eyes off the ten foot, thousand pound gator underneath him. Bubba was feeling ornery today for sure. His tail whipped back and forth as Trent struggled to trap his head so that Bubba's jaws wouldn't take him out.

"We gotcha!" Trent heard a moment before Granger Fox, one of Trent's best friends and the town's sheriff, leapt on Bubba's back. "Get his tail, Kord!" he ordered his deputy.

"I got this!" Edie called out before a nearly finished knitted scarf was wrapped around Bubba's jaws and a tablecloth from the diner was shoved over his eyes.

Only then could Trent look up to see if Skye was safe.

SHE WAS GOING TO DIE. She was sure of it. She could see the headlines now: *America's Sweetheart Eaten by Alligators*. The door to the diner burst open and suddenly Trent was there with a man who looked to be as large as the gators surrounding them.

Then a skinny man shot forward, Trent leapt on the large alligator, and Skye slammed her eyes shut, not wanting to see the man she'd fallen in love with be eaten by an alligator.

"Get back, Big Bertha. They don't have your baby."

"That's the biggest knife I've ever seen," Karri gasped and Skye opened her eyes. Oh my God. Trent was on the gator's back, then two cops jumped on. She turned her head and the skinny guy in baggy clothes was protecting them with the largest hunting knife she'd ever seen. The big man wearing a hat with COCKS blazoned across the front and a little guy who looked at least a foot shorter and a hundred pounds lighter than the COCKS hat guy ran past them. The little guy broke off to the left and when Big Bertha turned her head, COCKS guy leapt on her.

She and Karri screamed again and clutched at each other. People were wrestling alligators in front of them and behind them and Skye didn't know what to do.

"Someone go find that baby so Bertha will calm down," COCKS hat yelled. The diner emptied out and the skinny guy with the gigantic knife turned and smiled at them.

"Howdy. I'm Skeeter. Anne Bonny said you have the spirit of the wolf," he said to Karri, whose mouth fell open in surprise. "And she said to tell you that you better not hurt Trent or she'll haunt you until your dying breath."

"I'm sorry. Did you say Anne Bonny? The pirate I played in *Love's Dangerous Waters*?" Skye asked even as she kept her eyes on Trent and the two men holding down the big gator.

"Yup. She said you did her justice, but that she'd never wear makeup, especially during a sword fight. Oh, and your Southern accent needs work. A lotta work."

Skye finally had to turn to look at Skeeter. "You mean, *you* say that?"

"No, Anne says it. She lives here in Shadows Landing along with some of the other pirate ghosts. It's their home. They founded the town after all," Skeeter told her as Karri turned to him as if forgetting the gator battle raging around them.

"That's fascinating. Tell me more. How did she know I had the spirit of a wolf?"

"Found it!" a little old lady wearing a cat sweater yelled. She held up a small alligator and Big Bertha went nuts.

"Edie, run the baby down to the river," the COCKS hat man yelled out. A pretty woman in her early thirties with knitting needles in her hand reached forward, took the baby gator, and sprinted for the river while Big Bertha battled the two men to get free.

"Skeeter, move the women to the diner. Everyone else, inside the nearest building!" COCKS hat man yelled.

"Sure thing, Gator!" Skeeter called out as he turned the women toward the diner.

"You also talk to alligators?" Karri asked, now sounding doubtful. Skeeter laughed.

"Nah, that would be crazy. I only talk to ghosts. Gator is the name of the big guy in the COCKS hat. Right this way, ladies. And welcome to Shadows Landing."

6

Trent used all his strength to keep Bubba from breaking free as the people scattered inside different buildings. Granger and Kord were grunting with exertion as the big gator battled them.

"Trent!" Skye called out as Skeeter yanked her hand and pulled her past him at a run. Karri eyed them all with a look somewhere between being impressed and thinking she was in the middle of a bad dream.

"I'm okay. Get inside so we can release him," Trent yelled back to Skye as she struggled with Skeeter.

"Is that Skye Jessamine?" Kord asked as he pushed up to get a better look and let out a low whistle of appreciation. Bubba's tail slammed into his chest hard the second he was loose.

Trent could feel Granger rolling his eyes. "One day a woman is going to bring you to your knees and you'll beg her for monogamy. I'll laugh when she tells you to take a hike."

"I'm just making up for your shortfalls." Kord leaned

back down and grabbed Bubba's tail. "When was the last time you had a date? Right, Trent?"

"I agree with both of you," Trent said as Edie finally came back into view now sans baby gator. "I'll laugh when a woman gets Kord wrapped around her finger. I also agree with Kord that you need to date. You used to date all the time and don't use the accident as an excuse. Every woman in town would jump at the chance to date you."

"Says the man who ran away from Skye Jessamine."

"Y'all have no game," Kord snorted as Edie ran past them and gave him a thumbs-up.

"Okay, guys," Gator yelled. "On the count of three, let go and haul your asses inside!"

Trent focused on Bubba as Gator counted down. It looked as if Skye had come to him, so one way or another they were going to hash this out—if he didn't get bitten by Bubba first, that is.

"Three!" Gator yelled.

Trent, Granger, and Kord rolled off Bubba and leapt up in perfect synchronization.

"Here, boys!" Skeeter held the door to the diner open and they rushed inside.

Trent closed his eyes and took a deep breath. When he opened them, Skye was flinging her arms around his neck, and just like in his nightly dreams, she was in his arms once again.

Trent pressed his face into Skye's neck and held her as she lost all semblance of being calm, cool, and collected. Skye started rambling with a mixture of tears and sniffles, and all Trent could think about was how good it felt to have her back in his arms and in his life.

"Shhh, sweetheart. It's okay. Big Bertha is back at the river with her baby and Bubba is—" Trent looked out the window and saw Bubba staring back at him. "Mary Jane, can you get me an order of chicken and waffles for Bubba?" The waitress nodded and hurried off to get the chicken frying. Bubba loved his breakfast and would go back home after he had a snack.

"I was so scared, Trent. Two alligators downtown, a man with a hunting knife that was bigger than he is *and* who talks to ghosts, and then I don't even know about that Gator guy."

"Skye, I don't mean to sound harsh, but what are you doing here?" Trent asked and noticed the entire diner was quieter than the ghosts who haunted it.

"I thought I'd come for a visit." Skye smiled up at him, but he wasn't fooled.

"And where's your boyfriend?" Edie asked for him as she crossed her arms over her chest and stared Skye down in the perfect imitation of a big sister.

Skye's nose wrinkled as if smelling something bad. "I don't have a boyfriend. The last man I was with was Trent."

"No one likes a fibber, dear."

Skye turned to see the grandmotherly, plump Miss Ruby right behind her with the plucked-chickenlike Miss Winnie standing next to her. They looked as if they would grab her by the ear and wash her mouth out with soap if she lied.

"It's not a lie. I'm not that good of an actress. I swear."

Miss Ruby gave her the stink eye and several of the younger generation took an automatic giant step back in fear. "I may be old, but I know what I saw on my gossip shows. And they show you all over Mason Hemming. Not that I blame you, but just don't be fibbing about it or we'll have a problem."

"I swear I have never been with Mason. I think the movie studio leaked those photos to make it look like something was going on. It's their oldest trick to drum up interest in a movie. If you could see the whole photo, you'd see it's not what it looks like. There's only been one man to have my attention and that's Trent. Who hasn't even texted me back after a night together. What kind of manners are those?"

Miss Winnie's chicken wing of an arm shot out and smacked Trent on the back of his head. "That is no way to treat a lady!"

Okay, so she wanted to do this here. Fine, to hell with the nondisclosure agreement. He'd have it out once and for all in the middle of the diner with half the town watching. "You're right, Miss Winnie. It was rude. Do you know what else was rude? Waking up after the best night of your life to find her manager standing at the bedroom door and telling me I was just one in a long line of blue-collar men Skye liked to play pretend with. He then shoved a nondisclosure agreement in front of me and threatened to take everything I ever worked for from me if I ever told anyone about our night together." Trent stared down in helpless anger at Skye's shocked, wide eyes. "There, are you happy? I broke the NDA so are you going to take my life's work from me now?"

Skye's head shook and the look of shock was very real. She reached out and touched his hand. Even as Trent wanted to be mad, he craved her touch. "Trent, I don't know what to say. But I have *never* asked Lenny to do that. Not only that, but what he said just isn't true."

"Trent, she's telling you the truth." Karri added quietly.

"So, let us get this straight. You two had a moment that was then taken away from you by this Lenny guy?" Trent and

Skye looked at each other and nodded before Miss Ruby continued. "Trent, being a stubborn man, refused to reach out so you finally came here to get answers?"

Trent saw the corner of Skye's lip disappear as she bit down on it nervously. "Yes and no."

"Child, you better be getting to the point," Miss Ruby demanded.

"I've been trying to talk to Trent, and I did want to see him to get to the bottom of what happened." Skye paused and then looked up at Trent. "I guess we just did that."

"We did. Now I'm pissed at myself for not doing what Karri said and talking to you." Trent took a deep breath and looked over at the people surrounding him. "Skye, these sweet ladies are Miss Ruby and Miss Winnie. Then that's Mary Jane walking out to feed Bubba his chicken and waffles. This is my friend, Granger. He's the sheriff here and my other friend, Kord. He's the deputy. You met Skeeter and these two are Gage and Maggie Bell."

"We're brother and sister," Maggie said, giving her a smile and answering the unasked question of their common last name.

"And this is my very good friend, Edie."

"Don't worry, the rest of the town will be here as soon as Bubba leaves," Edie said as she looked up from her phone. "And I loved you in *Love's Dangerous Waters,* although whoever was your history person didn't know Anne Bonny very well. And, bless your heart, your Southern accent . . .," Edie cringed.

Skye laughed and Trent saw her shoot a smile to Skeeter. "So I've been told."

"Wait for us!"

Trent groaned and flipped Edie the bird. "You texted my family?"

Edie didn't look upset. Instead she just smirked.

"Were we not supposed to do that?" Kord asked. "I did it when I was hanging on to Bubba's tail."

"Yeah, I texted them too," Granger said with a shrug.

His family came pouring in from the diner's back kitchen door instead of waiting for Bubba to move so they could enter through the front. It had been Tinsley who had called out, but Harper was leading the charge and she looked pissed.

Harper stopped directly next to Skye and forced Skye to turn to look up at her. "Give me one reason I shouldn't kick your ass for the way you used my cousin."

"I told you on the text chain about the NDA and how Skye didn't know about it," Edie told her and Trent was finally thankful to have her here. "However, we're just about to learn the real reason she's here."

Harper crossed her arms over her chest and stared at Skye. Karri stepped up to her friend's side and returned the stare impassively. Harper raised one eyebrow. "You want to join in? One or two asses to kick don't matter much to me."

"Harper," Gavin said in that typical older brother warning voice. A voice Trent knew when Wade used it on him. It was why he and Harper were so close.

"I'm waiting for an explanation," Harper said, ignoring her brother.

Skye took a deep breath and Trent saw her reach for Karri's hand. Whatever it was, she needed the strength of a friend to tell it. "I've been getting these threats. No big deal normally, but then those images leaked of me nude, although those weren't me! Well, not the first ones. The ones on your table," she said to Trent. "Those were all fake. The next ones were through my bedroom window without my knowledge."

Tinsley pushed past Harper and pulled Skye in for a hug. "How horrible. You must feel so violated."

Skye nodded and swiped at the tears in her eyes. Trent's heart broke right then and there while all his protective instincts roared to life. He wanted nothing but to hold her and dry her tears. "I'm sorry. I should have known. I know we were only together a short time, but I knew you'd never do something like that silly table dance. What's being done to protect you? You're not here with just Karri, are you?"

Skye took a deep breath and nodded. "Just Karri and me. No one, and I mean, *no one* knows we are here. Please tell me no one posted about me being here? I was planning on keeping a low profile until the gator thing happened."

Everyone shook their heads letting Skye know nothing had been posted.

"You played Anne Bonny. That makes you part of Shadows Landing," Skeeter said as everyone nodded in agreement.

Trent went to open his mouth but Skye stopped him. "There's more." She told them of the attack, of her staff wanting her to take the movie role and use the leaked photos for the movie, and about how she went against their wishes and contacted the FBI. "So, I guess I did leave something out. Agent Shaw knows I'm here and so does an Agent—"

"Castle," Karri filled in for her.

"He's good people," Granger told her in full cop mode. "I'll let him know you're here."

"You know him?" Karri asked with a little blush to her cheeks.

Skye looked from her friend to Trent and gave him a

smile that said she noticed the blush too and they'd talk about it later. In that moment, Trent could breathe again. The connection that had been so strong between them was back. He hadn't missed his chance and he was not going to waste this second chance.

"He's friends with our cousin in Kentucky," Gavin answered. "When my wife was in trouble, he helped us."

"Us too," Trent's brother, Wade, said.

Harper rolled her eyes. "Okay, so he helped my husband and me too. He's a good guy. And going after someone with a lacrosse stick and shoving them out the window is pretty badass. You can stay. For now."

"Harper," Gavin groaned at his sister as Skye laughed.

"What can we do to help?" Edie asked.

"I was hoping Karri and I could hang out here until I knew who was behind the attack and the leaked photos," Skye asked not just Trent, but the entire town gathered around her.

"Of course you can, child," Miss Ruby said as if insulted she'd even asked.

"We protect our own," Miss Winnie told her matter-of-factly and Trent was grateful for their acceptance of her. Skye had told him how much she missed that small-town feel and they were giving it to her now. They had no idea how much it meant to her, but Trent did.

"Normally I'd welcome you to stay at our bed and breakfast, but we're full up," Maggie told her as she glanced to Trent. "And you might want to change your hair. While I wouldn't worry about the town, I can't guarantee our guests won't spill it." Skye looked around in fear and Maggie smiled gently at her. "Don't worry, they're not here. They're all in Charleston for a festival."

"I have some hair color," Georgina offered. "If you stop

by Harper's bar, I can turn you blonde or give you some blonde chunks that will change up how you look."

"Thank you," Skye said with all the feeling she had. "Everyone, thank you."

Tinsley turned and smiled at Karri. "Hi, I'm Tinsley. I'm Trent's cousin and I live near him. Do you want to stay with me? I have a spare room. Then Skye can stay with Trent."

Karri and Tinsley shared a smile and Trent knew they were setting them up, but in this case he was happy for his cousin to interfere. "That works for me. What about you?" Trent asked Skye.

"I just can't say thank you enough," Skye told everyone. "But I'm starving. Any chance I could get the Bubba special?"

Granger looked down at his phone and then back up at them. "Agent Castle will be here after work today to meet with you. Let's get you settled and then we can meet over at Harper's before Castle gets here. Georgina can do your hair and then we'll meet with Castle. Welcome to Shadows Landing, Miss Jessamine."

Granger walked out the door and then all chaos erupted. Introductions and questions about the movies flew all around him. One thing that didn't move, though, was Skye. Trent held her hand in his and kept her by his side. He let her become part of the town, all the while thinking how he could make up for being a cowardly jerk for not calling her sooner.

7

Skye felt as if she were among friends. No one was treating her differently than they did each other. They were curious about the movies and loved hearing her stories, but not because they wanted to sell magazines. They made her feel as if she were part of the town and they wanted to get to know the real her.

There were so many introductions she knew she'd never remember everyone's names. Next to her, Karri was similarly becoming part of the town, and on Skye's other side, Trent stood quietly or chatted with his own friends while still holding on to her hand.

"Here you go, hon," Mary Jane said, handing her a plate of fried chicken on top of waffles and smothered in syrup.

"Thank you." Skye smelled the food and her mouth watered.

"You know that is not a Lenny- or Jim-approved meal," Karri said as she winked at Skye and pinched off a piece of the waffle.

"I won't tell if you don't," Skye said to her best friend

who was moaning with pleasure after sampling the fried chicken.

"Deal," Karri said, turning to Mary Jane. "How did you get it fried like this?"

"Don't you know how to fry chicken?" Mary Jane asked as if she'd never heard such a thing.

"Well, I've had to limit my cooking to low-calorie, low-carb, dairy-free, gluten-free, and sugar-free foods for Skye's Hollywood diet," Karri told her.

Suddenly all eyes were on her and there were several audible gasps. Someone started crying.

"Bless your heart," Miss Ruby said with a pitying look.

"You poor child," Miss Winnie said as she dug around in her purse and pulled out a slice of apple pie in a plastic container. "You better eat this. Then you'll feel better. A good slice of apple pie fixes everything."

Skye was forced to drop Trent's hand as the apple pie was shoved at her. She really shouldn't . . . but then Trent pinched off a piece and held it up to her lips. She opened her mouth and his fingers caressed her lip as he placed the morsel of pie in her mouth. "*Oh my God*," Skye groaned in a very sinful way. Trent's eyes darkened in passion and it was then she realized she sounded as if she had climaxed, which she might have since that was the first bite of real sugar she'd had in years.

"I told you my apple pie could make you see God," Miss Winnie said saucily to Miss Ruby.

"We'll just see about that," Miss Ruby harrumphed. "It's a bake-off and Miss Skye will judge it."

Skye looked over to Trent as the place emptied so fast she was left alone holding the piece of pie and the chicken and waffles. "What just happened?"

Karri looked around the now empty diner and shrugged.

"It's a bake-off. Everyone is running home to make their best baked goods. These will be secret family recipes going back generations. This is great. I've never gotten to be the recipient of a bake-off. We're going to have so much food at our house," Trent chortled as he rubbed his hands together with glee.

Our house. That had to mean he was open to giving them a chance, it just had to.

AN HOUR later Karri was unpacking at Tinsley's house and Skye found herself looking up at a two-story house with a large verandah. The flowers lining the verandah surprised her. She didn't know why, but when she thought of Trent she thought of him chopping down trees, not planting flowers.

Large old trees lined the property and kept the hot sun from the yard. A barn sat to the right of the house with a style of windows she'd never seen on a barn before.

"That's my workshop," he told her when he saw her looking at the barn.

"Can I see it?"

"Sure, but it's not very interesting." He set her bags down and dug a set of keys from his pocket as they walked over the paved driveway toward the locked barn doors. "I like these doors because I can open them up wide if I need more natural light or if I want fresh air. Fall is the perfect time to work with them wide open."

Skye noticed that he was nervous as he unlocked the door. She wondered how many people got to see his workshop. She knew Karri hadn't gotten to see it when she came.

Trent pushed open the door as Skye looked about in

wonder. A massive metal industrial fan hung from the top of the barn. Exposed ductwork led out of the back of the building. The inside walls were painted white. The floor was beige epoxy with little flecks of color. And while it was clearly a workspace, it was organized, bright, and comfortable.

"It smells so good in here." Skye took a deep breath and inhaled the scent of the freshly cut wood. She looked around and saw giant planks of wood, whole tree trunks, and all of it was organized. "What is all of that?"

"I have them organized by natural woods, planks, solids, and manufactured woods. Then I divide each section by type of wood—pine, mahogany, teak, and so on. That way I can find what I need easily. Then those large padded loops hanging from the ceiling belong to this guy." Trent walked over to the wood and she saw a control panel near the wall. "I can't lift some of these pieces so I have a small crane in here. I use the padded straps so I don't damage the wood and then I can move it to the equipment I need to use on it."

"This place is amazing, Trent. It's state-of-the-art and who would ever know it was sitting in the woods of the small town of Shadows Landing?" Skye walked around looking at everything. She ran her hand over the rough raw wood and then the smooth sanded pieces.

"I'm glad you like it." Skye heard the roughness to Trent's voice and knew that it meant a lot to him.

"I don't like it. I love it. What's back here?" Skye asked as she pointed to a small room and then the back door.

"That's a small office and then this back door slides open so I can have the barn completely open." Trent opened it and she heard the hum of machinery.

Skye walked outside and saw what looked like an

extension to the barn about ten feet by ten feet with a little peaked roof on it. "What's that?"

"It's the mechanical room. There's a door that leads into it from inside the barn as well. It houses the air conditioner, air purifier, and humidity regulator so the wood doesn't warp."

"I'm beyond impressed. I'd have this door open all the time so I could be inspired by this view." Skye took a deep breath and savored the lack of air pollution and the smell of the outdoors.

"I'm glad you like it. Let me show you the house."

Trent took her hand again and Skye loved how he seemed to do it without realizing it. He picked up her bags and took her up the steps of the front porch. "Oh, you have one of the swings that were featured in the magazine! I tried to buy one, but you were all sold out."

Skye dropped Trent's hand and rushed for the swing. It was perfect. The cushions hugged her as the swing rocked her. Trent chuckled as he opened the front door and dropped her bags inside.

Skye hurried inside after him, telling him she could live in that swing forever. Inside was masculine, but not obnoxiously so. There were lots of wood and stone features with natural colors on the walls and for the furniture. "Oh my gosh. The paintings are insane." The natural color scheme allowed the paintings to pop. They were full of color as they showcased the best of nature: pictures of flowers, the ocean, and trees—all done with bright colors and a palette knife.

"Is that a good insane or bad?" Trent asked as she heard the seriousness to his voice. Did she say something wrong?

"Good. These are amazing. You have good taste."

Trent let out a breath as he picked her bags back up and

headed upstairs. "Good, I'm glad I won't have to tell Tinsley you hated her artwork."

Skye raced up the stairs after him. "Those are your cousin's?"

"Yup. She has a gallery on Main Street and her art is starting to get noticed. She has sold some to big clients in Atlanta and then she got back from a showing in Paris a couple of months ago."

"I can't wait to see her gallery." Skye followed Trent down the hall.

"My room is at that end. That door is the linen closet. This one is your bathroom, and then your room is on this end." Trent pushed open the door and set her bags on a queen-sized bed. A Tinsley painting hung over the bed that was covered in a brown and cream comforter. There were side tables next to the bed, a chest on the opposite wall, and a rocking chair by the large windows overlooking the backyard. "Is it okay? I don't have guests very often."

"It's wonderful, Trent. I absolutely love your home." Skye leaned up and placed a lingering kiss on his cheek.

"I'm glad. Get settled and I'll be downstairs."

Trent left and closed the door behind him. Skye walked to the window and crossed her arms over her chest. She was safe. For the first time she wasn't looking at the news, she wasn't holding strategy meetings, and she didn't have to dodge the paparazzi. She felt freer than she had in years.

Skye unpacked her things, texted Karri and found out she loved it at Tinsley's house, and cleaned up in the bathroom before going downstairs. She didn't see Trent in the living room so she moved to the back of the house. The kitchen was cute. The dining room had been converted into an office, but it was what was off the kitchen that had her smiling. There sat Trent in a sunroom. The large windows were slid open, revealing screens to keep the bugs out.

"Hey, how is everything?" he asked when he saw her.

"Great. This room is so comfortable." There was a large television on one wall, a couch and two recliners with a coffee table in front of them. The couch was the perfect spot for a nap with the breeze coming in.

"I'm glad you like it. As much as I like having you here, what's your game plan? Are you really going to hide out here until the stalker gets caught?"

Trent patted the seat next to him and she sat down with a sigh. "I'm not really sure. I honestly just needed to catch my breath and find some way to take control of my life. I feel as if the Hollywood spotlight has stripped me of myself. I have no control over anything. Look what Lenny did to you. Speaking of which," Skye took a deep breath and looked into Trent's green eyes. "Tell me he didn't ruin any chance we have to be together."

Trent was silent for a moment and then he reached for her. "I was an idiot. I shouldn't have signed the NDA. I should have gone right back upstairs and talked to you. Forgive me for being a stubborn jerk."

"Of course I forgive you. I knew there was something special between us. You have to believe me when I said that night was the first time something like that had ever happened. Call it fate, love at first sight, chemistry . . . whatever it was, it was there. I don't want to give up on it unless you didn't feel it."

"I felt it, Skye. I still do. If it didn't mean anything to me, I'd have told you to screw off. But it meant so much to me I couldn't tell you to stop texting, even though it hurt so much thinking what we had shared meant nothing to you."

Trent leaned across the arm of his chair. Skye held her

breath and hoped she was right that Trent was about to kiss her. His lips brushed against hers and tingles shot through her body before he placed his lips fully on hers and kissed her deeply. It felt like coming home. It felt right. It felt as if fireworks were exploding. It was like they were the only two people in the world. At least until the front door opened and Tinsley called out, "We're here!"

8

Trent groaned as his cousin walked into his house without knocking. He pulled back enough to look into Skye's eyes. Her eyes mirrored the desire and relief he felt. He should have listened to everyone and cleared the air much sooner. Then they could have had all this time together.

One kiss changed everything. Forgiveness. Understanding. Hope. It was all conveyed in that kiss. Skye smiled at him and cupped his cheek with her hand. "Now we have this settled, promise me to always talk to me first, okay?"

"I promise. The same goes for you. No lies or secrets between us. If something is bothering you or you're scared or have great news—whatever it is, we tell each other."

"Deal." Skye leaned across and kissed him quickly on the lips. "It's even sealed with a kiss."

"Trent! Skye! Are y'all here?" Tinsley called out.

"Back here, Tins," Trent answered without taking his eyes from Skye. "I'm glad you're here."

She smiled and he felt it in his heart. "Me too."

"There you are!" Tinsley appeared with Karri. Trent saw

her eyes go from him to Skye and down to where they were holding hands and then back up to his. "It looks as if y'all have been busy making up while I was getting Karri settled."

"Finally!" Karri said with an exaggerated eye roll that made Skye giggle and Trent chuckle. He'd get Karri alone later and apologize for his rudeness. She'd tried to help him and he'd brushed her off. "Come on, Tinsley said she'll show us around town before we meet with her family at Harper's bar. It used to belong to a pirate!"

"To be fair, most of downtown used to belong to one pirate or another," Trent pointed out.

"I don't remember reading about any of that when I studied for my Anne Bonny role," Skye said as she stood up.

"You probably didn't. Shadows Landing was a pirate safe haven and not really known to most people because they didn't want it known. While we do get some money from tourism, we like our little hideaway," Tinsley told them as they walked out of the house.

Trent pulled out his phone and sent a text to Skeeter, the town's ghost expert. Skeeter knew the history of Shadows Landing by heart, even more so than Stephen Adkins, the local historian.

"I'll drive!" Tinsley called out and Skye instantly reached for the car handle.

"Hey, Karri. Why don't you ride with me?" Trent asked. Now was the perfect time for that apology.

TRENT HAD FORGOTTEN some of the historical facts about the town's founding even though he grew up here. He found himself enjoying Skeeter's tour of downtown Shadows Landing just as much as Skye and Karri were.

"Reverend Winston!" Skeeter called out as they entered

the church. Trent saw the middle-aged clergyman with warm umber skin and his hair in soft coils look up from where he was practicing his sermon.

"Good afternoon. You've brought some new faces with you today. Welcome! I'm Floyd Winston, the pastor here at our beautiful church."

"Thank you," Skye said, smiling as she looked around. "My name is Skye and this is my best friend, Karri. Skeeter has been kind enough to take us on a tour of your town."

"Then he brought you to the right place," Reverend Winston stepped from behind the podium to join them in front of the altar. "I would think that the woman who played Anne Bonny would be particularly interested in the church's history as Anne donated several of the items herself. It's such a shame the screenwriters didn't come here so they'd get their facts right."

Karri hid a laugh under a cough. That sentiment had been expressed by just about everyone Trent had introduced her to today.

Trent slid his hand into Skye's as she looked around the church and asked, "Anne Bonny really was here?"

Skeeter and Reverend Winston shared a laugh. "She wasn't just here. She supplied some of the weapons and signed the decree ceding the church to the town along with Blackbeard, Black Law, Peg Leg Tom, and others. The history of the church is a fascinating one. It was built by the pirates and given to the town with the caveat that they'd be allowed to bring in their booty from the river using secret tunnels under the cemetery and furthermore, that this would always be a sanctuary to all in need, even if they'd broken the law by smuggling."

Reverend Winston turned toward the altar and picked up

a candlestick. There was matching one on the other side of the altar. He turned the candlestick upside down, grabbed the jeweled base, and pulled. A long narrow dagger slid free from inside. "These were donated by Anne Bonny. She believed women should be able to protect themselves. See, when the pirates sailed off to the high seas, the town consisted almost entirely of women and children. The founding pirates didn't want them to be defenseless, so the women were armed. The church still holds an armory and the women of Shadows Landing are still taught self-defense here."

"Fascinating," Karri said, completely engrossed in the story.

Trent felt as if he were hearing this all for the first time, based on Skye's excitement. She and Karri asked questions as Reverend Winston and Skeeter showed them around the church and told them more stories.

Trent's cousin Harper was already texting him that everyone was at the bar by the time they finished the tour of the church.

"Thank you for the tour and the fascinating history. I'd forgotten some of it," Trent said as he shook hands with Reverend Winston.

"Goodness, I'm going to be late for dinner. I look forward to seeing you again on Sunday."

Trent didn't let go of Skye's hand as they walked out of the church. Luckily it was just a short walk across the street to Harper's bar. They were almost at the door when a government SUV pulled up.

"Skye," Trent said to stop her from walking into the bar. "Agent Castle just arrived."

The door to the SUV opened and Agent Peter Castle slid out, his suit wrinkled. Not wrinkled as if it had been balled up and thrown in a corner somewhere, but wrinkled from a long day's work in it.

"I was right," Karri whispered to Skye who nodded in agreement.

"Right about what?" Trent asked.

"That he's hot." Karri fluffed her hair and moistened her lips as she watched the agent cross the street.

Trent looked at him to see what Karri was talking about. Castle was a couple of years older than Trent. He matched Trent's height of a little over six feet and had dark brown hair cut in that typical agent cut. He was clearly in shape. His face was clean-shaven. With the dark sunglasses that matched the dark suit, Trent could understand why Karri was suddenly standing up straighter and looking at him as if he were sex on a stick.

Trent looked at Skye. Instead of preening for Castle, she appeared nervous. Trent gently squeezed her hand. "It's okay. He's a good guy. We all know him and trust him."

Skye nodded but leaned closer to him. Trent dropped her hand and moved his hand to her waist. She leaned all the way against him and Trent felt her body tremble slightly with nerves.

"Hey, Trent. Sorry if I'm late."

"No problem. Peter Castle, this is Skye Jessamine and her best friend, Karri Hill."

Skye held out her hand and shook Peter's, but Trent noticed that Peter's eyes had already turned to look at Karri before he even turned to shake her hand too. "It's nice to meet you both. I was talking to Agent Shaw on my way over here and he's busy trying to track down any kind of surveillance near your house to see if he can find the man who attacked you."

"Thank you. I appreciate all he's doing to find out who's

behind this." Skye took a deep breath and turned to look up at Trent. "Am I right in that your family and everyone in the bar will want to know what Agent Castle has to say?"

"Heck yeah," Skeeter snorted as Trent chuckled.

Tinsley bristled. "That's not true," she paused, looked at the bar, and cringed. "Okay, so it might be true."

Trent glanced behind him and saw half his family in the window watching them.

"It's up to you," Agent Castle told her and Trent was grateful the agent would do what Skye wanted instead of what his family wanted.

"It's okay. You and Agent Castle can go to my house and talk if you'd rather make it private." Trent gave her that option and then left it up to her to decide.

"No, I think I'd rather have everyone hear. They all know why I'm here. This way we can be on the same page."

Trent pulled the old, thick wooden door of the bar and held it open for the group. He heard the welcome shouts from the patrons, but there was no rush for pictures or even a disruption to whatever debate was going on.

Two tables were filled with his family, and they greeted Skye and Karri as they made room for everyone. Trent headed to the bar and asked Georgina to put Skeeter's next two drinks on his tab. Skeeter had refused to charge them for the tour so Trent thought this was a good way to repay him.

"In that case," Skeeter said with a smile as he moved into his regular stool next to Gator and Turtle, "I'll take some of the good stuff."

Trent turned back and saw that Karri was seated next to Castle while Skye was next to her and saving a seat for him. When he sat down, Skye and Karri were telling his family about their tour around town.

Agent Castle cleared his throat and focused the attention to Skye. "I've talked to Agent Shaw in L.A. Your people are pissed off big time that you brought in the FBI. They're spinning these leaks to get you some movie role. They're also pretending they know where you are. So, do they know?"

Skye reached under the table and laced her hand with Trent's. He rested their clasped hands on his thigh as she shook her head. "No. I haven't even looked at my phone. It's turned off, actually. Agent Shaw put some encryption device on it, but I was too worried to even turn it on."

"One sec." Agent Castle pulled out his phone and sent a quick text. A second later he was nodding his head. "You're safe to turn it on. No one can see if you've read an email or received a text. There's no way the phone can be hacked. It's this new program developed by some wonder kid."

Trent felt Skye's knee began to bounce nervously. "Are you sure?"

"Absolutely."

Skye reached into her back pocket and pulled out her phone. She powered it up and the text messages were like a strobe light as they flooded her phone. Each one made Skye's stomach knot a little tighter.

"Geez," Savannah said with a little laugh. "I now don't feel bad about how much I text."

It helped to lighten the mood as Karri turned on her phone and began to stare at the tsunami of emails coming into her account and her own text messages. "My mom has been trying to get in touch with me. I'd better call her and let her know we're okay. Is that safe to do, Agent Castle?"

"Yes. You can use your phone as you normally do without worry of it being traced."

"Thank you," Karri said with a little smile that Skye recognized as Karri's flirtatious smile. Interesting.

"I'd better go with you. You know your mom will have twenty questions for us," Skye pushed back from the table and instantly missed the warmth of Trent's touch.

"Stay close. I'm going to talk to Sheriff Fox about security for you."

"Security?" Skye asked, stopping. "I'll meet you outside, Karri."

"I want someone with you at all times." Agent Castle didn't look as if he'd budge on that and Skye didn't know how she felt about it. In L.A., yes, she wanted that. But here she wanted to be normal. It had been the most perfectly normal day and she'd loved every second.

"I'll be with her," Trent told Agent Castle with a no-argument tone.

Agent Castle looked between them and then to Sheriff Fox who shrugged. "Trent's capable. But," Sheriff Fox paused to get their attention, "any time Trent is busy or unable to be with Miss Jessamine, either Deputy King or I are to be called and will stay with her until Trent's able to take over."

Skye moved to talk but Sheriff Fox slowly shook his head to stop her. "Further, either Deputy King or I will be stopping by numerous times a day to check in."

"I'd go farther than that and ask that Miss Jessamine attach GPS sensors to her purse and phone that will allow me, Agent Shaw, and Sheriff Fox know where you are at all times."

Skye sucked in an angry breath. No narrowed-eyed look from the men was going to keep her quiet now. "Now wait a minute. That's a little much. You know where I will be and who I am with at all times. Do you really need to track me? And isn't that what Agent Shaw took *off* my phone? Won't that just allow someone bad to find me?"

"May I offer a solution that may ease your mind?"

Skye looked over as a man leaned forward from the corner. He was wearing a suit even her agent couldn't afford. His face was sexy in the hard cut of his jaw, but his eyes were just as hard and that made him appear to be a man who wasn't to be messed with.

"Who are you and why should I listen to you?" Skye demanded. She was surprised when his full lips tilted up into a hint of a smile.

"So, you do have some backbone."

"Ryker," Trent snapped and the man shrugged as if the reprimand meant nothing to him. "This is my cousin Ryker Faulkner."

"And, again, why should I listen to you?" Skye asked again, not impressed with his alpha act. She'd been around sleazy, manipulative casting directors and producers. She managed them and she'd manage this man too.

"Because one of my companies is a specialty tech company that works hard to not be known by the general public," he said easily as he laced his fingers together and looked over at her as if she should know what that means.

Skye raised an eyebrow as if saying, *yeah, so?* and was pleased to see the faint smile return to Ryker's lips.

"So that little brand-new program Agent Shaw put on your phone developed by some young wonder kid? That's from my company."

Agent Castle let out a low whistle, but the sheriff looked annoyed. "What the hell, Ryker? Do you not tell us anything anymore?"

"I'm telling you now."

The sheriff flipped him off and Ryker's smile was broad and genuine. Goodness gracious. That man was hotter than sin and looked as if he knew every sin imaginable in the best possible way.

"So, what does this secret tech company have to do with keeping Miss Jessamine safe?" Agent Castle asked.

"We have our own GPS smart trackers. They'll program to her trace DNA. If someone else touches it or tries to remove it, we'll get a notification. They're small, so you can put them in your shoes, your underwear, your phone case, your purse . . . everywhere. You can even swallow one. However, they also have the ability to be turned into a listening and recording device if needed. Either we turn them on and listen, or we can set a perimeter that will automatically alert us and go live with sound should you leave that area. We're also working on voice activation with a select password. That's still in the works, but soon you can say a chosen word and it'll automatically start recording and notify us."

"So, a wire?"

Ryker gave a little snort. "A wire with unlimited range. You could be in France and we could still activate it and listen. These run off of private satellites so distance isn't even a factor."

"That's a little scary," Skye told him with all seriousness. "I don't want people listening to me at any time they want."

"The product isn't known. My team isn't known. Unlike FBI trackers, no one can hack them or will even know they're there. They don't show on scans and aren't subject to jammers. Further, if you place one near your body, like on the inside of your bra strap, I can even program them to set off a notification if your heart rate spikes, such as if you're in danger."

"Or if I'm working out."

Ryker shook his head. "We're a little smarter than that. It won't go off during sex either." Skye knew she blushed, but that didn't stop Ryker from continuing. "If it'll make you feel better, only I will monitor you. If there's any trouble, I can share it with Granger and Castle. I don't know Shaw so I'm not sharing anything with him. Deal?"

"Deal," Castle and Granger quickly said.

"I'll think about it," Skye said. Ryker gave her a slight nod to indicate he knew she was serious about it.

Skye was about to go meet Karri when the front door was flung open and Karri raced inside. "We have a big problem."

9

Skye didn't even have time to ask before Karri was shouting for the entire bar to shut up. Miraculously everyone did. The TVs were turned off, dart games paused, and beer mugs set down. Heck, people even stopped chewing their food. Karri then pressed the unmute button and held the phone out.

"Sorry, I'm back. What were you saying?" Karri asked into the phone. Skye looked at it and saw the caller ID showed that it was Karri's mom.

"Did your order for new fabric come in? I was hoping it would arrive in time for the Hisatuh ceremony. But, I'm sorry, I was telling you before I can't talk right now. Some men from L.A. came to talk about my daughter."

"What about her?" Karri asked.

"They're doing a story on her and Skye's friendship. We're talking about how they met, where they'd travel to on spring breaks, and even the relationship our family and Skye's family have developed. I talked to Skye's mother just a moment ago and she's being interviewed too. Isn't that something? I'm so proud I could burst. Look, I'll see you soon to work on the Hisatuh ceremony. Bye."

Karri hung up and everyone was quiet for a moment except for Agent Castle who looked up at Karri with worry. "If I'm not mistaken, Hisatuh translates into *treacherous little winter* and that ceremony isn't performed this time of year."

Karri's eyes shot open wide. "That's right. It's a warning. The people she's with are treacherous. How did you know that?"

"My grandmother is Oneida."

Skye was just as surprised. Karri's Onondaga Nation was one of the present-day Six Nations. Oneida was another one. "What clan?"

"Bear. I read that you're Wolf."

Karri put her arms across her chest and stared down at him. "You did a background search on me?"

"Of course I did or I wouldn't be very good at my job." Agent Castle turned his gaze to Skye. "Change your mind yet about the trackers?"

"You read my mind. They're looking for me."

"Who is?" Ellery asked into the quiet. "I'm sorry, pregnancy brain. I don't feel as if I'm following."

"I think that's the perfect question," Skye told her. "We don't know who they are or who sent them. However, what they don't know is Karri's mom is horrible at technology and always leaves her laptop open and never covers the camera. So, hotshot, you think your little tech company can get a look inside?"

Ryker's lips turned up into a slow, full smile. Karri cursed under her breath from where she stood next to Skye. "I think I like you, Jessamine."

"Jury's still out on you, hotshot. Let's see what you've got."

. . .

IT TOOK him one text and less than two minutes before they were all looking at a live stream of Mrs. Hill's living room. Two men sat on the couch as Karri's mom fed them food and talked about how sweet Skye and Karri were to her and the entire Onondaga Nation.

"Screen—"

"Already sent it to you," Ryker said as Agent Castle's phone pinged with an incoming text message. "I'm recording this too and will send it to you when they're done talking."

"So, where would Karri and Skye go if they want to unwind?" one of the men asked.

"The beach or for a hike. They love the Redwoods in California. Nature is very important to them both. I'm sorry, gentlemen, but I need to wrap this up. I hope I answered all your questions. Do you have my phone number? You can call if you think of anything else."

"Thank you, Mrs. Hill. We'll do that."

Skye felt her brow crease as she watched the men. "Something seems familiar about them."

"You know them?" Agent Castle asked as the screen went dark and Ryker went back to working on his phone.

"I feel as if I do. Or at least I've seen them before."

"The one on the right is Enzo Bruni and the left is Ace Hinton. They are employed as security experts with Star Power Private Security out of Los Angeles," Ryker read from his phone.

"Wow, okay, hotshot, you earned your name," Skye told him before closing her eyes and thinking. Star Power Private Security. She let her mind go back. "I remember how I know them. They did security for the movie that comes out next month. Did the movie studio hire them because they think I won't do the press tour?"

Ryker typed into his phone and then shook his head. "So far we can't determine who hired them. I'll let you know when I find out."

"They were also the private security Lenny recommended to you for bodyguards," Karri reminded her.

"Do you think it's okay for me to call my family?" Skye asked Agent Castle and Ryker. She didn't know how, but he'd become the head of her security team without even realizing it. At least he was head of her technological security.

"Yes, but don't give any indication of where you are. Not the time it is here, not the season, not the sound of the water. Nothing," Agent Castle informed her.

"Okay. I'll call them right before bed. That way they won't worry about me. They've texted me, and so has my agent, my manager, my PR person, and my lawyer. Oh, and Mason. I guess I didn't have as many friends as I thought."

"How could you?" Karri asked, "Lenny kept you away from everyone. I swear, half the time he probably made up those mean things he says he heard other actresses say about you."

"Should I reply to them?" Skye asked Agent Castle. She didn't want to get into another fight with Karri over this, especially when she was starting to realize that Karri had been right about Lenny manipulating her.

"A simple text that says that you've gotten their messages but need some time to disconnect. Then thank them for giving you your privacy. Isn't that in every PR comment?" Agent Castle asked with a little smile and Skye began to like him even more. It was just snarky enough to let them know she was pissed.

"Do that, and then I think we all need some drinks." Harper stood up and looked over at her and Karri. "What's your drink?"

"I got used to rum and Coke when I was filming Anne's movie. That feels appropriate today," Skye said as she wrote out the text and began to copy and paste it to her team.

"Sounds good to me too," Karri said, and then the whole table heard her belly rumble.

"I'll order some barbeque from The Pink Pig too," Harper said with a wink to Karri.

"Don't you have food here?" Karri asked as she handed her phone over to Agent Castle. "Here, go through these and see if anything looks interesting."

Karri walked off with Harper, who was talking about how she wanted to serve bar food but only has part-time help on the weekends so that's when she does it. Skye didn't need to see her friend to know Karri's mind was already on food she could make here without the dietary restrictions Skye was supposed to be following.

"They're all writing back demanding to know where I am," Skye said with a tired sigh. This had been her life because *they* had been her life. Now she didn't even want to talk to them. The other night at her house had pissed her off beyond belief. She'd been threatened over a movie role and now she'd begun to see past manipulations. She was trying to take control over her own life now and someone was trying to stop her from doing that. As far as she was concerned, all of Hollywood could shove it at this point.

"Don't respond," Castle told her and then leaned forward. "So, I didn't see anything about a boyfriend when I ran Karri's background."

Skye put down her phone and turned her attention to Agent Castle. "That's because Karri doesn't have one. So, you're Oneida? Do you visit the area around Seneca Falls in New York much?"

"According to my grandma, not as much as I should. My mother isn't a member, and I grew up away from my grandma. We're close, but not as close as if I'd been able to live nearer. Then, being with the FBI, I've traveled around too." Skye really looked at Agent Castle. He was attractive. He was strong. He was smart. He was calm under pressure or he wouldn't be the head of the Charleston office. Skye glanced at the bar and saw Karri peeking over to catch glimpses of him. Interesting indeed.

"What about you? Girlfriend?"

"I broke up with my last girlfriend about eight months ago."

Skye leaned forward as the table talked around them. "So, what do you want to know about Karri?"

TWO HOURS later Skye was stuffed with the best barbeque she'd ever tasted in her whole life and more than a few drinks. She'd hugged Karri goodnight before Tinsley drove her home.

Trent followed behind Tinsley's car, but pulled off into his driveway. Skye took a deep breath of air filled with the scents of fresh moss, flowers, and a hint of salt. She had put away her phone and gotten lost in the night with her new friends as all the tension melted away.

Ryker told her he'd be back tomorrow with what he needed to get her set up. Until then, she was determined not to fall into a pointless cycle of *what-ifs* and simply enjoy the night. Tomorrow was soon enough to let reality back in.

"I'm going to call my parents," Skye told Trent as she crawled onto the large porch swing.

"I'll grab us some fresh apple cider and meet you back out here."

"Thanks. That sounds great." Skye waited until Trent went inside and then called her mother's cell phone.

It rang and rang and Skye was worried her mom wouldn't pick up when she finally heard a hesitant, "Hello?"

"Hi, Mom!"

"Baby! Oh my gosh, what is going on? Why are you calling from an unknown number? There are men here, baby. They said they were reporters but reporters don't have guns on under their suit jackets."

Skye's heart fell and reality crashed into her like a ton of bricks. "Karri talked to her mom and she said the same, minus the guns. Are you okay? Did they hurt you?"

"I'm fine. Karri's mom gave me the heads up right as they pulled up to the house so I pretended you were still in L.A. Are you in L.A.?"

Skye hated not answering her mother, but now, more than ever she had a reason to do exactly what Agent Castle had told her to do. "I can't say. Just know I'm safe. Did you get a picture of the men who talked to you?"

She heard her mother sigh and heard her father tell her to put it on speaker. "Baby, are you okay?"

"I'm safe and unharmed, Dad. That's all I can say right now. Did either of you get a photo of the guys who came to visit you?" Skye asked again. Maybe Ryker and his mystery wonder kid could find out who these guys were too.

"No," her mother said. "I was too nervous trying to pretend that I wasn't nervous to even think about it."

"I grabbed a picture of the license plate as I drove the tractor by," her dad told her and Skye's heart rate picked back up.

"What is it?" Skye asked, moving her phone to speaker

and pulling up a text to Trent. She typed in the plate number, the make, and the model of the SUV they were driving and then sent it to Trent.

"Skye," her mother said the second her father stopped talking. "What is going on?"

Skye leaned back against the cushions and sighed. "I wish I knew. I'll find out though. I have my phone so you can still reach me. Let me know if the men come back or if anyone calls you."

"Call us?" Her mother said with a serious laugh that showed it wasn't funny at all. "We've been getting calls from Lenny and Jim almost every hour. I can't believe that they don't know where you are. Half the time I can't even get in touch with you because of the stranglehold they have on you."

"Wait, what?" Skye asked, sitting up quickly as Trent walked out the door with two mugs of hot apple cider and a blanket over his arm. His phone was also in his hand and his brow was creased in a way that said he knew something was up and he was trying to figure it out.

Skye held out the phone and pressed speaker once again. "What do you mean, Lenny and Jim put a stranglehold on me so that half the time you couldn't get in touch with me?"

The line was quiet and then her father cleared his throat. "Well, most of the time we'd call and he'd answer your phone and tell us you weren't available. And we came to surprise you for your birthday when you were on set and he turned us away. He said you were too busy and in the middle of a really important scene and that we'd be a distraction."

Skye would have dropped the phone if Trent hadn't reached out to take it from her. He sat down next to her and put a supportive arm around her. "I didn't know. I swear. I always want to talk to you or see you."

Skye's mother gave a relieved sob and Skye's heart broke at the sound of her father comforting her. Skye turned her head slightly to see Trent's jaw tight in anger. He too had his own bone to pick with Lenny. Skye had felt controlled and manipulated, but this was worse that she ever imagined.

"Mom, Dad, I promise I'll get to the bottom of all this. I'm safe, but I'm not sitting back doing nothing. I'm done letting other people control me."

"There's my girl," her father said with pride. "You give 'em hell, and if you need us we will come to you any time, anywhere."

"We love you with all our hearts and you know, the farm is big enough to bury some bodies. Shoot, we can feed them to the pigs if we have to. Although, I have to admit, that'd be really gross."

Skye felt the first tear fall as she laughed. "Thanks, Mom. You two are the best. I'll call or text soon, okay?"

"Okay. Goodnight, sweetheart. We love you," her mother said before the line went dead.

Trent reached over to hang up the phone and then set it down. Instantly she was in his arms and pulled onto his lap. He didn't say anything. He just held her as she cried. "I can't believe Lenny did that to my own parents and I never realized."

Trent was quiet for a second, but then said what she'd been thinking. "He's an asshole."

Skye nodded against Trent's strong chest. She took a deep breath to center herself. "I don't like who I've become."

"Skye, you're an exceptional woman who has accomplished a lot in a very short time. How old are you?"

"Twenty-nine."

"And how long have you been acting?" Trent asked, already knowing the answer.

"Seven years." Skye took a deep breath to calm herself. "It's not a professional thing. I know I'm a damn good actress. What I'm talking about is the farm girl who got into college on a lacrosse scholarship. The girl who took no shit from anyone. The girl who knew what she wanted and went after it, but was always there to be a friend to someone who needed one. *That's* what I lost. My independence. I don't make my own choices anymore, not even what shirt to wear or what kind of car to drive. The second the spotlight shined on me, everything changed."

Skye finally felt good talking about it, but she knew many would kill for what she had. She was proud of what she'd accomplished, but she'd started off on her own and somewhere along the way she'd gotten lost in the blinding bright lights.

"What's stopping you from taking back control?" Trent asked. It was a simple question, but the answer wasn't so simple. Or was it?

10

Trent handed Skye the hot cider as he held on to her. She fit so perfectly in his arms that he never wanted to let her go. She'd been quiet since he'd asked about taking control over her life. She'd laid her head on his shoulder and he could practically hear the thoughts racing through her mind.

He didn't push her to talk. Trent knew she needed this time to think things through. Instead, he handed her the cider and let her sip it, holding her as he slowly ran his hand up and down her arm. Trent's own thoughts turned to Skye's situation. He had talked to Aunt Gemma numerous times and there were never any stories of paparazzi or scandal. Of course, Aunt Gemma was an author, not an actress, and Uncle Cy would kill anyone who dared look at his wife the wrong way.

Trent's mind kept going back to Lenny. He was the gatekeeper. He was the one who turned Trent away, the one who turned Mr. and Mrs. Jessamine away, and as Skye's personal manager, he had his hand in every aspect of her life. Could it be as simple as firing Lenny?

"Thank you, Trent," Skye said as she sat up. She leaned

back so she could look at him as she spoke. Trent's eyes dipped to her lips and then made their way back to her eyes. She was hurting and he felt bad for even thinking about how kissable she was. Memories from their night together flooded him, but he pushed back against them to stem the tide. He needed to focus on her needs, not his wants.

"For what?" Trent asked as he moved his arms around her waist and linked his fingers together.

"For reminding me that the power is within my reach. I just have to take hold of it. I can still get great roles without whoring myself out to the likes of Tony Ketron. There are tons of A-list celebrities who maintain a private life. It's time for me to stop sitting back and acting the part of a trained circus animal. I'm going to talk to Karri in the morning and start taking back my life."

Skye leaned forward and placed a lingering kiss on his cheek. He felt her warm lips and his whole body responded. Trent wondered if Skye felt that spark too when her hands came up to touch him. It was even better than their one night together. This connection they had ran deeper than he thought either of them could understand.

Skye rested one hand on his chest and he knew she felt his heartbeat as her fingers splayed out and pressed into his muscles. Her other hand slid behind his neck as she absently ran her fingers through his hair. Then she looked up at him in such an intense way that Trent felt as if she were trying to read his soul.

"I'm not running, Skye. Not ever again."

"Good. I'd hate to chase you down and club you over the head. You'd be heavy to drag back home." Skye deadpanned as Trent's lips tilted up into a grin.

"You can drag me home any time you want. No concussion necessary."

Skye shimmied off his lap and stood up. Trent looked up at her and he knew his life was about to change. They'd moved fast last time, but not this time. If this feeling of forever was true, then Trent was going to take his time doing it right. He'd been given a second chance and he wasn't going to ruin it.

"Tired?" Trent asked as he picked up their now empty mugs.

Skye yawned in response and slapped her hand over her mouth. "That wasn't very romantic," she laughed afterward.

"Come on," Trent said as he stood and took her hand in his. "Let's get you to bed."

He knew it wasn't the kind of bed Skye had intended when he took her to her guest room. Instead, he told her he'd be back after she got ready. Trent trotted down the stairs and got two glasses of water before heading back upstairs and into his bedroom. He stripped off his clothes and pulled on a pair of lounge pants that hung low on his hips before he brushed his teeth and washed his face.

When Trent knocked on Skye's door, he heard her call for him to enter. She was sitting on the edge of the bed in an old Syracuse lacrosse shirt that stopped at the top of her thighs. She was so beautiful it almost knocked him over. Beauty wasn't red carpet fashion. Beauty was a freshly washed face in nothing but a T-shirt. Skye's long hair hung loose and she had one leg tucked under the other. Her bare leg swung gently as she waited for him.

Trent didn't miss the way her eyes traveled over his bare chest and downward. Taking a deep breath, Trent did the hardest thing he'd ever done before. He walked over to Skye, leaned down, and placed a sweet kiss to her lips before pulling back the covers. Skye slid underneath them and silently watched him move around the room turning off the lights. Trent grabbed the blanket on the back of a chair and walked over to the bed.

Skye rolled over onto her side and watched as he lay down on top of the comforter with the blanket. "I'm not *that* tired," Skye said with a little laugh as Trent rolled onto his side to face her.

He studied the way moonlight caressed her face and reached out for Skye. She immediately snuggled closer to him. Trent held her as she used his arm for a pillow. "Our relationship always seems rushed. I don't want to rush. I want to savor. So, how badly are you missing your sushi?"

He felt Skye laugh against him as they talked. As the hours went by, the moonlight traveled across her face, down her body, and when they finally fell asleep, dawn began to glow through the window.

∾

Skye stretched as she slowly cracked her eyes open. She immediately reached out for Trent and sat up quickly when she didn't feel him next to her. They'd stayed up all night talking. Talking to Trent was almost as good as foreplay. Almost. He listened, he asked questions, and he laughed at all her silly little stories. She felt valued and that was beyond sexy.

Skye looked around and slid from the bed. The air was a little chilly, but nothing the blanket Trent had slept under couldn't help. She grabbed it and wrapped it around her shoulders like a shawl before heading downstairs. "Trent?"

Skye paused and listened. In the distance she heard machinery and knew where he was. She didn't bother with shoes as she hopped out the back door and walked over to his workshop.

The door was cracked and she leaned forward to look inside without disturbing him. She saw him in his work clothes of jeans and flannel shirt. He had on goggles and gloves as he maneuvered a large saw. Skye was so engrossed in watching him work she didn't hear the people approaching behind her.

"I remember having a butt like that. I miss that butt."

Skye spun around to find Miss Ruby and Miss Winnie standing there holding two baskets of food.

"You could get them butt implants," Miss Ruby said to Miss Winnie.

Miss Winnie's face perked up as Skye tried to move the blanket to cover herself more. "I could get a personal trainer. You think your trainer would get my butt back?"

Skye tried not to laugh since she couldn't tell if Miss Winnie was joking or not. "I'll fly him out here for you when this is all over."

"Aren't you a doll?" Miss Winnie looked so excited that Skye found herself deciding she would actually do it for Miss Winnie. She wondered what Julio would think of training an eighty-year-old woman who strongly resembled a plucked chicken. "We brought you some food. Just ignore the pile of pies and cakes by the front door and start with ours. After all, we know we'll win the bake-off."

Miss Ruby nodded and looked Skye over. "You could do with some meat on your bones." Well, that was the first time since she went to Hollywood that she'd been told *that*. "We also know how Trent can get when he's working and we didn't want you to starve to death so we brought you more than just apple pie."

Skye reached out and took the baskets from the ladies. "Thank you. You both are so kind."

"Pish posh. We have ulterior motives," Miss Ruby told her.

Miss Winnie bobbed her head. "We told Mitzy Coburn we could get you to come to knitting club tomorrow. She didn't believe us, but my apple pie has been known to make people do all sorts of things."

"That's right," Miss Ruby said with certainty. "It's been known to make people strip down naked and take selfie pictures with it. We figured it could get you to knitting club."

"Knitting club? I don't know how to knit."

"Don't worry about that," Miss Winnie told her with a dismissive wave of her hand. "While we all knit, we also have some drinks and gossip. That's the real point of knitting club. And it's not all old ladies. Why, Edie Wecker will be there and I believe you've met her. She's a friend of the Faulkners."

Skye tried to remember not only everyone she'd met, but also everyone Trent had talked about. "Is she the widow?"

"Bless her heart, they were so in love and then her husband was murdered on a mission for the SEALS. She came back home and we take care of our own. We got her into the knitting club and she's thriving. Hog-tied a man earlier this year and everything," Miss Ruby explained. "Knitting club can be empowering."

"Well, maybe I can learn how to knit scarves for my parents," Skye said, not really knowing how to address the hog-tying comment so she just let it slide.

"Yes! We'd be happy to teach you and your friend Karri. Have Trent or Tinsley drop you off at five tomorrow night at the church," Miss Ruby instructed.

"I'll see you then. Thank you for the food," Skye told them as the duo waved their goodbyes.

Skye looked into the shop. Trent was still working and looked as if he were in the zone. His gaze never wavered from his work as he slowly carved pieces of wood into the vision he had in his head.

The aroma of apple pie was strong enough to distract her from Trent. Skye glanced down at the baskets and then checked her surroundings. No one would know. She hurried to the kitchen and opened up the baskets. She pulled out a casserole, some fried chicken, and homemade mac and cheese before she found what she was looking for—the apple pie.

Skye placed it on the kitchen table reverently and went in search of a plate, knife, and fork. She hadn't had dessert for breakfast since college. It had been too long since she'd indulged and, after all, Miss Ruby did say she needed meat on her bones.

Skye cut a large slice and looked around as if she were breaking the law. When she saw Trent was still in his workshop, she dug in. Apples, sugar, and cinnamon exploded on her tongue and she moaned as if she were climaxing. Goodness, they weren't lying about the powers of their apple pie.

Skye was halfway through when she heard a gasp.

"Do you know how much sugar that has in it?"

Skye turned her head and took a deliberate bite as Karri stared in surprise. "I don't care. If I never get another role in my life but have this apple pie, I can die happy."

"Oh, is that Miss Ruby's or Miss Winnie's?" Tinsley asked, stepping past Karri and cutting herself her own slice.

"I don't know and I don't care so long as I get more."

Skye held out her fork to Karri who looked as if she'd just caught her lover cheating on her. She rolled her eyes and grabbed the fork. "It can't be *that* special. An apple pie is an apple pie. I mean, I grew up in apple country."

Skye looked at Tinsley and they shared a grin. This was not some average apple pie. Karri looked annoyed at even having to take a bite. Then her eyes flew open in surprise before she closed them and moaned with pleasure. Her eyes popped back open as Skye and Tinsley giggled.

"So, just a regular apple pie, right?" Skye teased.

"I feel as if I just had a very intimate experience with that pie. I have to get the recipe. And you're right. It's worth every pound it puts on you." Karri rushed forward and sliced a large piece for herself.

Skye finished her last bite and looked at the pie. Would it really hurt to have another slice?

"Is that apple pie?"

Skye looked up as the back door opened. Trent and Ryker walked inside. She decided right then she wasn't going to give up her second slice to Trent, no matter how much she was falling for him.

Skye placed a second slice on her plate and grinned up at the men after claiming her pie. "Miss Ruby and Miss Winnie dropped it off."

Trent grabbed two more plates and cut slices for himself and Ryker. "What did you have to do for it?" Skye looked up as Trent sat next to her. "Unless you're lucky, there's usually something attached to it. They want to know your secrets? They want to be in your next movie? They want to know about our relationship?"

Tinsley's head snapped up from where she was licking the plate. "Relationship? I'd like to know the answer to that."

Skye turned to Trent and blinked innocently. "So would I."

"I like you enough to share my apple pie with you."

Trent grinned and held out his fork with a big hunk of pie on it.

"Should we book the church?" Ryker asked so dryly that Skye couldn't tell if he were joking or not. It was only Trent's smirk at him that told her that Ryker had actually cracked a joke. "Want to give me your phone, purse, clothes, and shoes so I can get your GPS trackers on?"

Skye ran upstairs and grabbed her bag. When she came back downstairs, she found Ryker threading a needle. "Are you seriously going to sew these yourself, hotshot?"

Ryker just glanced up as he pulled the thread through the needle and held out his hand. Skye shrugged and handed over her bag. She was used to designers, stylists, and photographers handling not only her clothes, but also her body. Ryker pulling out her bra wasn't embarrassing to her. Trent, on the other hand, looked as if he wanted to snatch the bra from his cousin's hand.

Tinsley cleared her throat and then looked over to Skye. "How are you handling work while you're here? Or do you just have downtime between films. I don't know how that works."

Karri groaned and pulled out her phone. "I guess I'd better check. I had rescheduled some meetings the other day. Then I've told others that Skye has laryngitis and needs to do all interviews via email. Usually she's very busy with promotion, auditions, and meetings."

Tinsley looked to her with sympathy. "Are you missing many auditions?"

"A few, but they weren't for parts I wanted." Skye didn't feel guilty about it either. "My team wants me to be in every movie—even better if it's a franchise. It doesn't matter if I hate the role. I want to audition for your aunt's movie. Gemma Davies's newest book is being turned into a movie, but my team wants me in this Tony Ketron film instead. I'm going to reach out to the casting director and see if they'll let me audition via video conference."

Karri cursed and everyone at the table stopped what they were doing, even Ryker. No one said anything as Karri read an email on her phone. Skye's heart felt as if it were in a vise being squeezed tighter and tighter the more Karri frowned.

"We have a problem," Karri finally said, looking up at the table full of people.

11

Trent had lost all sense of time until Ryker had come to his barn. He'd spent half the night talking to Skye and the other half holding her in his arms. The emotions it triggered had him slipping from the bed early this morning and into his shop. One of his clients had wanted a romantic feel for their bedroom furniture. Trent woke up that morning knowing exactly what to make.

Then he'd had an enjoyable time eating pie for breakfast and laughing with Skye, Karri, and his family. However, those four little words, "we have a problem," stopped all the happiness he was feeling. His hand went straight to Skye's as they looked at Karri with dreaded anticipation.

She finally looked up from the phone. Her eyes that had always been a bright warm brown were now dark and cold. Anger radiated from every inch of her body. "It's not just one thing. Every interview request has changed from talking about your career to talking about the nude leaks. Apparently, Bernie isn't even trying to get them taken down now. He says it's out there and there's nothing to be done. Lenny is pissed you're not responding to him. Rebecca is following Bernie's lead and spinning the PR to embrace the leaked photos as test shots for Tony's movie."

Trent felt Skye go rigid under his hand. The slight tremor that ran through her body broke his heart. "Wait, are you saying your own lawyer won't go after the places publishing the illegally obtained photos?"

Karri and Skye nodded. Karri looked ready to kill someone, but Skye looked ready to crumble. Then she sucked in a deep breath and lifted her chin. When she looked around the table, her kind eyes had transformed. He almost didn't recognize the resolute person next to him. "Does anyone know a good lawyer? I'm tired of not having control of my life. The first step is to get rid of Bernie and go after every website, magazine, and television station that put up my photo."

She might look cold and hard, but Trent had been wrong. It wasn't coldness from shutting down. No, it was steely resolve. Skye was preparing to break free. Trent turned to Ryker as he put down one of Skye's bras that now had a GPS unit in it. "What about Olivia?"

"Who's Olivia?" Skye asked immediately.

"Olivia Townsend is one of my lawyers," Ryker said, not looking up as he typed into his phone. "We'll meet at Harper's for lunch."

"I don't need an elite corporate lawyer. I need a down and dirty ballbuster." Skye's body started to vibrate with anger under Trent's hand. "No. Not just a ballbuster, but someone who will castrate everyone involved and shove their balls down their throats."

Ryker looked up from the shoe he was now sewing the GPS unit into. "I think I was mistaken about you, Jessamine." Tinsley blinked in surprise along with Trent. Ryker didn't admit to being wrong—ever. "Also, you'll love

Olivia. If she didn't know how to rip a man to pieces leaving him crying in a huddled mess on the floor, she wouldn't be one of my lawyers. I never play nice. Never."

Trent was sure Olivia could help but then it struck him. "Won't people know Skye is near Charleston if Olivia represents her?"

"Olivia is in the New York office this month finalizing a big deal for me. She's getting on a private jet as we speak. All addresses and phone numbers will be from the New York office," Ryker told him as he moved onto a pair of jeans. "Bring everything you have to the bar. Every copy of a contract, every email, everything."

Trent saw Karri working on her phone and then turned the phone around. A picture of Olivia filled the screen. She wore a blood-red suit and pristine white blouse. Her arms were crossed over her chest and her lipstick matched the suit. Her blonde hair was blown out, giving her a softness that hid the tough-as-nails interior. "Is this her?"

"Yes," Trent told her with a nod.

"She's so pretty and nice looking," Skye said as she studied the picture. Ryker snorted. "You're sure she—"

"Yes," Trent, Ryker, and Tinsley said at the same time.

"Okay then," Skye said. "I look forward to meeting her. What do we do in the meantime?"

"Savannah suggested we stroll downtown and maybe stop at Bless Your Scarf Boutique. She thought you might not stick out as much in some local clothing. The blonder hair does help, but the clothes will too," Tinsley suggested.

"Sounds fun," Skye said as Trent thought about what she'd been wearing. He didn't know clothes, but he knew she needed at least one University of South Carolina or Clemson T-shirt and also one of those sundresses the women all wore. Then with a hat and some sunglasses, Skye would blend in rather well as a local.

"I'll text the girls now. Plus, Darcy found some cool new sunken treasure that has just arrived and said she'd give us first look at it," Tinsley told them as Skye stood up.

"I'll run and change. This sounds fun. We'll meet you all at the bar at noon," Skye said before she hurried upstairs.

"How bad is it really?" Trent asked Karri.

"I don't know what you mean," Karri tried to respond innocently, but Trent and Ryker nailed her with a disbelieving look.

"I know there's more. So, what's really going on?" Trent asked Karri again.

"How could you know that?" Karri was trying to avoid answering Trent's question and that alone told him there was more to it.

"When you sit back and watch instead of participate in every conversation, you notice things. Things like the way your fingers tightened on the phone when you were reading the emails before you even got to the one about the photos," Trent told her.

"What he said," Ryker grumbled as he used his teeth to bite off the thread. "Tinsley, take these to Skye and have her wear this bra and these shoes today. They're all ready for her."

Tinsley got up and called to Skye. Now it was just Ryker, Trent, and Karri in the room. Trent crossed his arms and leaned back in his chair waiting.

Karri huffed as she flopped back in the kitchen chair. "It's not just Bernie. The whole team is going rogue and I don't know if I can stop them. I don't know if anyone can. Rebecca, the head of PR, is telling news outlets that Skye is unavailable because she is in the hospital due to exhaustion.

That's code for drug overdose. That's how they're explaining her absence. Then Tony Ketron emailed demanding Skye wax until she's completely bare down there because she's too disgusting to be in his movie until she's quote: 'shined and buffed.' Then he offered to do it for her to get it just right for the movie, so they capture the artistic purpose of the movie correctly." Karri rolled her eyes.

Trent felt like breaking the table in half. Even Ryker looked affected. Trent looked to his cousin. "Olivia handles it or I will," Trent said to Ryker through his clenched jaw.

"She will or I'll help you take them all down."

Trent looked up at Ryker and saw that he wasn't just saying it. Ryker was ready to take down Hollywood right along with him. "Thanks, cousin."

Ryker nodded his head in response and slid back in his chair to stand up. "I have a conference call. Karri, why don't you tell Castle and Granger of our appointment with Olivia? I'll see you both at noon."

Ryker strode out the door and it was Karri's turn to pin Trent with a look. "You care for her, don't you?"

"Yes," Trent answered instantly.

Karri nodded and went to work on her phone. "Agent Castle and Sheriff Fox will meet us at noon. Agent Castle asked for Low Country. What does that mean?"

"There are two barbeque places here: Low Country and the Pink Pig."

"It'll be hard to beat the Pink Pig. That was really good. But there's no burger place or something like that?"

Trent shook his head. "We have the diner. They have a burger, but it's nothing special. Mostly it's Low Country cooking. Shrimp and grits, gator—"

"Alligator?"

"It's fantastic. You deep-fry it and put it on a salad and

you'll never be the same again," Trent told her as they heard Tinsley and Skye walking down the stairs.

Karri leaned forward and dropped her voice. "For what it's worth, I think you're good for each other. You count her celebrity as a negative. And while that's a refreshing take from a guy, it's also an inescapable fact of life for her, it's never going away. You need to find a way to reconcile that if you wish to move forward with Skye."

Karri left Trent with a lot to think about as the women went into downtown with Kord ready to trail behind them. Karri was right. As much as he loved being with Skye, he wasn't experiencing her daily life. She was experiencing his. For him to know if they'd be able to have everything he'd been thinking about, he needed to stop tethering her to Shadows Landing. If he did that, he was just as bad as Lenny and the others trying to force Skye to be something she wasn't. It was time to let Skye fly and see if they could soar into the future together or if it was just her time to shine.

12

Skye had a blast at Bless Your Scarf. She ended up with two dresses, a sweatshirt, cute lounge pants, a college ball cap, and a handful of accessories. The group had grown to include Ellery and Darcy as they went to Darcy's museum. Kord was with them, but he'd blended into the background and she'd completely forgotten about him until they left the store and he trailed after them.

Darcy told Skye and Karri about how she met her husband, Trent's brother, Wade, and how they had discovered one of the largest sunken treasures ever to be found. Skye stared in wonder at the jewels, the ancient trunks they'd filled, and the pictures of the sunken pirate ship. Darcy was a badass. There was a movie right there. While Wade played a role, it was Darcy who was the heroine of her own story. But then Darcy also told them about Olivia Townsend and how she'd helped them.

"I wonder how she feels about public castration?" Skye mused absently. Ellery snickered and Savannah blinked in surprise.

Darcy laughed as Karri shook her head. "What is it about you and men's balls?"

"I have a better question," Skye continued as they walked down the street toward Tinsley's gallery. "I mean, we kick a guy in the balls, roast his balls, cut off his balls, feed him his balls . . ."

Karri groaned and rolled her eyes, causing everyone to crack up. "Again with the balls. What's your question? If we can deep-fry them?"

"Sure you can," Darcy said with a nod. "What do you think Rocky Mountain oysters are?"

A collective groan went up among the ladies before they broke out in laughter at the strangeness of the conversation.

"See, this is my question," Skye said through the laughter. She was having a great time. She couldn't remember the last time she had more than just Karri to laugh with. "What about women?"

Ellery cocked her head. "What about women? Aren't they busy cutting off and deep-frying said balls?"

Skye giggled again and shook her head. "I mean, what's the equivalent for a woman? Deep-fried boobies?"

Everyone stared at her and Skye wondered if she'd been too much herself with her new friends, especially when Ellery clutched her belly. But instead of chiding her, Ellery laughed. In fact, she laughed so hard, her little rounded belly bounced. Tears sprang from her eyes as she used one hand to grab onto Savannah who was next to her.

Karri took a deep breath and held up her hands in surrender. "Okay, that was a legit question."

"Right? See, if I want Olivia to go after Rebecca, do I tell her I want her to punch her in the tits? It just doesn't have the same effect." Skye looked over at the building that housed Tinsley's studio and gallery on the first floor and

Savannah's interior design company on the second. Skye glanced inside the window and all laughter stopped. "Is that new?"

Tinsley looked through the gallery window and nodded before unlocking her door. "I just hung it last night. Do you like it?"

Skye took in the painting, full of color. It wasn't fully abstract, but the knifing technique used to provide texture gave it that appearance. She could make out grass, the large oak trees festooned with Spanish moss, water, a vibrant evening sky, and then what looked like a sailboat. Along the shore were people and boxes that shone with jewel tones.

"Oh, Tinsley," Savannah gasped.

"It's stunning," Ellery told Tinsley seriously.

Meanwhile, Tinsley looked embarrassed at the attention. She shouldn't be. The large piece spoke to Skye and she instantly knew what it was. "This is how Shadows Landing started, isn't it?"

"It is," Tinsley said, opening the door so they all go inside to see the painting closer.

"It reminds me of one of those live photos where everyone is moving just a little and they freeze for the perfect picture," Skye told Tinsley, hoping she was explaining it well. "It looks like they're somehow frozen in motion, if that makes sense. I wouldn't be surprised to see the tree branches swaying."

"Thank you. These were the paintings that sold best in Paris, and I have to admit they're the ones I have the most fun making. I love being inspired by what's around me," Tinsley told the group as they all praised the painting.

Skye walked around the gallery and was drawn to several of the pieces. The watercolors were in soft contrast to the knifing work, but they both seemed to reach out and grab Skye.

"Tinsley," Skye said quietly as she drew Tinsley aside. "When I have access to my accounts again, I want to buy several of these. Would you mind holding them? I can put some cash down for a deposit or I have a watch that's worth fifty thousand dollars you can hold on to. I have the cash with me now, but I'd prefer to hold on to it since I need to pay Olivia."

"You don't have to buy anything," Tinsley protested.

"Tinsley, I know I don't have to. I want to. They speak to me. They reach out and pull me in. It's not a choice. I have to buy them. I promise I'm good for the money."

Tinsley laughed then and nodded. "I have a good idea of much you make from the papers, so I know you're good for it. Show me what you want and I'll put a Sold sticker next to them."

Skye put the last sticker on when the sound of an approaching helicopter echoed down Main Street. Darcy looked out the window and then back at the group. "Olivia's here."

"Good, I'm starving and some barbeque sounds delicious," Ellery said, making a beeline for the door.

Skye followed the group out the door. Karri looked at the town as if she were contemplating something. "What is it?" Skye finally asked after Karri started murmuring to herself.

"Nothing, it's silly."

"I talked about balls for ten minutes. Nothing you can say is possibly as silly. What is it?" Skye prodded.

"I love being your chef, but what was my dream?"

"To have your own kitchen. I'm sorry. I know I've been holding you back." Skye knew it was true the moment she said it. At first Karri had worked with her to use it as experience on her résumé. But then Skye's career took off and Karri turned into a full-time chef and a personal assistant. They'd been going nonstop since then and Skye felt like the absolute worst friend for not letting Karri chase her own dreams.

Karri shook her head. "You know me well enough to know I would leave if I wasn't happy. However," she said, pausing and looking around the town, "I like it here. I like the people, the slow pace of life, and the fact that eating apple pie is X-rated. It's not pretentious here."

"No, it's a lot of things, but pretentious is not one of them. I like it here too," Skye admitted.

"There are no good places to eat something besides barbeque and diner food. I wonder what would happen if I asked Harper to let me cook a few nights at the bar?"

"That's not exactly fine dining, Karri."

Karri shook her head. "I know. L.A. is upscale. Here it's not about price of the food to show off, but the taste of it. I've been flooded with ideas for menus since I arrived."

"Then ask her. Or I can ask Trent if he thinks Harper would be up for it."

"Let me think on it some more." Karri looked down the street and her mouth dropped. "That's your lawyer? She was gorgeous in the online photo, but here she looks as if she should be walking a catwalk."

The helicopter was in the intersection at the end of Main Street. Olivia Townsend was strutting toward them in high heels and a tight, royal blue pencil skirt. Her white blouse fluttered in the wind created by the helicopter blades, but her hair didn't dare move.

"She sure does."

Skye looked over her shoulder to find Kord, Granger, and Peter Castle standing behind them.

Granger rolled his eyes at his deputy who was practically drooling. "I'm going to laugh my ass off when some woman knocks you on *your* ass and then leads you on a merry chase."

"Likewise," Kord said with a grin to his boss. "Here, Olivia. Let me help you." Kord took off at a slow jog to meet the lawyer and take her briefcase from her.

"Is there romance brewing there?" Skye asked as she then noticed the meaningful glances and blushes flying between Peter and Karri. Well, well, well.

Granger grunted and opened the door for Skye to walk through. Boy, was Hollywood getting it wrong! Granger was old Hollywood. Back when men weren't juiced up on steroids or dressed in joggers and loose T-shirts that didn't look as if they'd been washed. No, the men of Shadows Landing— Trent, Granger, Ryker, Castle, Kord—reminded her of the men of the past; just as the town itself was a throwback to the past. These men reminded her of the old western stars who rode a horse, shot a gun, and escorted a lady across the street while looking ruggedly handsome at the same time.

Something about that and seeing Tinsley's painting had all the creative juices flowing. Skye pulled out her phone and did a quick note to herself about some ideas for movie roles to keep an eye open for. Olivia was standing behind her and Trent was next to her by the time she was done with her notes.

"You looked deep in thought," Trent said, lowering his voice. "Is everything okay?"

"More than okay. I've been inspired. I know how I want

to approach my audition for Gemma Davies's film. I sent an email to the casting director this morning and should hear back soon."

"That's great. Are you sure you don't want me to put in a word with my aunt?"

"I'm sure. I'm going to get that role, and I'm going to get it on my own."

Trent nodded his head in acknowledgment before turning to Olivia, who was shaking hands with Ryker. "Olivia, this is Skye Jessamine. Skye, this is Olivia Townsend."

"Thank you for coming," Skye told her. "Before we begin, do you feel capable of castrating any man standing in my way?"

Olivia didn't blink. Her eyebrows didn't so much as twitch. "I have a dull knife I use to make sure it hurts more."

"And what about women who are in my way?" Skye asked.

"I punch them in the tit with rings on so it hurts even more."

The men looked uncomfortable, but the women broke out in laughter. Skye grinned and only then did Olivia let loose with a smile of her own. "You're hired."

"Excellent. This is going to be fun." Olivia took a seat at the table and pulled out a contract. Skye read it over. Her eyes blinked twice at the retainer fee, but if Olivia could fix these problems, she'd pay double. She signed it and handed it back to Olivia.

"Excellent. I looked over all the documents Karri sent me. My first question: did you ever sign an agreement with your lawyer? I didn't see it anywhere."

Skye shook her head. "Jim, my agent, hired him. In fact, Jim hired everyone." Olivia frowned, then pulled out a piece of paper and handed it to her. "With your permission, I'll email this to him immediately."

It was a letter of termination of representation. Skye picked up the pen Olivia handed her and signed it. Olivia pulled out a little wireless scanner and scanned the document. Seconds later it was sent.

"Now, let's get those photos down and scare the shit out of anyone who published them or is thinking of publishing them. How does a two hundred and fifty million dollar lawsuit sound?"

Skye blinked at the sum. "Really high."

"Not so high when you break down your annual income. It's all explained in the brief I've written."

A thick binder was presented to her. Skye opened it and saw her name listed as the plaintiff and a very long list of defendants. "How did you get this done so fast?"

"I'm the best. You're not paying for me to doodle. Now, before I file this, read it over and then tell me what happened from the very beginning."

13

TRENT READ the brief over Skye's shoulder. It was more than good. It was the ballbusting suit Skye had wanted. It was a take-no-prisoners statement to send a big message in bright neon lights: Don't mess with Skye Jessamine.

After reading the entire binder, Olivia asked Skye and Karri to start at the beginning. Skye told Olivia how she was discovered, her move to L.A., how she hired Jim . . . everything. Three hours later, Skye looked up from the revised document. The rest of Trent's family had gone, but Granger and Castle stayed. They took notes quietly and asked questions occasionally.

"Where do I sign?" Skye asked after she'd read the revised suit.

"Here and here. I can file this electronically, and I already have people in my New York, Washington, and L.A. offices on standby to serve the defendants as simultaneously as possible."

Skye signed and then Olivia got to work scanning the documents and working on her laptop. Skye finally took a deep breath and sat back in the chair. Trent could practically see the weight lift off her shoulders.

"Miss Jessamine, I think you need to see this," Georgina called out as she turned the volume up on the daily gossip news show that just came on.

The perky anchor who'd interviewed Skye numerous times looked into the camera with a breaking news logo next to her head. The logo disappeared and was replaced with a picture of Skye and a second picture of Tony Ketron. "We have breaking news that Skye Jessamine, America's Sweetheart, is taking on an edgy new role in Tony Ketron's upcoming film. The contracts were just signed and insiders say that after Skye's racy photos, stripping for the gritty Ketron film won't be a problem."

Skye's whole world stopped, yet she felt the rest of the world racing by her at the speed of light as she sat frozen in place. She struggled to breathe as anger strangled her until she felt Trent's hand cover hers. She hadn't realized her body had turned ice cold until his warmth brought her back. Skye blinked her eyes to see everyone looking grim-faced around her.

"I assume you didn't sign said contract," Olivia said, her voice even and calm.

"Correct. I would never sign it and my whole team knew that."

Olivia nodded and pursed her perfectly pink lips. "You need to fire not just your attorney, but your entire inner circle including your agent, manager, and PR firm."

Skye felt deflated and embarrassed as she told Olivia about her lifetime contract with Jim and his agency.

"Never say never in the law. I'll tear that contract to shreds and then make him eat it one piece at a time. Now, with your permission, I'd like to release a very strongly worded response after I notify everyone that your legal representation has been changed. Give me fifteen minutes and I'll have that woman reading our statement before the end of the show."

"Go for it," Skye said, sounding defeated. Olivia stormed from the table with her cell phone to her ear and began snapping orders like a pissed-off drill sergeant.

"I knew they wouldn't like me trying to break free," Skye muttered as she leaned into Trent for support.

"They don't have a hold over you, Skye. You have to see that," Trent told her. "A contract to hire Jim, but there's nothing in place for Bernie or whoever your PR firm is. It's time to clean house. Let Olivia do her thing while you start picking your own inner circle."

"Know anyone in PR?" Skye said dryly, but Trent looked at Ryker and slow smiles spread across both faces. They were thinking the same thing.

"We sure do," Trent said, feeling excited as he pulled out his phone and typed away. "This is our aunt in Kentucky. She's mostly retired, but she runs PR for the family's interests. Her firm went from just her to a fulltime mid-sized staff."

"Morgan Davies," Skye read as she took his phone. "What does she know about Hollywood? It's a very different world out there."

"She reps the family. Aunt Gemma, my cousin Sydney McKnight who owns Syd, Inc., The Daughters of Elizabeth Foundation, several Derby-winning farms, and a professional football team coach, plus her firm handles the entire team. They're equipped, but Morgan is scarier than Olivia when she's pissed off," Trent explained.

Trent watched as Skye looked between him and Ryker, who nodded. "I've hired her myself, Skye," Ryker told her.

Trent looked to his cousin who shrugged. That was news to Trent. Of course, everything Ryker let them know was news since he kept more secrets than the priest in a confessional.

"Okay, hotshot. I trust Trent and he trusts you. So far you've given me no reason not to trust you. I'll ask Olivia, and if she signs off on it, I'd like to talk to Morgan and see if we mesh."

"If who meshes?" Olivia asked as she strode toward them in quick, sure steps despite the four-inch stiletto heels she wore.

"Ryker and I recommended our aunt Morgan Davies to head up Skye's new PR team."

Olivia actually rolled her eyes in frustration. "I'm annoyed I didn't think of that first. Morgan Davies is one tough, badass bitch in the absolute best way possible for you. Plus, her husband is a silver fox. It shows she has good taste."

Skye and Karri laughed as the men shook their heads.

"Want me to call her?" Trent asked.

"Yes, please," Olivia answered for Skye. "If Skye likes her and hires her, then I can run the press release by her before sending it off."

Trent scrolled through the long list of Davies contacts until he found Morgan's cell. She answered it on the third ring. "Trent! Did you get my thank-you note for the porch swing? Miles and I are just loving it."

"I did, but that's not why I am calling. I need PR help. Well, my girlfriend does." Trent swallowed and glanced at Skye. She was staring at him, but with a happy little smile on her face so he was hopeful he hadn't overstepped.

"Girlfriend!" Morgan yelled excitedly in the phone. "Tell me everything. I can't believe it. I have the scoop on my mother-in-law. In her senior citizen *face!*"

"Dear, you do realize you're a senior citizen too now," Trent heard Uncle Miles say in the background.

"Do you want to live to see your grandchild born?" Morgan shot back.

"You're a very sexy senior citizen," Miles's deep voice said, followed by some kissing noises.

Next to him Skye was trying to cover a giggle. "I like her," she whispered.

"I heard that. So, who are you and why do you need help and you'd better be good enough for my nephew. Also, my husband wants you to know that by providing your name you fully consent to him running your name through every database known to man or woman, and some that aren't known, to find out all your secrets."

"I'm very good at hiding bodies," Miles called out and Trent groaned.

"That's good to know, Mr. Davies. How do you feel about being paid to cut someone's balls off?" Skye asked as the men crossed their legs and Karri rolled her eyes.

"I don't do it for the money. I do it for the pleasure of seeing the person who hurt someone I love scream in pain."

Skye was smiling broadly and she probably thought he was joking, but Trent wasn't all that sure Miles was kidding. He'd been Special Forces and was a tough-as-nails businessman. Though he did turn to goo when talking about his daughter and her upcoming baby.

"So, what's going on and how can we help?" Morgan asked, bringing the talk away from actions that would result in jail time.

"Morgan, meet my girlfriend, Skye Jessamine. Skye, my aunt Morgan and uncle Miles Davies."

The line was quiet until Skye said hello.

"Well, this makes sense now. I can't believe your PR

person is using the leaked pictures to push your new role," Morgan said calmly and fully in business mode. Gone was the caring aunt.

"I didn't accept that role and everyone on my team knew I refused to take any part in a Tony Ketron movie. And I'm certainly not exhausted or in a hospital somewhere. I'm pissed off in South Carolina!" Skye's voice began to rise as Olivia stepped onto the call and filled Morgan in on what had happened so far.

"You're doing the right thing," Morgan told her and Trent could see Skye relax a little. "You need a team you can trust. I do things differently. One, I'm not taking new clients. But since you're almost family, I'll take you on. However, you hurt my nephew and all I can say is, after thirty years of marriage I know several of my husband's tricks for hiding bodies. Second, I won't tell you what you want to hear. I'll tell you what you need to hear. Third, I don't do high maintenance. We treat each other with mutual respect and we'll get along fine. And fourth, I charge a lot."

"I'm fine with all of those conditions," Skye said. "Now, I want to make a statement. I'm in control of my own life now and I'm stepping away from the lights to lead a more private life."

"Will you still be doing movies?" Morgan asked, and Trent could hear her taking notes.

"Yes. I just want to be in control of who my team is, what roles I take, and I am tired of being paraded about like a trained poodle. I want a private life when I'm not promoting a movie. My old team wouldn't allow that."

"I have a statement ready," Olivia said. "I'm emailing it to you. We want it read live on air right now."

"Got it," Morgan said. "Let me tweak it while you send a

notice of termination to your current PR firm. I'll handle it from here."

"Skye, here's the notice of termination," Olivia said, sliding a paper over for her to sign.

Olivia scanned and emailed the document. "Done."

Minutes later, Skye's phone was blowing up. "Based on the texts I'm getting back, they've received the notices."

Morgan chuckled over the phone, and Skye leaned closer as if she could see what Morgan was laughing at. "This is one hell of a statement. I like it. This is going to be fun. I enjoy these types of campaigns."

"When my wife grins like this, I almost feel sorry for whoever you're going after," Miles said in the background, and that made everyone around the table laugh.

"Leave this all to me, Skye. Trent can share my number and we'll check in daily. Olivia or I will field all questions that come to you. This will be a bloodbath, but I guarantee we'll be the ones left standing. Now, I need to get to work."

The line went dead and everyone was left in silence. "Ryan said his family was different. I am just beginning to learn the depths of that statement," Castle said into the silence.

"I like them," Karri said with a big smile on her face. Trent had to agree. Over the last few years, the Shadows Landing family and the Keeneston family had grown close after more than a generation of estrangement.

Trent saw Skye's phone light up and glanced down at it. It was a text from Lenny ripping into her for firing Rebecca and Bernie. Next one came from Jim claiming she was in violation of her contract and he'd sue her for every penny she'd ever made.

Anger rose to the surface, but then Castle interrupted them. "Shaw found the man who attacked you."

"Who is he?" Skye asked, instantly rigid. Trent put his arm around her as Castle put the phone on speaker and pulled up a picture.

"You're on speaker, Shaw," Castle told him.

"Skye, can you tell me anything about this photo?" Shaw asked.

Karri and Skye looked at the picture and frowned. It was the back of a man dressed in black getting into a black SUV.

"I can't tell," Karri said as Skye shook her head.

"I can't tell either. It might be him, but I can't tell from this angle."

"I found video of him through some of your neighbor's security cameras. I can't prove it was him who entered your house. What sticks out is that I was able to ID the SUV. It's owned by Star Power Private Security."

"The same group who sent people to talk to our parents?" Skye asked.

"That's right. And the same company that does a lot of off the books things for the rich and powerful in Hollywood."

"Who hired them?" Trent asked after introducing himself.

"We don't know yet. What we can determine is that when things are off the books, they aren't paid in the usual way. Sometimes it's cash, sometimes it's a stock transfer, and sometimes it's providing a trade for something Star Power needs. They claim all these on their taxes as gifts. When asked what they were for, their standard reply is that they are a thank-you for good service," Shaw told them. "Right now we can't prove otherwise. But based on their taxes, they received gifts from the who's who of Hollywood."

"Are you going to arrest them?" Skye asked and Trent could hear the worry in her voice.

"We don't have anything to arrest them on. They lied to your parents, but they didn't hurt them. They're still hanging out in both Iowa and New York watching your parents, but doing so from the public road. They're not doing anything illegal."

"What are you doing then?" Trent asked.

"We're trying to find out who the man in the SUV is. We've also put our own guys onto every Star Power security guard we know of. Further, we have people in Iowa and New York to make sure your parents are safe," Shaw told them. "I don't want to haul them in for questioning. I want to see if they'll lead us to whoever hired them."

"So they're out there looking for me?" Skye's voice had gone from worried to almost dead-sounding. There was no emotion in her as she stared down at the phone sitting on the table.

"Yes, but that's why you have Castle with you. Castle, I need you in Shadows Landing to check in daily. I also need locals to do protection and surveillance."

"Sheriff Granger Fox here. We're on it. Castle can send you my contact."

"Miss Jessamine, look!" Georgina said as she pointed at the television. Harper was already turning the volume up.

The anchor of the gossip show looked directly into the camera as they posted a picture of Skye from her last red carpet. "We have breaking news straight from Skye Jessamine's new team. We are breaking the story here first. Miss Jessamine has fired her longtime attorney and hired Attorney Olivia Townsend of New York as her new lead counsel. Further, we have received evidence that Miss Jessamine and Miss Townsend have been very busy serving some of the biggest online gossip sites, news outlets, and media for posting the illegally obtained images of her to the tune of two hundred and fifty million dollars in damages.

"For the record, our show and network refused to post them. You can read the entire statement on our website, but Miss Jessamine says in part: '*I take my privacy seriously and won't let criminals profit from trying to humiliate me. What you did was wrong and illegal, and I'm standing up for all women who have had some creep snap a picture up her skirt, through her window, or any other time her consent wasn't given. Let me set the record straight: I do not consent to the publication of illegally obtained or doctored photos of myself. Everyone is now on notice. I won't tolerate it and I will come after each and every one of you for publishing private or doctored photographs of me.*'" The news anchor kept her eyes on the camera as she finished reading the most relevant part of the press release.

"Miss Jessamine goes on to say: '*Further, it appears my old team colluded to use these images to force my hand into starring in Tony Ketron's newest film. I'll say what no one else wants to because I'm no longer afraid: Tony Ketron is an abusive, sexist, misogynist and I refuse to have my name attached to him in any way.*'" The anchor took a deep breath and then pressed her finger to her ear. "We're getting word that several A-list actresses are already responding online. Gina Toussaint is the first among the several who have just sent out messages of support. Her post simply reads, '*I support Skye Jessamine. #IwillneverworkwithTony.*'"

Skye watched as snapshots from several of Hollywood's top actresses' social media accounts were flashed across the screen with the same general message.

"In further news, it looks as if Miss Jessamine isn't done shaking things up in her inner circle because this press release came from the office of Morgan Davies Public Relations and not Miss Jessamine's longtime PR firm. Stay tuned for more tomorrow or follow us online for up-to-the-minute updates on this developing story."

The show ended and Harper turned the television volume down.

"Well, that should make things interesting," Shaw said over the phone. "Stay on your toes. You're not playing their Hollywood game right now, and I expect to see some retaliation. I'll check in soon."

Castle hung up and everyone was quiet for a moment. Skye was just trying to remember how to breathe. Suddenly Harper placed a shot of bourbon in front of her. "I thought you might need this. That was badass, ladies. Badass." She handed Olivia a shot too.

"My phone is exploding," Skye said after taking the shot. Texts from her friends and fellow colleagues flooded in along with threats from Lenny, Rebecca, Bernie, and Jim. Mason sent a supportive text that was so touching it almost made her cry. She was doing the right thing, no matter what happened next.

"Olivia Townsend," Olivia said, moving to put her phone on speaker. Bernie's voice filled the room as he called Olivia every horrible name in the book. The viler the threats, the wider Olivia's smile got. However, no one else at the table was smiling. The men looked ready to rip Bernie to shreds. Harper looked as if she'd gut him. Karri was wide-eyed, yet Olivia kept quiet as she listened. "Are you done with your little tantrum?"

"You bitch. I'll show you—"

"Let me tell you how this is going to go, Mr. Ganoti. You're finished acting like a petulant little child. You will cease and desist all contact with *my* client Skye Jessamine. You will close your mouth and keep it closed or I will close it for you. Do you understand me?" Olivia's tone was ice-cold as she spoke calmly into the phone.

"You can't touch me. You're nothing but a nameless associate. I'm calling your boss and when I'm done with you, you'll be begging me to let you practice law again," Bernie threatened and Skye was shaken to her core that this was the man she'd trusted.

Olivia winked at her and then looked back at the phone. "Go ahead. This nameless associate will be the one stringing you up by the balls with barbed wire if I find out you've said one negative or confidential thing about my client. Or worse, if I find out you had anything to do with those leaked photos or the fraudulent contract my client allegedly signed with Tony Ketron. Did you, Bernie? Did you tell Jim he could sign Skye's name to the Tony Ketron contract? If you did, I'm coming for you. And unlike other attorneys, I don't go straight for the kill. I like to play a little first. Do you want to play with me, Bernie?"

"You don't want to tangle with me, little girl," Bernie spat, but now he sounded less sure of himself.

"On the contrary, Bernie. I'm happy to tangle with you. Like Skye, I'm not afraid of men like you. You amuse me until you don't and that's when I stop playing. Don't talk to my client. You've been warned." Olivia hung up on him and smiled at Skye. "Well, that was fun."

Karri burst out laughing and broke the silence. "Barbed wire?"

Olivia shrugged. "Skye wanted to know what I'd do to a man's balls."

Granger shook his head as he looked at the women. "You gotta show some love to the balls. They're sensitive."

Even Olivia laughed at that. "I'm heading back to New York. I'll call you daily. Make sure to check your email. I'm sure I'll have things for you to sign off on." Her phone rang again. "Look, I bet this is your agent."

Olivia stood, and as she walked out of the bar, Skye heard her say hello to Jim. It was a strange feeling, having someone else fight her fight, but looking around she had a new team now—a team she could trust. And she wasn't going to let them fight alone.

14

THE DOOR to the bar opened and a large, dangerous-looking man walked inside. He nodded to the table and went straight to the bar. His dark hair was pushed back from his forehead and his leather jacket looked broken in.

Skye watched as the man leaned over the bar, wrapped his hand around the back of Harper's neck, then pulled her to him. His lips covered hers in a hot and heavy kiss that left Karri gasping and Skye averting her eyes.

"Are you staying for dinner?" Skye heard Harper ask a minute later.

"Can we do a late dinner? I have knitting club in a couple of minutes," the rumbling voice said. It was his comment, not the deep masculinity of his voice that caused Skye's head to pop up.

"Knitting club!" Skye stood up quickly as did Karri. "Excuse me, sir, where in the church does this knitting club meet?"

"*Sir?*" Harper snorted. "Skye, this is my husband, Dare Reigns. Dare, this is Skye Jessamine and her friend Karri Hill."

Dare winked at Harper and then strode toward the table. It was then that Skye saw the tote bag with knitting needles sticking out of it hanging from his hand. "America's Sweetheart is into knitting?"

"We got bribed with apple pie to attend, but it sounds like fun," Skye answered.

Dare spun to look at his wife, clearly upset. "Why don't I get apple pie?"

Harper rolled her eyes. "You get casseroles, pies, brownies, cakes, cookies, and more from them. Plus, Aunt Marcy sends you your very own apple pie every month."

"But not Miss Winnie's or Miss Ruby's apple pie." Dare looked as if someone just kicked his puppy. His face was long and his bottom lip threatened to roll out into a full pout.

"Men and apple pie. You'd better hurry or you'll be late. Then Miss Mitzy won't make you those chocolate cookies with peanut butter chips that you love so much."

Dare winked at his wife and then motioned with his arm for Skye and Karri to follow him. "Let's go, ladies. Knitting club is going to be a good one tonight."

Karri didn't look convinced, and for that matter, Skye didn't feel convinced either. How good could a knitting club be?

Skye greeted Edie, Miss Ruby, and Miss Winnie, and then was introduced to the cat lady, Miss Mitzy, before meeting everyone else in the knitting club. She and Karri had just taken their seats when the women began to pull out their projects.

Skye felt her brow crease as Karri leaned over toward her. "Are those what I think they are?"

"They can't be," Skye whispered as she took in the half-completed knitted penises. Skye looked around and saw penises in all colors, and someone with matching male and female squares, but she didn't know what they were. Then she looked over at Dare and saw a knitted nipple.

"What kind of knitting club is this?" Skye whispered to him.

"This month we're doing erotic knitting."

"You're knitting a boob?" Skye asked. Her head couldn't wrap around what she was seeing.

"It's going to be a nursing cap for Ellery's baby," Dare said with a snicker as Skye put it together. When nursing, it'll look like a boob and not a baby's head. And then this is Harper's Christmas gift." Dare reached into his bag and pulled out a long soft pink scarf with a breast on each end. He wrapped it around his neck and the breasts fell right where they were supposed to be. "Think she'll like it?"

Skye relied on all her acting skills to smile pleasantly and nod. Karri, meanwhile, couldn't stop the "What are those?" that blurted out of her mouth.

A gray-haired woman held up the anatomically correct male and female squares. "They're potholders with nude people on them, dear. Do you not cook much?"

"I'm a chef," Karri sputtered back as she leaned closer to look at them. "Those are incredibly detailed."

"Thank you," the little old lady said with pleasure.

"You're a chef? Here," Mitzy said, handing over what looked to be a knitted dildo. "Just put this on the pot handle and you won't burn your hand."

Skye pressed her lips together tightly as she tried to keep the laughter down.

"It's a penis," Karri stated as she rotated it in her hand.

"I'm glad you know one when you see one," Mitzy said

dryly as she went back to work on another penis potholder, but this one seemed to have a cat on the shaft.

"I made these for my wine bottles," Miss Ruby said lining up a series of flesh-colored penises that ranged from black, to tan, to beige.

"Miss Ruby, why is the penis you're working on green?" Skye asked, taking in the one color that stood out in the lineup.

"I don't exclude anyone in my wine toppers. That includes aliens," Miss Ruby said with such surety that Skye had to bite her lip hard to stop the laughter.

Miss Winnie rolled her eyes. "Ruby swears she saw a green alien coming out of the river last night. Now she believes in aliens."

"I'm telling you, Winnie, he *was* an alien. What else is green from head to toe?"

"How do you know it was a he?" Skye asked and noticed that everyone, even Dare, was leaning forward with interest now.

"I could see, you know, *it*. And *it* was green."

"What was this alien doing?" Dare asked Miss Ruby.

Miss Ruby's needles flew as she added to the shaft of the green penis. "It was like he was watching us to learn about us. He was in the shadows of the tall grass by the river. When he saw me watching him, it was like he just vanished. One second he was there and the next he was gone. I walked closer to see him, but there was no evidence he'd ever been there."

"Was there a boat nearby?" Dare asked while Skye shivered hearing Mitzy's story. Something about it was creepy.

Miss Ruby shook her head. "No boat and no car. Also,

there was no spaceship that I could see. I think he teleported."

Skye saw Dare glance over at her and the creepiness factor grew. "You don't think he was looking for me, do you?"

Dare didn't respond, but the tightening of his jaw and the texts he sent out didn't make her feel any better. Even Karri looked a little worried, but Miss Winnie was showing her how to knit while Dare helped Skye get started on her scarf.

THIRTY MINUTES LATER, Skye was discovering the calming benefits of knitting. Her needles moved rhythmically as she listened to Miss Mitzy talking. "I told my son, bless his heart, that having a child of his own was payback for all he put me through." Dare snorted next to her as he worked on knitting the nipple of his hat. "Well, I laughed and laughed when he asked me to watch J.R., my four year old grandson, last weekend so he and his wife could have a date night. Apparently J.R. had snuck out of his room during naptime and gotten into the glue. He smeared it all over the floor and walls. He then threw glitter on the wet glue and snuck back into bed. His mother's hysterical screaming woke him up later. They asked him if he knew anything about it. With glitter covering his entire body, he batted his big brown eyes and said, "I made it for you, Mommy. Surprise! I love you."

The other grandmothers chuckled. Skye and Karri grimaced. Dare cleared his throat and shifted uncomfortably. Dare didn't appear to be the glitter type.

"So, they said they need a break," Mitzy continued. "I tried to remind my son of when he was that age and he took

Sharpies to the living room wall and furniture. Then he accused me of finding the glitter situation funny."

The women all made disapproving noises and shook their heads in a way that instantly made Skye feel bad for whatever was coming next in the story for Mitzy's son.

"That's no way to speak to your momma," Miss Winnie clucked. "What did you do?"

"I told J.R. about penises and vaginas," Mitzy said with a proud smirk. "J.R., bless that sweet boy, waited until they were in the middle of the grocery store to point at a woman and holler, 'Vagina!'"

Skye gasped as she choked on a laugh.

"Then," Mitzy continued with glee, "he saw a group of college boys and screamed, 'Penis, penis, penis!' as he pointed to each of the three boys. The horror in my son's retelling was glorious."

"I think I like being called a dick better. Penis is too formal. What about you, Fox?"

Skye saw Karri's head snap around and Skye followed to see who had just spoken. There stood Sheriff Fox and Agent Castle. Neither looked horrified by the story. Actually, they looked amused.

"*Dick* is a much more versatile word. Dickhead. What a dick. Don't be a dick. Just doesn't sound the same with penis." Granger managed to say that with a straight face and Skye had to give him full props for that.

"I find the same to be true for vagina as well," Mitzy said, not even looking up from the dick potholder she was making. "But I couldn't very well teach my grandson to say *pussy* as he points to a woman. That's just bad manners. Although, I did tell him to call his cat a pussy just to irritate my daughter-in-law. Gives me joy every time he calls, 'Pussy! Here, pussy, pussy.'"

A strangled choking sound came from Dare as he tried to cover it up with a cough. Karri covered her face with yarn as her shoulders shook. Skye turned to pound Dare on the back and used it as a cover for her own laughter. When she looked over Dare's shoulder, she saw Castle and Fox struggling. Their shoulders were shaking, their faces were red, and finally Granger just turned to face the door as he bent over and dragged in deep breaths as his whole body shook with laughter.

Miss Ruby nodded her head. "That was smart of you. She deserves that. It's not right not to let the grandmother pick her own name."

"Pick your name?" Skye asked, still struggling for composure after the pussy incident.

"That's right. When my grandson was born, I couldn't wait to be called Mimi. I've been planning it ever since my son got married. Then, out of nowhere, I go to meet my grandson, and my daughter-in-law looked up at me from the bed holding my grandson and says, 'J.R. meet your Gaga.' She didn't even let me pick what to be called and then stuck me with that name."

"Bless your heart," Miss Winnie said with a sympathetic shake of her head. "A horrible name to be saddled with. I'm sure you're not tolerating that, though."

Mitzy shook her head. "Of course not. I had him calling me Mimi before he was eighteen months old. Mimi doesn't play that game. However, I invited her to join our knitting club even though she hasn't been gracious in defeat. It's why I wanted to have Skye here. I want to say Skye Jessamine knitted with me when my own daughter-in-law said knitting was only for old Gagas."

A chorus of angry "Bless her heart," echoed around the

room. Skye suddenly felt angry for Mitzy and strangely protective of the stranger.

"I'm sorry," Granger said to Mitzy and for once didn't sound so serious. Instead, he sounded heartfelt. "I'll pull Karen over the next time she's in town. A ticket should piss her off."

Mitzy's sad frown turned into a smile. "You're such a sweet boy, Granger."

"Thank you, ma'am. Now, why we're here is because we heard there was an alien sighting."

Miss Ruby repeated her story and held up the green penis. "It was about this size and color."

Castle cleared his throat and dropped his voice. "Today has been a very strange, very anatomical day."

"We looked at where you told Dare you saw him in the park. From that vantage point, he could have a clear view of Main Street," Granger said, trying to stay on point.

"That's right." Miss Ruby nodded her head. "I told you, I think he was observing us."

Castle, Dare, and Granger turned to look at Skye and she knew then the creepy feeling she'd gotten was telling her she'd been found. "Do you think they know I'm here?"

"I think they're trying to figure that out. My guess is Lenny gave them Trent's name and they're here to watch the town to see if they see you," Castle told her. It made sense, but now the safety she'd felt was gone and it hadn't even been a week yet.

"You think some Hollywood guy sent an alien to find Miss Skye?" Miss Ruby asked, setting down the green knitted penis.

"I think they sent a person dressed in a dark green wetsuit to find her. My guess is there was a boat a little offshore. They didn't want to tip their hand and let Skye or Trent see them, which is what's really worrying me. I think you and Trent should spend the night someplace else tonight."

Edie looked up from her knitting with a grim expression. "What about Ryker's guesthouse? His place is a fort. It should be the safest place."

"Great idea." Granger was already texting before Skye could protest. "Ryker says Trent knows how to get in. He's out of town for a couple of days."

"We can take Skye to the guesthouse and Edie can take Karri back to Tinsley's," Miss Winnie said, not bothering to look up from her knitted G-string.

"I'll stay with her and make sure no one follows them when they leave," Dare said. "But now we need to get back to our knitting."

Skye watched as Granger shook his head with amusement. "Got to get your gossip in?"

Dare looked up and a cold smile crossed his face. "I heard something interesting about your love life."

Granger spun Castle around to face the door and pushed him forward. "We're outta here. Call us if you need us. Skye, Karri, we'll check in with you tomorrow. 'Night, ladies."

Everyone was quiet for a moment until Miss Winnie finally set down her knitted underwear. "We didn't say anything about Granger's love life. I didn't even know he had one."

Dare looked up from his knitted nipple. "He doesn't. But his reaction told me otherwise."

"That was interesting," Miss Ruby said with a raised brow. "I believe we've been letting Granger get away with flying under the radar for way too long."

"Granger is a very handsome man. Why isn't he dating?" Karri asked as several white and gray heads snapped up.

"Handsome, huh?" Miss Winnie said as she wiggled her eyebrows.

"If you like that brooding type, which I don't," Karri added hastily.

"Agent Castle doesn't brood," Edie added with her own bit of mischievousness to her voice.

"No, he doesn't," Karri said, focusing back on her work before looking up and nailing Edie with a stare. "I can't help but notice you and Granger are both single and around the same age."

The white and gray hairs snapped their attention from Karri to Edie as if this were a tennis match using gossip instead of balls.

"I am not single. I am widowed," Edie replied.

Karri set down her knitting and reached over to Edie. She placed her hand on hers and waited until Edie looked her in the eyes. "I've heard your husband was a wonderful man. I'm sorry that you lost him and that it hurt your heart. But, you are still drawing breath. Your heart is still beating. It's bruised, but like all bruises, it will heal over time. Don't give up on life when you still have so much to live for."

Tears shone in Edie's eyes as the other widows in the room nodded their heads.

"You may have a point, but that point doesn't lead to Granger. I've known him my whole life. He's like a brother to me."

Karri straightened up and put a stern look on her face. "Well, that's fine and all, but you'd better not eye Peter. I'm not above beating up on a widow for taking the man I'm into."

Skye almost dropped her needles in surprise. Karri was very private and usually was easily embarrassed. Yet in this group of women ... and Dare, she had just laid claim to a man. Suddenly a laugh burst from Edie's mouth and mixed with a shaky cry. She wiped a tear from her eye as she continued to laugh. Karri joined her and soon the whole room was laughing.

Skye was shocked at how easily Karri fell into conversation with the knitting club. The remaining time flew by as the voices flowed around her and her needles clicked rhythmically. Skye couldn't remember ever being so relaxed as she felt being part of this group. When it was time to go, she found herself lingering as she talked with the ladies and instantly promised to meet next week. That's when reality hit. Next week? Would she even be here next week? And why did the idea of leaving Shadows Landing fill her with more dread than the idea of not going back to Hollywood?

15

"What do you mean, you think they found Skye?" Trent didn't know how this was possible, yet here were Granger and Peter in his shop telling him that's exactly what they think had happened.

"Unless you really believe it was an alien by the waterfront, it means they tracked you down and are hoping that you will lead them to Skye. Lenny knew you two had a night together. My guess is, based on knowing Skye for just a short time, her potential relationship with you scared Lenny," Granger told him as Peter nodded in agreement.

"Why?"

"It's classic abusive behavior—manipulate and isolate. He made sure he was the only man in Skye's life. As soon as you came along, he got rid of you. I have no doubt in my mind that he hired someone to spy on you to see if you're hiding Skye."

Trent looked at Granger and then Peter. "What do I do? How do I protect her?"

"The change in hair color and clothing helps," Peter told

him. "But we need to hide her better. We don't think the man found anything or else there would be someone attempting to either take her or Lenny would be driving into town already. I think they're still trying to find her. It's actually classic law enforcement and military procedure. He arrived without anyone knowing. If he'd been a tourist and asked if any famous people ever came here, the town would have picked up on it and called Granger."

Trent agreed.

"What you do first is get the lay of the land. Coming and going from the park was the best strategy. He could watch the entire downtown. Gauge how many people were tourists and how many people regularly came and went during the day. Once he surveyed the town, he could determine how best to blend in. Since he wasn't walking down the street trying to observe anyone, I don't think he reached that point. Now the question is, will he come back to get eyes on you and your property?" Peter looked as if he already knew the answer.

"You think he will."

"I do," Peter confirmed. "He has a job to do and he's going to do it."

"That's why I asked Ryker to allow you to stay at his house for a couple of nights. While this *alien* is looking for you, Kord and I will be looking for him."

Trent took a deep breath and began shutting down and cleaning up his shop. "Okay. So I'll get Skye and take her to Ryker's guesthouse."

"No. Miss Winnie is going to drive her. No one will be looking for her in Miss Winnie's car. Edie is taking Karri to Tinsley's. It'll be hard, but I think we need to alter her appearance too."

"Why would it be hard, Peter?" Trent asked.

"Because she's so beautiful she kind of stands out." Peter stopped and cleared his throat. "I mean, her hair is dark and that's hard to change. You know?"

Trent and Granger smiled, letting him know they didn't believe it for a second. The all-business FBI agent was into Karri.

"Okay, what do you want me to do?" Trent asked finally.

"Pack a bag and all of Skye's stuff. I'll drop you off at Ryker's. You have a smart house, right?" Granger was already looking back at the house and Trent could see him thinking of something.

"Yes," Trent confirmed.

"I want you to turn on and off the lights from your phone to make it look as if you were home. In the morning I want you to sneak back on the property and be very visible through the day. Then get tucked in at night and sneak back to Ryker's. I'm hoping the man will check you out, see you working alone, and then see the house appear to have just you in it. If he thinks everything is normal here, he'll leave and Skye will be safe."

"I can do that. Give me thirty minutes and meet me at Tinsley's for pickup. Ryker has a fleet of ATVs. I can use one to come and go the back way."

Trent closed down his shop and headed inside while Peter and Granger left in separate cars. His guess was Peter wasn't really gone, but securing the area. Trent showed himself in the kitchen, but then made sure to close the blinds. He turned on the television and all the lights on the first floor while he went upstairs to pack. He packed a large duffle bag with a few of his things and all of Skye's things. He made sure the spare room looked as if no one had been in it.

He headed back downstairs and turned off the kitchen light and waited. He looked outside and didn't see anyone. He scanned the trees, his shop, and then slid into the shadows. He had disappeared into the woods in under ten seconds.

The darkness of the night didn't bother him as he made his way to Tinsley's. It was a hike, but one that wouldn't take more than fifteen minutes. He made sure to be as quiet as possible and stopped every so often to listen to the night. He never heard anyone following him so he picked up his speed until he got to Tinsley's.

Trent was standing five feet back from the end of the tree line as he watched Tinsley's house. He saw Granger's car parked in the drive, but Granger wasn't in it. A shadow passed by the house and Trent narrowed his eyes. He recognized the cowboy hat and slipped from the tree line.

"Granger," Trent said quietly when Granger almost disappeared around the side of the house.

"I was getting worried. Come on, let's go. Peter said everything looks normal on the street. I have Kord kayaking the river right now to see if he can find any boats anchored out of sight nearby."

The drive to Ryker's house had been something Trent had done more than a thousand times, yet this time felt different. Everything looked suspicious. The gnome in a garden, the palmetto flags that flew, and the deep shadows of the night all seemed malicious.

When they arrived at the gate that enclosed Ryker's property, Trent had to hop out of the car and enter his specific code. The heavy gate slid silently open and immediately closed behind them.

Don't drink my cognac.

Trent looked down at the text that had just come in from Ryker and shook his head. *I didn't know you kept any of the good stuff in the guesthouse.*

Ryker ignored the text but sent a temporary code with Skye's name on it. Trent thanked him and then sent it to Skye with instructions. The code would open the gate and the guesthouse door.

Granger pulled up to the guesthouse, which was just as big as Trent's home, and parked. "I'll check in on you tomorrow."

"Thanks, Granger." Trent grabbed the large duffle bag and walked toward the guesthouse. Lights automatically turned on as he approached. The keypad lit up and Trent punched in his code. The thick locks slid free and he opened the frosted glass and steel door.

Inside a tablet glowed on the wall. It controlled the entire house. Trent pressed the icons that turned on the lights and then the gas fireplace. There was a master bedroom downstairs and three bedrooms upstairs. Trent set the bag down in the living room and walked to the back of the house. He unlocked and pushed open the entire wall of sliding glass doors and walked out onto the patio.

He took in a deep breath of the cool air rolling in from the river and waited for Skye. Everything in him wanted to run to her, but he knew it was best to let Miss Winnie bring her to him. His girlfriend—he'd called her that with Aunt Morgan and Skye hadn't protested the title he'd given her.

Trent listened to the river rolling by in the distance. There was so much to say yet it seemed as if it were too soon. Protect Skye. Get her career back on track. Then, maybe, it would be time to discuss their relationship. He didn't like it, but that's what needed to be done.

Trent saw headlights shining through the front windows and knew Skye had arrived. Trent went to open the door but found Dare instead of Skye. "What are you doing here?"

"I used Harper's code. I'm ten seconds in front of Skye. I wanted to talk to you." Trent held open the door and Dare stepped inside. "Look, you're the best friend I have here in Shadows Landing. You're like my brother."

Trent was touched. It had always been Trent and Harper as best friends, but when she began seeing Dare, Trent knew he was being replaced. Or at least being pushed down a rung from best friend to runner-up. And while that may be true, he'd gained Dare as a friend.

"Thanks. Is something the matter? Is Harper okay?"

Dare looked over his shoulder and saw the headlights from Miss Winnie's car in the distance. "Harper's great. It's about you and Skye. She fits, bro."

"Fits?"

"Here. In Shadows Landing. She and Karri belong here. She's tougher than she looks, but she also feels more deeply than she shows. I wasted so much time when I got together with Harp because I thought it was the wrong time for a relationship. Don't make that mistake. That woman is in it for the long haul. Bro, she came to knitting club!" Dare said as if that explained it all. "Also"—Dare reached behind him and pulled out a 9mm— "take this. You see an alien getting too close, shoot him."

Trent took the gun and slapped Dare on the shoulder. He was a good man. "Thanks. How did you know I needed the gun and the advice?"

"That's what friends are for. Call me if you need anything. I'm good at undercover work." Dare winked at him and then left. He waved to Miss Winnie and Skye before driving off.

Trent looked around and opened the narrow entry table drawer to hide the gun. By the time he made it outside, Skye had already thanked Miss Winnie and was waving at the taillights headed back down the drive.

It was so natural to wrap his arms around Skye and pull her to him. He leaned back just enough to look into her face. "How are you?"

"I take it they told you about the alien?"

"Yes. We have a game plan on how to make it appear that nothing is out of the normal. Hopefully, he'll see I'm alone at home during the day and then leave us alone."

"Just let Miss Ruby show him the alien penis she knitted for him and he'll go running back to L.A. or wherever he came from."

"Alien penis? What kind of knitting class was that?" Trent asked with laughter as he led Skye inside.

"This month's theme was erotic knitting. I don't think I've ever had so much fun. Also, when this is over, I'm totally taking Miss Mitzy and her grandson to a movie premiere. Her mean daughter-in-law can suck it."

Trent burst out laughing. Dare was right. Skye fit—fit in his life, in his family, in his town, and in his heart.

"So, I'm your girlfriend, huh?" Skye looked up at him and batted her eyelashes. "Does that mean we're going steady? I already feel as if we're sneaking around. What if someone catches us making out under the bleachers?"

Trent tamped down his smile and played along. "I had my class ring all ready to give you, but if you don't want it," Trent shrugged. "And I wouldn't have made out with you under the bleachers. I was thinking of the bedroom where I'd slowly strip each article of clothing from your body. With each newly exposed area, I was going to kiss, lick, suck, and maybe if you're a good girl, nibble my way across every inch of your body."

Trent saw her chest rising and falling quicker as her eyes dilated with desire. "However, I'm a gentleman and would never dream of doing that to someone I wasn't involved in a relationship with. I'd only do that thing with my tongue and my fingers." Skye gasped and her cheeks flushed. She remembered the move he was talking about. "As I was saying, I'd only do that with my girlfriend who I hoped to have in my life for a very long time. So, let me show you to the guest room."

Trent made it two steps before he felt Skye leap on his back. He caught her instantly and hooked her legs with his arms. "What I'm hearing is not only do you want to go steady, but I might be promise-ring material."

Trent chuckled as he carried her inside and used his foot to close the door. "I'm saying you're already promise-ring material, but what am I to you?"

He felt Skye's head lower to rest against the side of his head. He felt her warm breath on his neck and the way her arms tightened over his chest. "You're the kind of guy a girl dreams about marrying. Does that scare you?" Her voice was a whisper over his skin. The thought of marriage used to have him running. Any mention of it felt oppressive. However, it felt entirely different when she said it. He felt excited for a future with her in it.

"Not with you," he answered with raw honesty.

Trent carried her upstairs. He felt too exposed to say another word until he set her on the bed. He turned to gaze down at her lying there. All teasing was gone from her features. Instead, she looked just as vulnerable as he felt.

"Don't be mad, but I have to ask."

"Ask what, Skye?"

Her eyes locked with his and Trent knew whatever she was about to ask was important. "Do you want to be with me because I'm, you know, 'America's Sweetheart,' because you want to be famous?"

Trent's answer was immediate. There was no thinking about it. "I like you in spite of it. I don't want America's Sweetheart. I want you, Skye. Just you. I don't care if you ever act again. But I know it's important to you, so I'll support you in every way you need me to. Does that answer your question?"

Skye nodded and he felt that he'd passed a very important test. However, it did bring up a lot more questions. Questions that they'd need to discuss sooner rather than later if they were to take this relationship as seriously as they were talking about.

"Trent?"

"Yes, Skye?"

Trent watched as she kicked off her shoes and scooted back onto the bed. She reached down and slowly stripped off her clothing. "Come make love to your girlfriend."

"You just want me to do that thing." He smirked at her as he pulled his shirt over his head. He didn't think she'd realized that she licked her lips as her eyes traveled over his chest and landed on his pants. He worked the button and zipper free and shoved them down.

"Oh yes, but I also have something I want to try." She licked her lips again and Trent groaned as he reached for a condom and tossed it on the bed for easy access.

"Ladies first." Trent's voice rumbled as he leaned down, grabbed her ankles, and pulled her toward him.

Joining with Skye was like coming home. The excitement of knowing you're near and then the feeling of welcome when you've finally arrived. The panting breaths, the sighs, and the tightness all felt like heaven. This was where he belonged. This was who he belonged with. Skye cried his name as she dug her fingers into his back and he was lost in her, around her, with her.

16

THE MORNING SUN slipped through the large trees outside and into the bedroom. Skye was used to her blackout curtains that shut out not only the morning sun, but also the world. That was why she found herself up so early.

Trent was asleep on his back and her head was snuggled into his arm with her back pressing against his side. They were both still nude from last night and she knew they needed to talk, but last night had been perfect. A thought stuck in her mind, though, and she wanted to talk it out. She would talk to Trent, but first she wanted to talk to Karri. While Trent was filling her heart and mind, Karri was still like a sister and always would be.

Skye reached for her phone slowly so she wouldn't wake Trent.

Are you up? Skye texted Karri as she snuggled back against Trent's warm body.

Yes. No blackout curtains. Although the sunrise is stunning.

Skye almost laughed out loud as she had the same thought about the curtains and the mornings. *You know how I talked about wanting a private life?*

Karri sent a GIF back of a woman saying, "Duh."

Skye smiled at her phone and took a moment to just breathe in the Shadows Landing air from the open window. She looked out at the sunrise, heard the birds chirping and the river flowing.

I'm at peace here.

That's all Skye needed to type. Karri would know what she meant.

Me too. So, we're doing this? Even if things don't work out with Mr. Hammer Hottie?

Skye looked at the text and knew right away what her answer was. *Yes.* The second she hit Send, she felt free. She'd made yet another move to take back control of her life. *But things are going to work out. He's the one. I know that too.*

There was a pause, then a GIF saying, "You go, girl!" came through from Karri.

Skye smiled to herself but her heart suddenly felt heavy. She didn't want to make this decision for them both. *What do you want? You don't have to stay with me. I can take care of myself now. Chase your dreams, Karri.*

Skye waited as Karri took a long time to respond. *I had a dream last night.*

Dreams were very important to Karri. This could change everything. Skye saw that Karri was already typing so she didn't respond. Instead, she just held her breath.

Let's meet for coffee at the diner and I'll tell you about it. It's too important for text. Tinsley is heading to her gallery in an hour. Want us to pick you up?

Skye looked over her shoulder and saw Trent silently watching her. "Mornin'," he told her with a smoldering look that told Skye this was going to be a *very* good morning.

No. I'll meet you there. I may need a little extra time.

Skye set her phone on the side table as Trent pulled her on top of him.

"Now this is a way to wake up every morning. I could get used to this."

"Good. You need to." She tried not to laugh at Trent's look of confusion.

"Things will go back to normal. This will be over soon and your life can go back to normal."

Skye shook her head as she placed her hands on his bare chest. She felt the muscles tense under her fingers. "I don't want my *normal* life back. I want a *real* life. I want privacy. I want love. I want it all. And I want it here, with you."

"What are you saying?" Trent asked as she began to wriggle against him. She saw Trent fighting to stay in control, but she didn't want him in control. She wanted Trent underneath her and completely out of control.

"I'm saying that regardless of what happens with my career, I plan on moving to Shadows Landing. Half of my movies are filmed in Georgia anyway. I've made my career now. I've established my reputation and I don't need to be in L.A. to pound the pavement for auditions anymore. I do believe Charleston has an airport and maybe Ryker will let me borrow his plane every now and then."

The smile on Trent's face left her soaring with happiness. That and what he did next with his tongue. It was good being Trent Faulkner's girlfriend. She bet being his wife would be even more spectacular and that was something she was beginning to want more than any acting award or role.

. . .

"What are you doing?" Trent asked as he got out of the shower.

"I love the chunky highlights, but I'm making my hair totally blonde so I can fit in here better. I'm going full South Carolina girl," Skye said as her hair was processed. The time was almost up as she slipped on a pair of cowboy boots and a cute white lace skirt.

"Pretty," Trent told her as he toweled off.

Yes, she could do this everyday for the rest of her life. "Can you help me rinse my hair?"

"Sure," Trent hung up his towel and walked nude over to her. "Bend over."

Too bad he was talking about putting her head in the sink and not what they did earlier. She wouldn't mind a repeat of that. Yup, she could definitely get used to this every day.

Skye held the towel around her shoulders together with one hand and bent over the sink. Trent turned on the water and only when it was warm did he start rinsing her hair. Her hairstylists certainly had never made her feel this way before. His fingers combed through her hair and seemed to caress her scalp in a way that sent tingles down to her toes.

"There you go," he said, turning off the water way too soon. She'd been lost in the feeling of his strong hands gently massaging her scalp and never wanted it to end.

"Oh shoot, I have to hurry." Skye saw the clock and realized she had fifteen minutes to meet Karri.

"For what?" Trent asked as he pulled on his boxer briefs.

"I'm meeting Karri at the diner."

"That's not a good idea," he told her.

"It's fine. I don't look like me," Skye bristled at the tone of voice he used.

"Skye, someone is supposed to be with you the entire time."

"Then have Granger or Kord pick me up in ten minutes. I know you can't take me because of your master plan."

Skye knew Trent wasn't happy, but he stalked off to make the call while she blasted her hair with the hairdryer. She used the diffuser and her hair had a relaxed, beachy vibe to it by the time she was done. She'd even tinted her eyebrows to make them a dark blonde and the effect was worth it.

Skye slipped on the navy blue, off-the-shoulder, bell-sleeved blouse with tiny white whales on it and checked herself out in the mirror. She picked up her black liquid liner and placed a small mole just above the corner of her mouth. That small mark in conjunction with the contouring makeup she'd done made her look completely different.

"Wow, you don't look like you," Trent admitted when he walked back into the bathroom, now fully dressed. "I'm going to drop you off at Gil's Grub N' Gas. You go inside and stay there until I leave and then five more minutes. Then you'll walk out and you'll see Granger across from the diner down the street. He'll be on the courthouse steps watching to see if anyone is following either me or you."

"Okay. Wait in Gil's for five minutes, then walk to the diner. Got it."

"I don't like this."

"It'll be fine. Let's go."

THERE WERE SO many things Skye wanted to talk to Karri about, she could barely contain her excitement. The drive to Gil's and the wait inside was making her impatient. However, it gave her time to pull out her new College of

Charleston cell phone case and replace the old one that she then tossed in the trash.

She also changed the lock on her phone and the settings on her texts so anyone looking couldn't see them if they came in while the phone was locked. Then, as much as she hated it, she needed to change the lock screen image from a picture of her and Karri to something else. Her five-minute timer went off and Skye pulled the College of Charleston baseball cap from her purse and walked out of the store after giving Gil a wave. She turned so she was facing the marina with downtown behind her and snapped a selfie that was mostly downtown with her face bent and showing off her hat. She added a filter and then made the picture her home and lock screens.

There! She was a South Carolina girl through and through.

Skye looked up and saw Granger sitting at the other end of Main Street as she began walking toward him. The only warning she got that something was wrong was when Granger suddenly leapt to his feet.

A shadow appeared behind her as she passed an alley and a hand clasped her shoulder. Granger took off running toward her, but then she lost sight of him as she was spun around to face a wide muscled chest.

"Skye?"

Skye looked up into the face of a man she recognized as one of Star Power Private Security guards who had worked on the set of her last movie. "Sorry, darlin', but my name is Emma Kate," Skye said in her best Tinsley impersonation. She wanted to run. She also wanted to ramble, but she took her time so the words came out slow as honey. "But you can call me anything you'd like." Skye smiled up at him from under her lashes and flirted with all she was worth.

He looked past her and she knew he saw Granger running toward him. "Who's he?"

Skye tossed a glance over her shoulder and as she looked back at the man she rolled her eyes. "Whoops, that's my boyfriend. He's the sheriff and a tad overprotective."

The hired man looked down at Skye and back to Granger. "Sorry to bother you."

"Any time, darlin'," Skye said with a wink as the man jumped into a car she hadn't noticed parked in the alley.

"Stop!" Granger yelled, pulling his gun.

"Baby!" Skye shrieked suddenly. "Nothing happened, I swear. He was just lost."

She saw the confusion on Granger's face as she rushed toward him and threw her arms around his neck. "Get his plates," she told him before she kissed his cheek.

"Dammit!" Granger cursed as he shoved her back. Skye would have been insulted, but she knew Granger had no idea what was going on. "You made me lose him."

"Look, you were about to blow my cover. He had no idea it was me," Skye said in her new Southern accent.

Granger cringed. "Why are you talking like that?"

"I told him I was Emma Kate and you were my boyfriend. I was doing my best Tinsley impersonation. He bought it. I promise."

"That's a *horrible* Southern accent. Why do actors always think they can do Southern accents?" Granger looked disgusted as he put his gun away and called in the license plate number.

Ouch. That hurt. Skye had been so proud of her performance.

Granger tossed his arm over her shoulder and pulled her against him. "Come on, Emma Kate. Let your *boyfriend* escort you to breakfast and teach you how to speak with a real Southern accent."

Skye looked up at Granger with surprise. "Why Granger Fox, you do have a sense of humor."

Granger winked down at her. "That's our little secret . . . darlin'." Somehow when he said it, it did sound completely different from her accent. When he said *darlin,* it sounded like pure sex.

"I see what you mean about my accent. And don't tell Trent I'm cheating on him."

Granger smiled slowly, "I'm sorry, ma'am. I can't do that."

"Impossible. You made the word *ma'am* sexy. You have no idea how much Hollywood would love you. Can I be your agent?"

"Not in a million years." Granger opened the diner door for her and Skye immediately saw Karri.

Her hair was longer and had dark purple and pink stripes in it, and when she turned to wave Skye over, her eyes were blue. It looked as if someone had a makeover last night.

Granger nodded to the table near the window. "I'll be right there if you need me. Castle is already on his way from Charleston and will be here soon, plus Kord will be over soon with the plate trace. Sorry, darlin', you're on lockdown."

"Holy smokes," Skye heard Karri say under her breath. Granger had dropped his voice to give her the full Southern gentleman effect and it was a panty-melter. "What did I miss?" Karri asked as soon as Skye sat down.

"A Star Power goon just stopped me, but I convinced him I'm a local named Emma Kate. Granger saw it all. He was watching me and I told the goon Granger was my boyfriend and that explained why the sheriff was suddenly running after him."

Karri looked nervously around. "This is not good."

"I know. It also means any taste of normalcy has been yanked from me. But we have it for this brief time so tell me about your dream."

Karri took a deep breath. "It was the most bizarre dream I've ever had, yet it all made complete sense. I dreamt I was on a pirate ship. The moon was full overhead and a woman was at the helm. I'm pretty sure it was Anne Bonny and she was the captain. Anyway, I'm on this ship, but no one else is on it so I walk up to Anne and ask her where we are. She tells me we are home.

"When I look out, there's land now. Not just any land, but in the moonlight, there's the present-day Shadows Landing. I'm confused and tell Anne that this isn't my home. She turns and looks at me and says that my wolf disagrees. Then I hear a wolf howl and look back out over the town. I see Main Street now and there's my wolf in front of that empty storefront between Harper's bar and Bless Your Scarf. Only this time it's not empty. It's a restaurant and it's mine. You're inside and so are Trent and the rest of the town. The wolf howls again and I see darkness creeping along the street straight for my restaurant."

Skye felt her heart rate speed up as she bent across the table and took Karri's hand. "What then?"

Karri took a deep breath and continued. "My wolf turned to attack the darkness, but I wasn't alone anymore. A big black bear and an alligator came and together we fought the darkness. When I thought it would defeat me, the bear saved me. Then the doors to the restaurant opened and everyone from town came out to fight alongside my wolf, the bear, and the alligator. We beat back the darkness, but only because we were together. When it was over, I turned and Anne Bonny looked at me with a smile. She said, 'This is your home, fight for it. And fight for the moon.' Then I woke up."

"Wow." Skye let out a deep breath and waited as coffee was poured and they placed their orders before continuing. "You said you know what it means?"

Karri nodded and leaned forward again. She dropped her voice so Skye had to lean close to hear her. "I'm the wolf, the gator is the town. Remember Bubba and Bertha?" Skye nodded. "And Peter is the bear. He's part of the bear clan."

"So he's going to save you?" Skye asked.

"More than that. Anne told me to fight for the moon. My mother always said to tell my wishes to the moon. No one knows that, but Anne did. Last night, before I fell asleep, I looked out at the moon and wished for love and direction in my life. Then I dreamt of Peter and the restaurant and this town."

The door opened and Karri's gasp caused Skye to turn around. Peter Castle stood there in a black suit with a black shirt underneath it looking for all the world like a black bear.

17

Trent rarely had the television on while he worked, but today he thought the noise would indicate he was home, especially since he wasn't using a loud saw. Instead, he was sanding a piece as he thought about last night. Skye was moving to Shadows Landing. Could his dream really be coming true?

"Hey." Trent looked up as Harper walked inside, a white paper bag in her hand.

"Are those my favorite muffins?"

"They are," she said, setting down the bag and opening it.

"What do you want?" Trent asked suspiciously, making Harper laugh.

"Nothing. I just wanted to see if you wanted to talk."

Trent bit into the muffin and rolled his eyes at Harper. "What do you want?" he asked through a mouthful.

"Fine." Harper grabbed her own muffin. "I wanted to talk about Skye. I know I've been wrapped up in married life and we haven't hung out as much. When I heard about Skye, I thought it was ridiculous. I thought *she* was ridiculous. However, I was wrong. I like her. I see how she's good for you. She balances you and you balance her. It's like Dare and me. Anyway, I know you don't need my approval, but I wanted you to know you had it if you were trying to decide if she fits in here. She does."

"She's moving here."

"What?" Harper almost screamed.

"She told me last night she's going to move here. She said she's made her mark in Hollywood so she doesn't need to be out there all the time now. She wants the privacy Shadows Landing gives her, plus, a lot of her filming is done in Georgia."

"That's great. Why don't you look excited?" Harper asked, zeroing right in on the heart of the matter.

Trent put down his muffin. He and Harper understood each other. They were more than cousins. They were best friends. However, that still didn't mean he liked talking about his feelings.

"I think I love her," Trent admitted.

"Think?" Harper raised an eyebrow in challenge.

Trent felt like tossing the muffin in her face. "No, I know I do. I have since I met her. It's stupid, right? Who falls in love the first day they know someone? I'm embarrassed to even admit it."

"It's not embarrassing, Trent. I admit I fell for Dare fast and hard. Great Aunt Marcy always tells us everyone in the family falls fast and hard. 'When we know, we know,'" Harper said in her best Great Aunt Marcy impersonation.

"True." Trent had to admit his aunt had been telling him the same thing recently. A lot. Like, every time they talked and it was written on every note she mailed with her monthly apple pies.

"So, are you going to tell her?" Harper asked before she popped a pinch of muffin into her mouth.

"I will. I don't know when, but I will when the time is right." Trent had wanted to tell her last night, but it just seemed as if too much was going on. She was busy restructuring her whole life. Plus, she'd been through enough recently. When he told her, he wanted it to be private, romantic, and something they'd share with their grandkids someday.

"Oh crap!"

"Are you okay?" Trent asked Harper as he stood up from where he was leaning on a worktable.

"No, look!"

Trent turned to look at the television. There was a picture of Skye with the word *MISSING* under it. He lunged for the remote and turned it up as a police officer stepped to the microphone.

"Let me first say the involved parties wished for this to remain a private matter for the police to handle. However, the public statement released yesterday has pushed this case forward and into the public eye. Yesterday afternoon, Skye Jessamine's agent, Jim Hexter, and her manager, Lenny Daniels, reported her missing after receiving a ransom note," the police spokesperson said, nodding to the two solemn men standing slightly behind him and to the side. "The major crimes division is in charge of the investigation and is combing through the threatening letters Mr. Daniels has provided to them.

"We believe the break-in at Miss Jessamine's property and the leaked photos were committed by this same perpetrator the other week, which caused Miss Jessamine to receive mental treatment from a private doctor. Mr. Daniels said he hasn't talked to the actress since shortly after the break-in. Mr. Daniels believes firing half her staff was an attempt to get his attention about the abduction. Both Mr. Hexter and Mr. Daniels have been in touch with Miss Jessamine's supposed new legal and PR teams. However, they claim the signed contracts are not signed by Miss Jessamine. Our investigators are currently meeting with them. Due to threats from the paparazzi, we were left with no choice but to come forward with this story. We are asking the public not to approach Miss Jessamine if you see her, but to contact us immediately."

A phone number appeared on the bottom of the screen, but Trent was already running for his car. Harper was only a half step behind him.

Trent was sure he didn't breathe until he flung open the door to the diner and had Skye in his arms. It was only then that he heard Peter Castle yelling into the phone, saw Granger and Kord take off out of the diner, and saw the tears in Karri's eyes.

"What's happened?"

"Peter's on the phone with Agent Shaw. After you dropped me off, one of Star Power's goons stopped me. I played it off as being a local named Emma Kate and the angry sheriff running at him was my boyfriend. I don't think he knew it was me." Trent crushed her to him. He needed to feel her in his arms to know she was safe.

"I'm so sorry." Trent heard Skye's muffled apology from where she'd pressed her face against his chest.

"For what?"

"For bringing this trouble to you and to Shadows Landing."

"We need to get you out of here," Peter said as soon as he hung up his phone. "There are tourists in town and the last thing we want to happen is for one of them to snap a picture of you."

"Is hiding really the only option I have?"

"Yes. For now. My friend Ryan Parker and a local attorney are racing over to Morgan's office to make sure she's safe and not being questioned without representation. Granger called Olivia, but then they got a hit on the car the Star Power man was in just outside of town. While they distract him, we need to get you to Ryker's house. Let's go."

"Here you go, hon." Mary Jane shoved a plastic bag the size of a shopping cart into her hand. "You need some comfort food. As soon as I saw the news, I told them to whip you up some biscuits and gravy for breakfast and some shrimp and grits for lunch. I also put in a whole pineapple upside down cake for you, bless your sweet little heart. If you need anything, you just call and we'll find someone to run it out to you, you hear?"

Skye hugged the waitress without any hesitation. "Thank you. You're all so kind. I'm sorry for any trouble this causes y'all."

Mary Jane cringed as did most of the people in the diner. "Bless your heart. Y'know some people just can't do the accent and that's okay."

Skye tossed up her hands as Trent took the bag from her. "Is it really that bad?"

"Yes!" came the resounding reply.

"If you can't be born a Southerner," Miss Ruby said as she reached out and patted her hand, "you can marry one."

Everyone sent her smiles and winks. Trent scowled at Harper who shrugged as if saying she had no idea what they were talking about. Not that Trent had mentioned marriage —yet.

"Can Karri come with us for the day?" Skye asked him

and he felt horrible. He didn't want to isolate her as Jim and Lenny had.

"Of course. You never have to ask that. Your friends are my friends." Trent bent and placed a kiss on the top of her head as Peter moved toward them.

"I'll drive you, Karri."

Karri nodded but watched worriedly as Trent placed his free hand on the small of Skye's back and led her from the diner. He whisked her into the car and had her safely in Ryker's guesthouse before she could blink.

Trent, Skye, Peter, Karri, and Harper filled the living room as Skye broke out breakfast from the diner and passed it around.

"It's my dream. The darkness is coming," Trent heard Karri whisper.

"What dream?" Peter had heard her too. Karri's face turned red and Trent wondered what kind of dream this really was.

"Karri had a dream that Shadows Landing was our home and that darkness was coming," Skye answered for her.

"Dreams are very important. My grandmother says that in our dreams, our past, present, and future can join to share their wisdom." Peter was staring at Karri, almost willing her to tell him the entire dream.

"I saw myself starting a restaurant in the space to rent next to Harper's bar. I saw all you inside of it and then I heard my wolf howl as darkness crept forward. I had to fight the darkness, but I wasn't alone. Others were there to help," Karri answered Peter's unasked question of what she'd dreamt.

Peter nodded and reached out to hold Karri's hand. "You're a wolf and your courage and loyalty are seen by this dream. I had a dream too. I saw the mist, but I also saw us fighting it together." Peter looked around the room. "All of us."

Trent felt a shiver race through Skye's body and looked down at her. "I'll tell you later," she whispered.

Skye's phone rang and everyone practically jumped out of their skin as the jarring sound echoed in the silent room. "It's Olivia," she said as she put it on speaker. "Are you okay?"

"I'm *pissed*," Olivia's voice came through loud and clear, as did her anger. "Those little assholes with major crimes tried to arrest me for kidnapping."

Trent almost felt sorry for them. He knew Olivia would not respond well to that sort of thing.

"This is Agent Castle. Agent Shaw of the L.A. office was supposed to call them," Castle told her.

"He did. But since he wouldn't disclose Skye's location, they said they couldn't stop the investigation. They want the press and publicity and I told them what they could do with both."

"I take it they didn't arrest you?" Trent wanted to hear what happened next.

"Of course not. They don't have a case. They're totally confused as to where Skye is and why she's missing. I refused to answer any question other than to say that my client was safe and had not been kidnapped. They wanted me to call you, but I refused that as well. If we have to, we'll go public. They wanted a video call and I didn't want them to hear or see anything that could give you away."

"Well," Skye hedged, "it might be too late. One of the Star Power goons found me today, but I don't look like myself and gave him a fake name. Granger came running at me so I told him he was my boyfriend."

Olivia let out a very unladylike snort of amusement. "I bet Granger loved that. Granger doesn't do girlfriends. Just be careful. I'm here on business for another couple of days and have a feeling this won't be the last I hear from them. If I need to prove you're safe, Ryker has a soundproof room in his house that I'm sure he'll let you use to verify that you're alive and well. In the meantime, I'm fighting Jim Hexter and Tony Ketron over the alleged contract. Both camps have made threats, but I think they think I'll swerve in this game of chicken. What they don't know is, I don't swerve. I decimate any obstacle in my way. I'll keep you updated."

Olivia hung up and within minutes Morgan was calling.

"Are you okay?" Skye immediately asked upon answering the phone.

Morgan laughed with amusement and Skye looked at Trent with worry. "I haven't had this much fun in years. The new attorney in town, Tandy Rawlings, was supposed to be here with me when I was questioned, but she got stuck in court. Henry Rooney came instead, and I know you don't know him, but he wears shiny suits. That should tell you everything you need to know. And he speaks only in awful pick-up lines just for laughs. However, he's brilliant. I just sat back and didn't say a word."

"So, what happened?" Trent asked.

Morgan laughed again. "The detective they sent was female and Henry started off by telling her he had a great idea on how they could use her handcuffs. When she ignored him and tried to threaten me with arrest, Henry turned to her and said the only law she was going to enforce was the law of attraction. Then he growled at her. It totally flustered her. Then she got stern and threatened me some more and Henry told her it was hot that she was playing bad cop and tonight he'd let her plant something on him while he showed her how to use his nightstick."

"That's not right," Karri muttered.

"That's Henry. I almost felt sorry for her," Morgan told them. "But she threatened me so she's lucky she only got some pick-up lines that are so bad they're funny and not a direct response from me or my husband. She gave up and left with the threat that she'd be back. Henry shouted after her that he'd have her on her back too. You have Olivia. I have Henry. I bet Henry got rid of the detective a lot faster than Olivia did."

Trent tried so hard not to laugh. Skye smacked his arm. "I'm sorry. I know it's wrong, but I can't help it. I was envisioning what would happen if Olivia and Henry met."

There was a moment of silence and then everyone laughed. Not just a little snicker either, but full-out belly laughs.

18

IT HAD BEEN two days since the media had gone forward with their #FindSkye campaign. It was sad how fast a routine could be established. Skye sighed as she closed the door to the guesthouse after kissing Trent goodbye for the day.

And thus day two began the same as day one. She and Trent woke up at five in the morning. They made love, showered, and then she kissed him goodbye. At eight, Tinsley and Karri would join her for breakfast. At noon, Miss Winnie and Miss Ruby would bring her lunch and sit with her for a while. Yesterday they brought Reverend Winston. Today it would be a surprise guest. Then Skye would work on knitting her scarf when Edie came over at three. Finally, Trent would be home at five. Kiss, eat, sex, repeat.

Skye hated feeling like a prisoner, but the media hunt for her was reaching epic levels. It didn't matter that she'd even had a videoconference with the L.A.P.D. from Ryker's soundproof room, they still wanted to meet with her in person. She and Olivia, who had conferenced in from New York, had denied their request. They were so adamant Skye was tempted to hire Henry Rooney just for giggles.

She took a seat on the back deck and waited for Karri and Tinsley to arrive. The ding of her phone told her she had a text. It was a strange situation to be in. She both dreaded being alone and yet every time her phone went off, she wanted to throw it in the river.

Court date set for end of the week on your contract with Jim. You don't need to be there. I'll castrate him for you and send you the video.

Gosh, she loved Olivia. Could it really be that easy? A court date on her contract and then she'd be free? Well, free of Jim, Lenny, and Tony. Not so free from whoever had been sending her threatening letters.

Skye pulled up her email and got to work on changing her passwords and authorizations to all her accounts. Olivia had discovered that Jim and Lenny had tried to get into Skye's personal bank accounts and promptly fired Lenny. He'd refused to leave, stating he wasn't Skye's employee, but Jim's. That was the excuse Olivia needed to get the emergency bench trial to rule on her contract. She'd told Olivia they'd shot themselves in the foot with the move.

"Hello! Emma Kate?"

Skye laughed as Karri and Tinsley announced their arrival.

"Mary Jane packed us full this morning," Karri told her with a smile as she set the gargantuan bag down on the outdoor table.

"It must be good because you're beaming like a kid in a candy shop." Skye looked at her friend and noticed the light blush, the big grin, and the happy sparkle in her eyes.

Tinsley gave a cute snort of laughter. "More like a woman in an FBI strip club where they let you touch the goods."

Skye whistled in surprise. "You and Peter?"

Karri sat down in the chair and the smile only grew. "Nothing happened. Tinsley's making too big of a deal out of it."

"It is a big deal!" Tinsley said with a faux pout as she handed out the food.

"He stopped by last night after he checked in on you and we talked some. That's all," Karri said in such a way that Skye knew that definitely was not the whole story. She glanced at Tinsley who rolled her eyes.

"Some? You talked until three in the morning and I found you two asleep on the couch this morning."

"You slept with him?" Skye knew Karri had been feeling lonely recently and to find someone she connected with made Skye so excited for her friend.

"Yes, but only in the most literal sense. We didn't even kiss."

"But you wanted to?" Skye pushed.

"Of course I wanted to. Everything in my entire body feels connected to him. Ugh!" Karri flopped back against her chair and tossed her hands up in the air. "What am I going to do?"

"Yo! Anyone here?"

Skye cocked her head at the new voice. Who was that?

"Back here, Harper!" Tinsley yelled.

"Does everyone have a code to this house?" Skye asked.

"Just family," Tinsley assured her.

Harper walked in looking none too happy about being up so early. Her hair might not have been brushed when she'd pulled it back into a sloppy bun, but it was the PJ bottoms that were a dead giveaway. Harper had rolled out of bed and come straight here. "Did something happen?" Skye asked worriedly.

"Yeah, someone woke me up. Coffee. I need coffee."

"It's in the kitchen," Skye told her. Harper shuffled off and returned a minute later with a giant cup of black coffee.

"Better. Dare got called into work. He's going to be undercover for a week or so. He knew better than to wake me up when he left. Suze Bell, on the other hand, didn't."

"What did Suze want?" Tinsley asked after filling Karri and Skye in that Suze had the large bed and breakfast next to Ryker and reminding them that Maggie and Gage were her kids.

"She owns the empty space between my bar and Bless Your Scarf," Harper dropped that bomb and then paused to chug some more coffee. "She wants to sell it. She got an offer from someone in Charleston but would rather it go to someone here. She asked me if I wanted to buy it."

Karri's face paled and Skye remembered that in her friend's dream, it was Karri who owned that space. "Are you going to buy it?" Karri asked in a studiously neutral tone.

Harper took another healthy sip of coffee. "I can, but I thought you might want first dibs on it. I actually had an idea. I want to serve food at my place, but I'm not set up for anything but bar food. That meal you cooked me yesterday was out of this world. What do you think about a little demolition and building a connector between the two?"

Karri sat up, no longer pale-faced but suddenly very animated. "A joint operation? I'd provide food to my own place and yours while you serve drinks to your place and mine?"

Harper nodded. "That's exactly what I was thinking. You do food, I do drinks, and everyone's happy. I was even thinking you could give my place its own bar menu. Gourmet burgers and such and then you can serve the upscale stuff at your place. I can create special drinks for your restaurant to pair with your specials too." Harper slid a piece of paper across the table. "Here's Suze's number. Let me know what you decide. If you don't want to do it, I'll buy it. I can also rent it to you if you want."

"Thanks, Harper. This means everything to me."

Harper grunted and got up. "I refuse to have morning meetings if we do this, though."

Karri smiled and Harper finished her coffee and stumbled from the house.

"Are you going to do it?" Skye asked her best friend. Karri had wanted her own place since college and now it was in her reach.

"I know it's not L.A., but the only other place I ever considered living was Syracuse. We've talked about it, though. I just have this feeling. Shadows Landing is where I'm supposed to be. Then there was that dream. I think I'm going to learn more and then decide. Excuse me. I have a call to make."

Skye and Tinsley watched Karri walk inside and close the door behind her. "You know, I've heard that old Mrs. Cramble is thinking of selling her house."

"Um, okay. Good for her." Skye had no idea where Tinsley was going with this.

"It's next door." Tinsley pointed toward Shadows Landing. Ryker had an old historical estate. You didn't see your neighbors what with the acres of land and the substantial hedgerows and trees planted all around for privacy.

"The one with the beautiful scrollwork on the gate?" Skye asked, sitting up now that Tinsley had her attention.

Tinsley nodded. "Want to go see it real quick?"

"Can I really?"

"Let me call her." Skye waited impatiently as Tinsley made the call. When Tinsley smiled and said they'd come by the back in ten minutes, Skye knew it was a go. "While you get your shoes on, I'll tell Ryker we're going to scale his fence so he doesn't call the police on us."

"How would he even know?"

"His fences have motion sensors on them. Motion sets off the video camera and sends the footage to Ryker's security company."

Okay, there was a lot more to Ryker Faulkner than Skye could fathom. "Let's go," she said, slipping on her shoes.

THE FENCE-HOPPING WASN'T graceful and she'd gotten a text from Ryker with the thumbs down emoji. However, just thinking of Ryker sending a text with an emoji had Skye and Tinsley cracking up.

Skye took in the large backyard, the big detached garage, the swimming pool, and the outdoor living space. It rivaled a home in the Hamptons except it oozed Southern charm.

A sweet older lady came out the back door and waited for them. Tinsley took the lead and made the introductions. When Skye shook Mrs. Cramble's hand, she didn't let go right away. "Thank you for being so kind to Mitzy. She's my sister and her daughter-in-law, Karen, is a viper. You made her feel so good by just talking to her at knitting club."

"Your sister is very kind. Why aren't you in knitting club?"

"I'm in needlepoint club. I could never get the hang of

knitting. Now, Tinsley said you wanted to see the house. Are you thinking of moving here?"

"I am, but it's a secret."

"Of course, dear. I've seen your hashtag all over social media. You poor girl. To be hunted like that?" Mrs. Cramble shook her head in disgust, but then perked up. "I hear you're staying with Trent Faulkner. He's such a nice young man. He's made several pieces for me. Do you think he'd be moving here with you?"

"I don't know, Mrs. Cramble. I sure hope so," Skye admitted and as soon as she said it she saw her life with him in it. She saw him in the garage working on his furniture and their kids fishing off the dock. The more Mrs. Cramble led her around the house, the more she knew it was meant to be. It had room for everything. It was big, historic, and yet homey.

"This sits on twelve acres. There're two docks. One straight down there that you can see from the house and another farther down. The second one has a boathouse and boat ramp on it. So, what do you think?" Mrs. Cramble asked after they ended the tour.

"It's beautiful. I'd like to talk to Trent. Even if I wanted to buy it right this second, I have to wait until this mess is cleared up. Would that be a problem?"

"Not at all. I wasn't going to put it on the market until springtime. Just let me know. It's been a pleasure to meet you. I know all the girls are looking forward to seeing you at knitting club this week."

"I'm looking forward to it too. Thank you for the tour. It's a lovely house."

"So, what are you going to do?" Tinsley asked as they crawled back over the fence and into Ryker's property.

"It feels right."

Tinsley nodded as if she understood and maybe she did. That was the thing about Shadows Landing. As long as someone didn't bless her heart in a bad way, it meant they understood her. There was no preening or fawning just because she was a celebrity because it was, well, home.

19

Olivia Townsend rode the elevator of her law firm's building in New York City down to the lobby. She'd been working on her arguments for Skye's court date in two days. Nothing was a sure thing, but breaking this contract was as close as you could get to a sure thing. It made her mad that people like Jim Hexter took advantage of young women like this. It was more than likely that he took advantage of all his young clients who were desperate to break into the movie industry.

The doors to the elevator slid open and her high heels clicked as she walked across the marble floor. It was rush hour and she was surprised to see a free town car. She lifted her hand and the driver who was taking a smoke break looked up and nodded. He ground out his cigarette and opened the back door. "Where to?"

Olivia rattled off the address of the firm's apartment where she was staying and leaned back to relax. She put in her headphones and turned on her audiobook. Time to unwind and then it was back to work once she got to the apartment.

They made slow progress but then the driver turned off the congested avenue and went through a side street. "Where are you going?" Olivia pulled the earbuds from her ears and looked around.

"Traffic is a nightmare. I'm taking a shortcut. We're not that far away now."

Warning bells went off and Olivia pulled her phone up as if she were working. "Thanks. I'm swamped with emails back here and the faster I can get out of the car, the faster I can stop feeling as if I'm going to throw up. I hate reading in the back of the car." She snapped a picture of the driver and emailed it to herself.

The side street turned into an alley and Olivia knew her fear was warranted. She dialed 911 as the car rolled to a stop. Her adrenaline kicked into high gear as she silently slipped off her shoes. She moved the phone into her left hand even as she heard the 911 operator pick up. "Why are we in the alley behind The Thirsty Taco? This isn't where I live," she said loudly. She hoped the 911 operator would pick up on her clues and dispatch police.

A man dressed in head-to-toe black materialized from behind a dumpster on her side of the car. He ripped her door open and was reaching for her before Olivia could try to escape out the other side.

"Don't hurt me!" Olivia cried. "Help!"

There was no way in hell they were getting her out of this car. Olivia gripped the shoe in her right hand and prepared to fight. The man in black reached for her and she stabbed the stiletto heel into his hand.

"Bitch!" The punch to the face came hard and fast. Olivia felt her head snap back and her eyes water. She struggled against the darkness as she felt the man's hands grab her ankles and begin to pull her from the car. The world snapped back into focus. She had to fight.

"Help!" she screamed at the top of her lungs as she pulled her leg back as far as she could and kicked. She didn't stop at that. She kicked and kicked and screamed and screamed, hoping someone would hear her.

The man smacked her feet away as if she were an annoying gnat and grabbed her computer bag. "I got her computer. Get her phone." This wasn't a standard robbery. They needed something from her electronics. She hoped the 911 operator had enough information because she ended the call and pressed the button to put her phone in sleep mode. Her phone was now completely locked down. No facial recognition or finger touch to open it. No, to open it, you had to have a six-number code that she changed monthly. They would never get it from her. Period. If they thought the code on her phone was tough, they were in for a surprise with her laptop.

Olivia tried to climb into the front, but the driver opened the other back door, fisted her hair in his hand, and yanked. Olivia screamed, her hands automatically coming up to hold his hand on her head to limit the pain. She was flung backward from the front to the backseat, then dragged like a rag doll from the backseat and out the door.

Olivia's butt hit the dirty ground hard. It jarred her, making her head throb even more as a hand that smelled of cigarettes was placed over her mouth. "Do you have her phone and computer?"

"I got the computer up but need the password. What is it, bitch?" the man in black asked as he bent down in front of her and put his mask-covered face in hers.

Olivia shook her head and lashed out with the best punch she could muster. The satisfaction of landing the surprise punch was short-lived. He punched her hard and fast in the stomach.

"What's the code?" he demanded again.

Olivia coughed and tried not to panic. She couldn't get any air. It was all gone. Her lungs burned, her head spun, and she thought she was going to vomit.

"Try the phone. Maybe she has a password app," the driver suggested. The man picked the phone up from where it had fallen in the backseat even as Olivia struggled to regain control of her mind. There was so much pain mixed with panic that she had to fight to calm down. She knew she had to be clearheaded to make it out alive.

The ski mask was back in her face as he held her phone in front of her. The driver gripped her head to make sure she didn't move. Olivia smirked when the phone wouldn't turn on with facial recognition. With a growl, the man in the ski mask yanked her thumb forward and placed it on the reader, but it still wouldn't unlock.

"Dammit. We have to get the phone and computer or we won't be paid," the driver cursed.

"I'll get it from her." The man in the ski mask stood and the booted kick to her side came as a shock, as if it were happening to someone else. Olivia's mind was screaming for her to run, to fight, to do something . . . but the booted kick came again and again.

She felt the masked man's hand grip her hair and pull her back up to sitting. Olivia couldn't breathe. She couldn't make sense of what was happening to her. "What's the password?"

"*Screw. You.*" It hurt as she gasped the words but they felt satisfying to say—until the punch to her face landed.

"Shit, sirens," the driver said. The increasing noise of the police sirens broke through the fog in Olivia's swimming head.

"You're lucky, bitch." Olivia didn't see the fist coming as her eye was already swelling shut but then blissful darkness overtook her.

∽

TRENT COULDN'T WAIT to get home. It was amazing how his own house didn't feel like his anymore at all because Skye wasn't in it. It was 4:53 in the afternoon. Close enough to the end of a workday. Trent closed down his shop and went inside. He changed clothes, packed a couple more things, and then snuck out the back. He walked over to Tinsley's house and used the ATV to drive through the woods, across North Cypress Lane, and into the back part of the Bell Landing farm. He drove the distance of the farm until he turned onto a path that led to Palmetto Drive. He looked both ways and when he didn't see any people or cars, he gunned the ATV and shot down the short distance to Ryker's house. He entered the code and could finally breathe when he entered the compound.

Edie's car was still parked in front of the guesthouse and Trent knew the sight that would greet him. He parked and walked inside. He looked the length of the house and found Edie and Skye knitting out on the patio. Home. He was finally home.

Edie glanced up and then Skye as soon as he opened the glass door to the patio.

"Hey, sweetie. You're home early," Skye said, smiling up at him. Trent placed a kiss on her lips and his hand automatically fell to her shoulder as he stood next to her.

His whole body relaxed with her touch as she welcomed him home. There was that word again. *Home.*

"I hit a good stopping point. Your knitting is coming along nicely," Trent told her.

Edie stood up and stuffed her things into her tote bag. "She's doing really well. The girls will be excited to see your progress at knitting club."

Trent wasn't relaxed anymore. "I don't think that's a good idea."

"Don't worry, Trent," Edie told him as she packed her knitting bag. "It's four days away. A lot can happen in four days. And if it doesn't, we can totally sneak her in through the back. No one will see her, I promise."

Trent wasn't so sure about that.

"Do you think we could have it here?" Skye asked. "There's enough room, isn't there?"

"That's a great idea! I'll run it past them. I'll see you tomorrow." Edie bent down and hugged Skye before patting Trent on the shoulder as she walked by.

Trent took a seat on the couch with Skye and pulled her against his side as she finished her knitting. The silence was comfortable and once again that warm feeling of being home wrapped around him and soothed him.

"How was your day?"

Skye didn't look away from her scarf as she spoke. "Busy if you can believe it. I have such good news, and I also have something I wanted to talk to you about. Let me just finish this row."

Trent watched the way Skye concentrated on her knitting. She was so focused on it that she probably didn't notice the tip of her tongue was peeking out between her lips.

"What's the good news?" Trent asked when she finally set down the scarf.

Skye's eyes were shining with happiness when she looked up at him. Trent automatically smiled at her joy. "Karri is going to buy the building next to Harper's bar and they're going to work together!"

"Wait, Karri's staying in Shadows Landing? And how are she and Harper going to work together?" Trent was not expecting this news. It was great, though. It might mean that Skye was serious about staying herself.

"Yes, she's staying. She had a dream that Shadows Landing and this restaurant were her home. Then Harper walked in this morning and told us the building was for sale and offered to make the drinks for Karri's restaurant if Karri made the food for Harper's Bar. Isn't that great?"

"Great? It's genius. Harper hates trying to come up with a menu. Now she can focus on what she loves and Karri can focus on what she loves. What's the other thing you wanted to talk to me about?"

Skye's whole demeanor changed. Worry clouded her eyes and dimmed her smile. Trent wanted to know what was wrong, but he wanted Skye to go at her own pace. Skye took a deep breath and then looked toward the property next door. "I'm afraid you'll think I'm moving too fast, and I know I am. I mean, we just started dating and I don't want this to sound as if I have any expectation of our relationship."

"Okay," Trent said slowly, not knowing where she was going with this.

"The house next door will be going up for sale in the spring. Tinsley took me over there and I met Mrs. Cramble. She showed us the estate. We had to hop the fence, but it was worth it. I want to buy it. However, I'll only do it after everything is settled and if you support my move to

Shadows Landing. This is your home. I want to make it mine too."

Trent's initial reaction was excitement. Then what she was really saying set in. She would move her whole life here. What if they broke up? What if they didn't? Now he understood why she looked nervous. This was a conversation that most couples had after they'd been together for a while, not just a week.

"I understand exactly what you mean. This is a huge step. Let's not even consider our relationship in this. Will moving to Shadows Landing make you happy?" Trent asked. "Really think about it. This isn't a big town. Remember what it was like growing up in a small town? Everyone will know everything about you. However, it's almost the farthest from Hollywood you can get."

Skye took a deep breath as he used his thumb to trace a gentle circle over her shoulder while he held her. "Yes. Both Karri and I felt it instantly. We were at peace here. We are happy and we love the residents. Somehow, in less than a week I feel as if I've been here for my entire life."

"If I weren't in the picture, would you buy Mrs. Cramble's house?" Trent asked next.

"Yes." Skye's answer was instantaneous. Then she took a breath and looked back at him. "But, I want to know if we're together long term, which," Skye paused and bit her lip nervously, "which I really hope we will be. In that case, could you see yourself there with me? For all that it's my house right now, I want it to be our house when we're ready."

He was ready now. He wanted to tell her he loved her. He wanted to rush headlong into forever, but the fear of Skye changing her mind and breaking his heart held him back. "I'd love to look at it with you. Why don't we set up a time with Mrs. Cramble to look at the house again in a couple of weeks? She's not putting it on the market until the spring, so we have time, right? That way we can get things settled with your career and not have to sneak over the fence. I'd love to see that, though. It's a tall fence."

"Don't worry, Ryker has it on camera," Skye said with a chuckle. "I was not at my most graceful."

"I refuse to believe it, but I'm totally asking Ryker for the footage." Trent loved teasing her. He loved her laugh as he pulled out his phone, but before he could fake-text Ryker, his phone rang.

"It's like he's listening," Trent said, turning the phone to show it was Ryker calling. "Hey. We were just talking about you and Skye's fence-vaulting skills," Trent said with a wink to Skye.

"It's Olivia." The icy tone in Ryker's voice changed everything in a split second.

20

"What is it?" Skye shot up and looked at Trent the second she felt his body go rigid. He moved to put the phone on speaker.

"Ryker, you're on speaker with Skye and me. What happened to Olivia?"

Skye felt as if an icicle had replaced her spine as she shivered with dread.

"She was attacked. She's not conscious yet. Surveillance shows she thought she was getting in her usual town car and she ended up severely beaten in an alley about fifteen blocks away. The police found my business card in her purse. The town car was still there. It had been stolen from the company under contract to provide rides to the firm. They took her phone and computer. But she was smart. She called 911 and the police were able to get to her within a couple of minutes."

"Is she going to make it?" Skye's voice trembled as ice shot through her veins.

The short time it took to hear Ryker's voice seemed like

an eternity. "Yes. She has broken ribs, a concussion, and a broken nose. She'll make it, though."

"Why did this happen to her? What can I do?" Skye felt so helpless and she didn't like it. She feared she already knew the answer to why this happened to Olivia. It happened because of her. "It's because of the court date for my contract in two days, isn't it?"

"We don't know," Ryker answered honestly. "The doctor is signaling me. I'll text with updates."

The line went dead and the tears that had been threatening froze as cold determination took hold of her. "This is because of me and I'm going to fix it."

"No. You're going to stay hidden here where you're safe," Trent ordered as he reached for her. His body was warm as he held her against him, but Skye wasn't thawing in her resolve.

Skye pulled out her phone and dialed. "I have to warn Morgan." The phone rang and then went to voicemail. Skye looked up at Trent, her eyes wide with worry.

"I'll call Miles," Trent said and Skye knew in that second he too knew this was all because of her.

∽

"Are you sure you don't need me to stay, Morgan?"

Morgan Davies looked up from her desk in Lexington, Kentucky, and smiled at her assistant. It was dinnertime and her assistant had a young family to get home to. "No, go on home. Thank you. I'm just working on these press releases until Miles gets here."

"It's so cute you two still commute to Lexington together. I hope Robby and I are still so in love when we've been married thirty-plus years."

"You will be," Morgan said with a smile. She heard her assistant leave before looking back down at the three Skye Jessamine press releases she'd been working on. One was to be used if Olivia was victorious in court in two days, one if she lost, and a third if the judge didn't rule immediately.

The door to her lobby opened again and Morgan called out, "I'm in my office."

She and Miles were planning on a romantic dinner out in downtown Lexington tonight. Her husband was a nervous wreck over the fact their only child, Layne, was pregnant. It didn't matter that the pregnancy was trouble-free and both baby and Layne were completely healthy. Morgan's rough and tough former Special Forces husband was a mess. He was reading so many pregnancy and baby books that he was seeing danger at every turn and she needed to distract him for the night.

A shadow covered her desk and Morgan looked up with anticipation at her husband. Her smile slid from her face, though, as she saw not her husband but a man in a ski mask with a knife in hand standing there.

"Bless your heart. You picked the wrong place to rob." Morgan stood slowly as she palmed the fountain pen Miles had given her for Christmas many years ago. She slowly pushed the cap loose and waited to see what his next move was. She knew that all he saw was a woman in her sixties alone in her office. She almost felt sorry for him. Almost.

"Where's Skye Jessamine?" the low, gravelly voice asked as he leaned forward threateningly.

"Oh, now this is interesting," Morgan said, widening her stance and rocking up onto the balls of her feet. She was ready to make her move at any second. "Why do you want Skye?"

"That's none of your concern, but do you know what is? The fact that if you don't tell me where she is, I'll kill you."

The lack of hesitation in his voice told Morgan he meant it. Her cell phone rang in the thick silence and drew their attention to where the phone sat in the middle of the desk.

"Who is Eugene Fitzwilliams?" the man asked.

It was the fake name she had Skye's number listed as, that's who. "My accountant."

His eyes drifted down to the phone and as he reached to pick it up, Morgan made her move. She sent the cap flying on her fountain pen as she stabbed it down into his hand. She felt the nib of the pen plunge through the man's skin and sink down into his palm. He screamed and fumbled with the knife in his free hand as he reached for the pen skewering his left.

Morgan grabbed the front of the man's shirt and smashed her head into his with a head-butt that sent him flying backward right as the door to her office was flung open.

"Hi, honey. Are you ready for date night?" Morgan asked her husband who had burst into the office like an avenging angel.

"Let me just take out the trash first." Miles sent her a wink that still made her body flush with anticipation. Dinner was suddenly off the table as a whole new menu was about to be served up.

Miles leaned down, grabbed the man around the neck, and hoisted him up. "Let's have a little chat about how to treat my wife. Not that she didn't tell you already, but I really want to drive the point home."

Morgan watched her husband haul the man out by the scruff of the neck and reached for the phone. Miles would handle it from here. She needed to talk to Skye.

"Morgan, you're in danger!" Skye blurted out the second the phone was answered.

"No worries, dear. It's all handled."

Skye looked to Trent who just shrugged. "I told you the Keeneston family was different," he whispered.

"Did something happen?" Skye asked, feeling as if Morgan was perhaps playing a joke on her.

"Yes, they made the mistake of sending only one person after me to find out where you are. Miles has him now. I almost feel sorry for him. We might look like grandparents, but you should see how many ways I can kill someone with a spoon."

"I want to be you when I grow up." Skye was sure she was living in a parallel universe. Morgan laughed and promised to teach her when they saw each other soon. "Soon?"

"Yes. I'm coming to Shadows Landing. We're all coming to Shadows Landing after this. They just made it personal."

"I have a better idea. This is about me. This is about trying to stop my contract with Jim from being thrown out. Well, I'm not going to be intimidated anymore. Let's bring the fight to them," Skye said with a slow smile as she looked up at Trent. "Do you think Ryker will let us borrow his plane to sneak into New York City?"

"I have a better idea," a deep voice said over the speakerphone. "We'll get you to New York for the bench trial while keeping all ties to Shadows Landing safe. I'll be in touch, but for now I have date night with my beautiful wife who stabbed a man through the hand with a fountain pen before head-butting him."

The sound of things crashing to the floor and then, "Oh Miles!" was heard before the line went dead.

Trent cleared his throat before looking down at his phone. "Ryker just texted that Olivia is awake. I'm telling him about Morgan. I'm also telling Granger and Peter."

Skye sat stewing. The more she thought about it, the angrier she got. She'd told Morgan her plan, but it was so hard to wait. She wanted those spotlights on her now so she could destroy the people behind this.

"I know you're ready to wage war, but we don't have the right ammunition yet." Trent gave her thigh a light squeeze, drawing her attention back to her.

"What do you mean?"

"I mean, we have an idea it's Jim and Lenny behind this, but we have no proof. Also, you've been getting those threatening notes for almost a year. Who is behind those? What if that person is the same one trying to hunt you down? What if Jim and Lenny were honest about receiving that ransom note? Or what if they're the ones sending them? We just don't know."

Damn. Trent was right. She had to find proof that they were behind this. "How do we find out who's behind the threats? The FBI is working on it and we have nothing."

"We give them time to do their job," he replied.

"I don't want to give them time. I want this over now. People helping me are getting hurt. What if you're next, Trent? I couldn't live with myself if anyone else gets hurt because of me."

Skye was up and pacing as Trent took a deep breath. "I like our idea for New York. Instead of going in full blast, let the trial do the talking for you."

"And then what? Come back here and hide?"

Trent stood up and cut off her pacing. "Come back here

and stay safe until we find out who is behind these threats. We sit, we plan, we make connections, and we wait. When we have the evidence, *then* you'll be able to take your revenge."

Skye took a deep breath. She felt like smashing someone with her lacrosse stick, but he was right. She needed to be smart, but she also wanted to make a statement in New York. A big one.

"You're right. But I *do* have an idea. I need support and you won't be able to give that to me in New York. It'll only take seconds to know I'm in Shadows Landing if you're seen there."

Trent nodded with his jaw clenched tight. She could tell he didn't like the idea of her out there in public without him. "I'll stay on the plane while you go to court."

Skye picked up her phone and began to text. "Sometimes I forget I have friends. I'll show them I'm not alone at the trial."

21

Trent knew Skye's plan for the bench trial was sound, but that didn't mean he liked it. However, watching the woman he was falling in love with find her confidence again was worth it. It would be hard to do, but he was going to have to move from protector to supporter. He knew just how to do that too.

Trent picked up his phone and sent his own texts. Within minutes, he knew Skye would be safe when she left him to make her stand.

"How is it going?" he asked Skye, who was still working on her phone.

Skye put down her phone and looked up at him as the setting sun's rays cast her in a warm orange glow. She took a deep breath and moved to lean against him. Trent opened his arms wide for her and felt as if the world was perfect when Skye was in his embrace.

"Really well, actually. I always felt so isolated, but I just needed to reach out. Turns out I have a lot more friends than I thought. Now if Miles and Ryker can get us to New York undetected, I feel pretty positive about the case."

Trent's phone pinged with a text and he glanced down at it. "Incoming," he said as he read Ryker's text. "Granger and Castle are coming in the gate now."

Whoever was driving must have been flying down the drive because Trent couldn't even stand up before there was banging on the front door. "I'll be right back." Trent kissed her forehead and yelled that he was coming to whoever was beating down the door.

It wasn't a surprise to Trent to see that it was Granger about to bust down the door. "Come on in. We're on the back patio." Granger's and Peter's faces were in full pissed-off cop mode. Their lips were pursed, their jaws tight, and their eyes cold.

"We have a plan. I'll let Skye tell you." Trent reached out and grabbed Granger's arm, stopping him from storming through the house. "Skye is beyond upset about what's happened and feels responsible. Don't be a dick."

"I'm never a dick," Granger ground out between his teeth. Then he stopped and took a deep breath before letting it out slowly. "Okay, so *sometimes* I can be a dick."

"She's trying to take control of her life. Let her." Trent blocked Granger and Peter until they both agreed. Skye was carrying around so much guilt for what happened to Olivia he didn't want them to break her. She needed to be built up now to believe in herself or she might shatter into a million pieces.

Trent turned and led them out onto the patio where Skye looked so little on the couch. She was nervously playing with the hem of her shirt as she waited for them.

"It's my fault Olivia got hurt," she said as she looked up at Granger and Peter. "But I won't allow it to be for nothing. I have a plan."

Peter took a seat in one of the chairs, but Granger just

leaned back against the door and crossed his arms over his chest as he listened to what Skye wanted to do.

"I'll go with you to New York," Granger told her when she was done.

"That's very sweet of you, but I can't have anyone from Shadows Landing there or they may make the connection to me staying here. This is my safe place until we find the evidence to connect Jim and Lenny to the threats. Only then can I—*we* move on."

"I'm working every lead on that evidence. I'm trying to find a link between Star Power and Jim, Lenny, or anyone on their team. I've had to escalate it up to cybercrimes to see if they can find any digital currency used to pay for these thugs to harass you," Peter told her. "And," he said, looking to Granger, "I agree that neither you nor I can go with her."

Trent saw Skye grimace. "It'll just be Karri and me. We'll do what we need to."

"Karri? Like hell." Peter jumped up from his seat and started pacing the same path Skye had trod not a half hour before. "We have to go. I'm not leaving you two to go alone."

"I'm going with them," Trent told his two friends. "I'm just staying in whatever transport Miles and Ryker arranged for us."

"Then we are too," Peter said as Granger nodded.

"They need protection in the city. We can do that. No one looks at the bodyguards," Granger tried to argue.

Trent smiled and that got his friends' attention. "Don't worry. I've got that part covered."

Neither Peter nor Granger looked convinced, but they agreed to escort the three of them to New York and then home. Trent didn't admit it, but it would be nice to have them along. It was going to be nerve-wracking letting Skye do her thing and not be able to be by her side every minute, but having Granger and Peter with him would help.

"I'm going to check in with Karri." Peter stopped pacing and looked down at Skye. "Don't worry. We'll keep you safe. I understand what you're doing and why. Now the rest is up to me. I won't let you down."

"I know you won't. Thank you for all you guys are doing for me." Trent watched as Skye stood and hugged Peter and then Granger. Granger looked so uncomfortable with any display of affection that it almost made Trent laugh.

"We'll check back in tomorrow. Call if there're any new developments," Granger grumbled before he and Peter left.

Skye took a deep breath and looked out over the river with a sad expression on her face. Trent sat down next to her and pulled her near. He wrapped his arms around her and nuzzled his lips against her neck.

"Trent, I have something I have to say."

Trent stopped the light kissing down her neck and looked into her serious face. "What is it?"

He saw the swallow working its way down her throat as she looked determined yet nervously up at him. "I feel as if I'm facing the executioner the day after tomorrow. Suddenly all the time I was envisioning between us has been narrowed down into a two-day window. Less than that, actually. We have two nights and one day together until my world might implode."

Trent gently pushed back her hair so he could look down into her face unobstructed. "Skye, your world won't implode. No matter what the court ruling is or what happens, we'll face it together."

Skye gave a weak smile and Trent moved to cup her cheek with his hand. He loved how she leaned her cheek against his hand and nodded. "That's why I have to talk to you. You've shown me the courage I have and by doing this myself I am taking control of my life once again. But there's one thing I have no control over now and that's my heart. Trent, I know it's crazy, but I fell in love with you the second I met you. No matter what happens in New York, I love you and I will always love you."

Trent felt as if someone had knocked the breath from him. He went to open his mouth, but Skye stopped him.

"I know it's too soon. I know I shouldn't be thinking of forever, but I can't help it. I had to have you know that you're in my heart and soul. I totally understand if I'm not in yours. I wanted to tell you before everything goes crazy." Skye paused and cocked her head a bit and then rolled her eyes. "Well, crazier than things already are."

Trent moved his thumb over her lips to stop her from saying whatever it was she was going to say next. "May I speak now?"

Skye nodded and Trent raised his other hand to cup her face. He looked down at her, begging her with his eyes to believe what he was going to say. "Skye, I love you too. I have from that first day together, even before the most amazing night of my life. When we sat down and were talking and laughing together, it was just *right*. I knew it right then. That's why it hurt so much the next morning when Lenny did what he did. It broke my heart."

Skye started to talk, but he shook his head to silence her. "I know it was all Lenny's doing. I wish I had seen it then. I should have fought for you, but I promise you from here on out, I will never let anything or anyone come between us ever again."

Trent saw the tears threatening to spill from her eyes and leaned forward to kiss her. He didn't want tears tonight—even happy ones. He wanted love to shine and with his kiss he tried to promise her that he'd love her forever.

The kiss turned from sweet and loving to hot and needy as soon as Skye ran her hand up and under his shirt. Trent wanted more—needed more. The way Skye was pulling his shirt off told him she needed it too.

Trent ended the kiss by pulling back as she slid his shirt over his head. She groaned in frustration as he stood up. But she didn't need to worry. He wasn't leaving her ever again. Trent bent down and kissed her hard and deep. Their tongues caressed each other and their lips demanded more. Skye flung her arms around his neck and Trent urged her to do the same with her legs around his hips.

Without breaking the kiss, Trent stood with Skye locked against him, lips to lips, chest to chest, hip to hip, as he carried her inside. He stopped at the closed bedroom door and pressed her against it. Trent couldn't stop his hips from surging forward and relished the demanding groan that came from Skye.

"I love you," she whispered as she clung to him, her breathing heavy as they looked into each other's eyes.

"I love you too." Trent slowed things down then and kissed her with all the love he had. He reached down and opened the door all while kissing her. He didn't set her down until they reached the bed. He wanted to make love to her now, so he took his time undressing her.

Trent climbed onto the bed and with every kiss down her body, he told Skye what he loved about her. Her hands possessed him as she wordlessly conveyed her love, her desires, and her wants as she drove him higher and higher. When they were both breathing hard with overwhelming need, Trent sank home and knew the woman in his arms was more than just a love but was *the* love of his life.

22

Trent had gone home to make a show of working but not before they made love again in the early morning light. Last night had been reverently done, but this morning it had seemed as if they'd let their passion instead of their feelings take the lead. She'd never felt sexier as he whispered all the things he wanted to do with her.

Skye had made him swear he'd hurry back so they could start on the long list of things that made her breathless just imagining.

After taking a shower, Skye poured a cup of coffee and padded out onto the porch. She took a deep breath of morning air and felt more focused than she had in years. She knew what she wanted both personally and professionally and she was going for it.

Skye picked up her phone and got to work. She was so busy getting things in motion for tomorrow that she didn't hear Tinsley and Karri until they were halfway through the house.

Her two friends made a pit stop in the kitchen for coffee and then joined her. Tinsley set a bag of muffins down on the table and smirked at Skye. With an incline of her head, she drew Skye's attention to Karri, who had a smile on her face Skye had never seen before.

"What's going on?" Skye asked her best friend.

"Nothing." She sighed happily.

Tinsley rolled her eyes. "Nothing? Oh, I guess it was nothing when I caught Peter Castle sneaking out of my house at four this morning?"

Skye gasped but was smiling. "Karri! Tell me everything."

Karri's happily glazed eyes finally focused on Skye and her own lips turned into a teasing smile. "It looks as if I'm not the only one who has something to tell."

Tinsley waved that off. "We already know she and Trent are in love. Now you and Peter? That's new."

"Is it true? Does he love you?" Karri asked as only a best friend who knew how much Skye had hoped for a relationship with Trent could.

"He does. We do. It's everything I ever dreamed and never thought would come true. And you?" Skye wanted the same for her best friend.

"We didn't sleep together, but he did spend the night again. He held me while I slept and it was . . . perfect. I never thought of myself as traditional until Peter. Is that crazy? I'm suddenly thinking of marriage and that my children will carry on the Wolf Clan and that I want to teach them all that my family has taught me."

"It's not crazy, it's love." Skye couldn't be happier for her friend. "When will you tell your mother about Peter?"

Karri let out a sigh. "I don't know. I was thinking after things are settled I could have them fly down here."

"They'll be excited for you, Karri. No matter who you bring home. If you love him, you know they'll love him too. I don't think this one will run, either. He's the one for you. He'll fight for you, just like in your dream."

"I think so too. I can show my parents the restaurant if they fly down. I know they just want me to be happy and to follow my dreams. Speaking of parents, have you talked to yours yet?" Karri asked.

Skye shook her head. "I didn't want to risk anyone overhearing and give away my location. I text them every morning and night and tell them I'm safe. I was thinking the same as you. I want to bring them here to meet everyone when it's all over."

"So, you and Trent?" Karri asked then.

"Are madly in love. Do you love Peter?"

Karri smiled and looked so content at the sound of that word. "I feel as if he's been with me in my dreams forever. I know it's silly but you've heard of old souls? It's like our souls are old together. Like we already have a history."

"That's not silly. It's wonderful."

Life was changing so fast for them both, yet it felt as if she couldn't move at all. Skye was stuck until the court ruled on her contract. Olivia had fought so hard to get the jurisdiction in New York and then to get ready for a bench trial as fast as possible. Now she wasn't going to be there. Olivia had texted that morning that all was taken care of. Skye wished they could go now. Tomorrow there would be darkness, but there would also be light. There was love and friendship, and Skye wasn't going to face it alone. They'd face tomorrow together.

Tinsley and Karri had left, and now Skye prepared for the biggest moment of her life. They wouldn't know it was coming, but she was going to face Jim down in court. The speech she had prepared was finally ready. She was ready.

The door opened and Skye glanced up as Trent walked in. "What are you doing here so early?"

Trent closed the door and joined her in the kitchen where she was eating a slice of apple pie for a snack. "I was dying for some ... apple pie."

"This apple pie?" Skye asked in her best seductive voice as she held up the remaining slice of pie in the dish.

"Yes, that pie," Trent said roughly, but his hand didn't reach for the pie, but for her center.

Skye's breathing suddenly picked up as her body heated. "What will you do for the apple pie?"

"Let me show you."

Oh goodness. Trent stripped as he walked toward her sitting in the kitchen chair. When he reached her, he kissed her hot and hard and pushed the straps of her dress down to her waist. His hands were on her breasts as he stood over her kissing and caressing her. Last night and this morning had been amazing but this was just panty-melting hot.

Skye reached around him and clasped his ass. Her fingers flexed into his muscles as she felt him reaching for the pie. She smacked his ass reflexively. "Don't you take my pie!"

He chuckled as he held the fork out for her before yanking it away and putting it in his own mouth.

"Ugh!" Skye smacked his butt again.

"I'll make it up to you." His hand moved to shove her dress up her thighs as he reached for another forkful of pie.

"I told you people will do anything for our pie."

Skye screamed at the sound of Miss Winnie's voice. At the same time, Trent spun around as if to protect her as silence descended on the kitchen for a long moment.

"Now, I haven't seen one of them in a long time, but I don't quite remember them being so big. Do you, Ruby?"

"You were with the wrong men, Win. But even so, that's mighty impressive. That's definitely blue ribbon material."

"Now I have a hankering for pie," Miss Winnie said.

Skye yanked up her dress and peered around a naked Trent as Miss Winnie licked her lips.

"Yes, this peach cobbler just isn't going to cut it. Now, where is the camera on this blasted phone?"

Trent reached for the nearest thing to cover himself, which happened to be the pie dish since his clothes were littering the kitchen floor.

"Here it is!" When Miss Ruby told Trent to smile for the picture, Skye was lost in helpless laughter.

"There!" Miss Ruby said with excitement. "That's going to be my new banner at the bake sale. I'll sell out in seconds and that will show Doris Jean who has the best apple pie."

Skye leaned around Trent as Miss Ruby showed them the picture. "You know, Miss Ruby, that's a good picture. Would you text it to me, please?"

"Skye," Trent groaned, but then looked at it. "That is a good picture."

"The smile you gave is the perfect touch," Skye told him. "And nothing is exposed except the apple pie."

"One, two, three," Miss Winnie counted out as she leaned forward and squinted at him.

"What are you doing?" Trent asked as he used one hand to reach around and grab for Skye.

"I'm counting those little ridges on your stomach. Four, five," she said as she got even closer.

"Don't forget that one, Miss Winnie," Skye said, pointing at his abs.

"Thank you, dear. Goodness. I miss being young." She

turned to Ruby with a laugh, "Remember when we all ate Kord's grandmother's brownies and went racing around town naked?"

Skye almost choked as she sidestepped over to pick up Trent's jeans and hand them to him.

"Oh yes. That was the best." Miss Ruby stopped at that thought. "You know, every time we ate those, we got naked somewhere."

"The Main Street dash, the river float, the ghost run," Miss Winnie ticked off. "Maybe we need to make those brownies again."

"That's what I'm thinking. Sorry to cut our visit short, Skye, but we see you're in good hands."

"Among other body parts," Miss Winnie said on a sigh.

"Let's get baking and then hand the brownies out to the men in town. We'll just sit back and watch what happens." Miss Ruby grabbed Winnie's hand and dragged her out of the house.

"Well, that was not how I saw this seduction going," Trent said as he zipped his pants. Skye walked over to the door and slid the side table in front of it. She reached back up and pushed her straps down slowly until she wiggled free of her dress.

"How about now?"

"I don't know," Trent said with a sexy grin. "I have the pie now."

Skye made her way back to the kitchen and picked up the fork. "So, which will it be?"

The pie went flying and Skye laughed as Trent lifted her quickly and set her down on the kitchen table. "I will always pick you. Every time. Even over apple pie." And Trent showed her exactly why he was a blue ribbon boyfriend.

23

A BLACK EXTENDED SUV showed up at Ryker's gate at four in the morning. It was still dark out and the air was heavy with the smell of the river and the sound of frogs and crickets. When Trent and Skye got inside, Granger, Peter, and Karri were already there. Ryker hadn't told them anything except to get in the SUV and that he and Miles had taken care of everything.

They were a quiet group as they drove into Charleston. No one felt the need to fill the space with small talk. Instead, some stared out the windows while others napped.

"This isn't the airport," Peter said, breaking the silence.

"Mr. Davies got you another kind of plane," the driver said, pulling into a designated gate at the Charleston Air Force Base.

The driver flashed a military ID and the soldier at the gate saluted. Skye looked at Trent who shook his head. "Sometimes I feel as if I don't know my cousin at all," he whispered to her, even though in the silence everyone heard him.

They pulled up to a large plane whose back was down

forming a ramp as cargo was loaded inside. "Here you go. There will be someone waiting for you when you land," the driver told them.

Trent opened the door for them and climbed out first. He held his hand out for Skye and she took it as they walked onto the plane.

"Right here, y'all," the pilot told them as soon as he joined them. He pointed to the few chairs and gave them a smile. "I was told not to ask who you are. You're the only people on the flight, so no worries. Ground crew is waiting for your arrival. It won't be that long a flight so off we go."

"Why does this feel like a horror movie where we fly into a parallel dimension or get dropped into the middle of a jungle to be hunted by some ancient evil?" Skye asked the group as they buckled in.

"I don't like not knowing, but I know we can trust Ryker," Granger answered. Skye looked over and saw Karri sitting with Peter and holding hands. Likewise, she and Trent were holding hands. Granger was the odd one out, and while he was emotionally closed off, Skye saw the tight jaw before he relaxed it and shut his eyes for the rest of the flight. Somewhere there was a woman who could break through whatever he'd built to close off his heart.

"Prepare for landing," the pilot's voice came over the intercom.

Skye looked out and saw the Atlantic Ocean before the pilot began his descent over land. "Where are we?" she asked as soon as they landed.

Peter had his phone out and pulled up the maps as they taxied on the runway. "Andrews Air Force Base."

"That's not in New York." Skye wondered what was next

as the plane's tail opened and the morning light slid in.

"No, it's in Maryland. He did say someone was meeting us. Maybe we're driving?" Trent shrugged and took her hand in his once again as they walked off the plane.

A drop-dead sexy man in a flight suit stood smiling at them from the bottom of the ramp. His brown skin was rich with warm copper undertones. His black hair was in a buzz cut and he had swagger just standing there.

"So, which one of you is related to Keeneston?" he asked with a grin that showed off his kissable lips.

"My family is, but I'm from South Carolina," Trent told him as he tried not to look confused.

"Ah, the cousins Dylan has talked about."

"You know Dylan?" Trent asked, and Skye was left wondering who Dylan was.

"Yup. I've worked quite a bit with him and Abby recently."

"Trent Faulkner," Trent said, holding out his hand and shaking with Mr. Sexy Pilot.

"Crew Dixon. I'm your HMX-1 pilot for the day. You're coming in under diplomatic papers today." Crew handed them all papers and when Skye read it, they said she was a diplomat of a country named Rahmi. "And I must say, you are way hotter in person, and I didn't think that was possible."

Crew winked at her and Trent wasn't amused.

"Do you have a favorite pick-up line too?" Skye asked with humor. She'd met enough men like that to know Crew wasn't the creepy kind.

"Pick-up line? That's for amateurs. I don't need pick-up lines. Normally I just pull an LL Cool J." Crew looked at her and slowly licked his full bottom lip. Yup, that would definitely work. Gracious.

"Wait," Peter said, interrupting Crew's display. "If you're HMX-1, that means you fly the president."

Crew just smiled in response and motioned with his hand to follow him. "The flight will only take ninety minutes. We'll land atop a private building. It's rare since New York City doesn't allow rooftop helipads, but this one has special permission and we've been cleared to land there today."

They followed him to the large helicopter and climbed inside. This was not like the bare-bones cargo jet. The inside had a couch and chairs covered in ivory leather. It was spotless and everything was state-of-the-art. "Is this one of the president's helicopters?" Peter asked as Crew strapped in.

"Yeah, but it's just a spare. We hardly use this one. Now, strap in and let's get you to New York."

"Who the hell is Miles and how did he and Ryker pull this off?" Skye asked Trent as the blades to the helicopter began to spin. "And where the heck is Rahmi?"

"Uncle Miles was Special Forces and I guess he still has contacts in that world. I'm also thinking I need to ask Ryker more questions about his businesses," Trent admitted as they all looked out the windows when they lifted off the ground. "My cousins in Kentucky are friends with the Rahmi royal family. It's a small island nation in the Persian Gulf, so I know that part."

Skye had met plenty of rich and powerful people. She was America's Sweetheart after all and that put her in the path of many such people. However, getting diplomatic papers and the president's spare helicopter? That was a type of power she'd never encountered before.

"Are you ready for court?" Karri asked once they'd been in the air for a while.

Skye took a deep breath and looked up from her phone where her notes were typed out. "I think so. Are you ready to be called if necessary?"

Karri looked to Peter who gave her a silent encouraging smile. "I think so. Peter helped me prepare last night."

Nerves rattled Skye's body and she bounced her knee to try to cover for them. "Then let's do this."

The New York skyline was familiar to Skye. She'd signed her contract with Jim here. She'd auditioned for numerous roles here as well. For as big as Hollywood was, she and New York were twin entertainment powerhouses.

The helicopter began to approach one of the tallest buildings along the skyline. As they grew closer, it was clear they were landing there. "What's this building?" Skye asked, but no one knew as they landed on the large helipad.

"Welcome to New York City," Crew told them as the blades slowed to a stop. "I'll be staying here and will be at the ready for a quick departure."

"Thank you, Crew," Skye told him as the door to the helicopter was opened. And waiting at the base of the stairs stood Ryker. His suit was dark and expensive. The rising sun cast a glowing light over his darkness, but there was no hiding that the man haloed in light was no angel. While Ryker might be her angel, he clearly danced with the devil and that devil stood about four feet behind him.

"What's up, Seb?" Crew smiled at the devilish man and slapped him on the shoulder.

"Good to see you again, Crew. How's that girl you were dating?"

Crew rolled his eyes. "You know I can't be tied down long. Just like you."

The devil gave a small shrug and then turned his penetrating stare at her. "Skye Jessamine, welcome to my building. I'm Sebastian Abel and this is SA Tech headquarters. I have a private car downstairs to transport you, Miss Hill, and the private security that Mr. Faulkner arranged for you to the courthouse. I have a floor here set aside for your private use. Agent Castle, Sheriff Fox, Crew, Ryker, and Mr. Faulkner can wait there. If there's anything else I can do for you, please ask one of my assistants who will be sitting at the front desk on the main level."

"Thank you, Mr. Abel. You didn't have to go through so much trouble, but it's very appreciated."

Sebastian stared at her seriously and gave her a short nod. "Ryker told me you were a fighter. That's the only reason I agreed. Good day."

The man turned on his heel and strode inside the automatic glass doors before disappearing into an elevator.

"How did you get Sebastian Abel to agree to this?" Trent asked Ryker before turning to Crew. "And how does a pilot know the world's largest tech giant?"

Crew shrugged and headed inside.

Ryker didn't bat an eye as he told them, "We do business together."

Ryker led the way inside the luxurious office tower. They were greeted by an attractive woman who asked if they wanted anything to drink before leading them down a floor and into an expansive conference room. Inside the room, they were met by a group of people Skye had never seen before. Well, the older woman looked familiar, but she couldn't place her.

She smiled but the salt-and-pepper-haired man behind her did not. "Skye! It's so nice to meet you in person. I'm Morgan Davies."

"Oh, Morgan!" Skye wrapped the older woman in a hug. "I didn't know you were coming."

"I was just dying to meet you, plus I figured I better be in court with you so I could put out a good press release and give you your talking points before you faced the media." Morgan turned to the glowering man who was slapping Trent on the back. "This is my husband, Miles. He's Trent's uncle."

Miles turned to her and shook her hand tightly. "Ma'am."

"Mr. Davies. Thank you for coming and thank you for the transportation."

"Miles will be staying with me." Morgan rolled her eyes. "Since I'm *in danger*." She used her fingers to make air quotes.

"Here." Miles shoved a thumb drive at Peter. "That's all the information I got from the man who tried to hurt my wife. He's employed by Star Power Private Security. He hasn't given over the name of who hired him yet, but he will. Doing it the *legal* way always takes longer," he complained, using the same air quotes his wife had just used.

A man in a suit so shiny it was practically iridescent shoved past Miles with a wide smile and a wink. "Enough about that. Let's talk about how Miss Jessamine is breaking the law with her sexiness."

Skye choked on a combination of a gasp and a laugh. Morgan let out a long-suffering breath. "Skye, meet your new attorney, Henry Rooney."

Henry took her hand in his and looked into her eyes. "I already know you're Hollywood's biggest star since I'm burning with love for you."

Skye sputtered. She couldn't even get out a hello because it was truly a horrible line. No wonder he made the detective run for the hills. It was strange, but there was nothing dangerous or scary about Henry Rooney. He was just a lovable goober.

A young woman with movie star looks stepped forward then. "I'm Tandy Rawlings. I'm also your attorney. I've just moved back to Keeneston from the city, but still hold my New York Bar license. We already have a plan set out for your trial."

"It's nice to meet you. Thank you for helping me." Skye felt a little better now. Tandy seemed as if she could cut a man's balls off with her perfectly manicured nail.

Morgan turned to the man and woman behind her. They were in matching black suits, but that's where the similarities ended. "This is Aiden Creed. He's married to my niece, Piper. He owns a security company and will be in charge of your personal protection while you're in New York."

"It's nice to meet you, ma'am. When Trent called we were happy to assist in any way possible." Skye wasn't expecting the deep English accent, but the way he was built like an elite soldier was a comfort. The woman beside him wasn't, though. She was pretty and petite and had a warm smile. "This is my associate, Blythe Kencroft. She'll be with you at all times."

Blythe's bronze-colored eyes met hers, and although she was small, she was definitely mighty. "Such a pleasure to work with you. I've heard you like to cut off men's balls. I'm always happy to assist with de-balling men who don't deserve them."

Skye laughed and the weight of the tension began to ease off her shoulders. She had a team around her—a team she felt she could trust. "Then let's do this."

24

SKYE ARRIVED at the courthouse fifteen minutes before her trial was to begin. There were only a few cameras outside since they weren't expecting anyone famous to show. Today was just a technical argument between lawyers. At least it was supposed to be.

"Ready for this?" Tandy asked. She might look like a movie star, but on the ride over they discussed Skye's case and she had even more brains than beauty, which was saying something. It was also surprising that under Henry's fondness for bad pick-up lines was a brilliant legal mind.

It was time to put her plan into action. The SUV drove around back where several cars with tinted windows were lined up and waiting. Aiden was the first out of their car, then Tandy and Henry. Next Skye slid out with Blythe right behind her and then Karri.

As soon as Skye exited the SUV, the other car doors opened.

Skye felt tears threaten as she faced all the people filling the entire area. There were more than thirty of them standing quietly all in matching black skirts or pants suits. The only difference was the color of the shirts they wore.

A woman separated herself from the pack and reached for a hug. "I hope you don't mind that I invited some more friends."

Skye felt the first tear run down her cheek. "Gina, Mason! I don't know what to say." Skye hugged her friend Gina Toussaint, the A-list actress who was the first to stand up for Skye in her fight against Tony and his horrid film, and then Mason, her frequent co-star and friend.

Skye looked over the group and saw writers, camera assistants, producers, actresses, and actors ranging from the top-earning A-listers all the way down to the D-listers who were struggling to break out. Skye took a moment and went to each person, thanking them for coming today.

Gina waited until Skye was done before turning to the group. "Ladies, let's show Hollywood we're tired of being taken advantage of, from degrading directors to unequal pay and representation behind the cameras."

Mason nodded and picked up from there. "Gentlemen, let's show them Hollywood's men support them in their goals."

Together they all walked into the courthouse. Tandy and Henry led the way and with Karri and Gina on each side of her, and Mason and Blythe behind her, Skye walked onto the battlefield.

Tandy called Karri's phone as soon as she walked into the courtroom. The phone sat on the defense table open so the group could hear the court proceedings from the holding room they were in. Jim's attorney, Bernie, argued that the bench trial should be delayed since Olivia Townsend was unavailable. Then they tried to challenge Tandy's standing in the court. Finally, there was a challenge to Henry's ability to participate since he didn't hold a New York license.

The judge ruled in Skye's favor and the trial went on. Tandy worked hard laying out affirmative defenses on why the contract was invalid on its face and called several expert witnesses. Tandy examined them and Henry questioned another expert before Jim and Lenny were called as defense witnesses. Skye listened with building anger while they lied about her signing the contract, about her excitement to do Tony's movie, and about how she gave them full authorization to sign her name for them. They tried to tell the judge that lifetime contracts were the standard with unproven actors since the agent and manager were investing so much into their young careers.

Then Tandy was up. Skye listened as her whole life depended on what happened next. Tandy started off slowly as if lulling Jim to sleep. She asked him about other clients, about other roles, about how and when he met Skye. Then she asked Jim how about this so-called authorization and Jim showed the power of attorney Skye had supposedly signed. "Did she tell you she wanted to do the Tony Ketron movie?"

"Of course she did. It's the role of a lifetime. Lenny heard it and testified that she wanted to do the film."

"Your honor, my co-counsel has some questions if you don't mind," Skye heard Tandy say.

The door to the holding room opened and Skye turned, expecting to see Aiden ready to lead them all into the courtroom, but what she saw brought tears to her eyes.

"So, you ready to shove his balls down his throat?"

"Olivia!" Skye gasped as she rushed forward. Behind her,

Aiden was holding onto her wheelchair. "I'm so sorry. This is my fault. How are you feeling? You shouldn't be here."

"Everything hurts like a bitch with PMS but I'm here to have some fun. Aiden, let Skye push me in," Olivia ordered. "All right ladies and gentlemen, let's do this."

Aiden gave her a sexy little grin, and Olivia winked back at him with the one eye that wasn't swollen shut. "Too bad you're married. All the good men are unavailable."

"Ain't that the truth," Gina muttered and the women all laughed. The men didn't seem as amused but stood up straighter as if they were ready to audition for the role of boyfriend.

Skye took a deep breath and hold of the wheelchair handles. If Olivia could come here today, then she could hold her head high and tell the truth to a roomful of people if necessary.

Aiden went first and very dramatically pushed open the double doors to the courtroom. Skye was rewarded by the gasps and smartphones suddenly pointed at her. There were no flashes, which meant they were live-streaming this to the world.

"What the hell is this?" Jim hissed at no one in particular as Skye, Olivia, and the rest of the Hollywood entourage surprised the entire courtroom with their appearance. The few reporters in attendance were instantly on their phones and texting frantically. The courthouse would be packed with journalists within minutes.

"What's this?" the judge asked as he couldn't stop looking at Olivia.

"I'm Olivia Townsend, lead attorney on this case. I'm here to question Mr. Hexter."

The judge looked back at Skye as she wheeled Olivia right up to the witness stand while everyone else silently filled every remaining seat in the courtroom. "And who are you? For the record?"

"Skye Jessamine. I am the plaintiff, Your Honor."

The judge's expression didn't give away a thing as he cast a glance at Jim who was trying very hard not to look nervous. "Skye! Thank goodness you're okay. After getting that note, we thought you were in danger."

"You mean you thought your jobs were in danger after I started firing all the people you forced me to hire?" Skye shot back. The judge banged his gavel and pointed for her to take a seat. Skye walked toward her table and Henry winked as he pulled out the chair for her while Tandy smiled serenely. Skye took a seat between them and was sure she hadn't taken a breath since she entered the room.

"Mr. Hexter, what is Star Power Private Security?" Olivia asked.

"They're a very well-known security company in Hollywood that protects studios, top actors, and industry personnel," Jim replied.

"Have you ever hired them?" Olivia asked.

"Yes. I'm sure everyone in Hollywood has at some point."

"What have you hired them for?"

"Objection!" Bernie said, standing. "Star Power Private Security holds no relevancy to Miss Jessamine's contract with Mr. Hexter."

"Your Honor, I ask for a little leeway. I think I've earned it after all I've gone through."

Skye waited for the judge to rule. He looked down at the bruised and battered Olivia and then nodded. "Overruled. Go ahead, Miss Townsend, but get to the point."

"Thank you," Olivia told the judge before turning back to Jim. "Now, why have you hired Star Power?"

"Mostly as bodyguards."

"Do bodyguards assault people, Mr. Hexter?"

Jim shook his head. "Not unless someone is a danger to one of my celebrities or myself."

Olivia nodded and glanced back at Henry who got up with a folder and walked it over to her. He stood at the ready and every eye was on the red folder he had in his hand. "Are lawyers a danger to you or your clients, Mr. Hexter?"

"I don't understand," Jim said with his eyes glued to the folder.

"Why then did you hire Star Power Private Security to assault, attempt to kidnap me, and steal my electronic devices, Mr. Hexter?"

The room gasped and the judge ordered everyone quiet.

"I did no such thing!" Jim yelled as Skye blinked with confusion. Olivia knew something she didn't. What was it?

Henry handed the judge the folder as Olivia spoke. "I'd like to enter into evidence the picture of the driver who kidnapped me. This is from my law office's security camera. I'd also like to enter into evidence the video of my assault from The Thirsty Taco's cameras that had been installed that morning. Pictures are included in the folder. Further, I'd like to enter into evidence the financial trail of digital currency from Mr. Hexter's private account to Star Power's VIP account the day before my attack."

"That proves nothing!" Jim argued. "I hired them for personal protection since I was worried after Skye's kidnapping, but apparently that was all a hoax for her to get the media's attention. I'll admit Morgan Davies is better at PR than Skye's old firm. There's no reason for me to hire someone to beat you up."

The judge looked them over as Tandy gave a copy to Bernie who objected, but the judge overruled him and allowed them into evidence.

"Henry," Olivia said as Henry picked up a remote and turned on the television to a blank screen. "Your honor, I'd like permission to enter into evidence this video that directly disputes Mr. Hexter's claims. May I play it?"

"Objection!" Bernie tried again.

"I need to see it before I can rule on it. Go ahead, Miss Townsend."

Skye clasped her hands together so tightly her knuckles turned white. The video started with a black screen and then suddenly showed Jim and Lenny staring at the camera. Bernie objected. Jim started yelling. Lenny went white.

"What is this, Miss Townsend?" The judge sounded angry and Skye didn't know what was going to happen.

"Your Honor, I was attacked by those two men hired by Mr. Hexter for the purpose of finding out what evidence I had regarding this case and destroying it. Specifically, the affidavit I had told them I had from Miss Jessamine appointing me as her legal counsel and denying that she ever granted Mr. Hexter power of attorney when, in fact, Miss Karri Hill was and still is Miss Jessamine's sole power of attorney. This video is proof of that, Your Honor."

"Illegally obtained evidence is inadmissible, Miss Townsend," the judge censored, but Olivia just smiled with her swollen lip.

"Oh, I know, Your Honor. But this isn't illegally obtained. Henry," she said as Henry handed the judge a piece of paper. "This is an affidavit from the SA Tech analyst I hired the moment I was conscious to log in to my computer remotely and film whoever opened it. Not only that, but you'll see the SA Tech analyst set up dummy files that the defendants thought they were deleting."

The judge's brow creased. "Are you saying this is video from your personal computer that was stolen?"

"Yes, sir. You'll see my desktop in a moment if you'll allow me to continue."

Over Bernie's objections, the video went on. It showed Jim and Lenny talking about the documents, searching for them. In the end, they deleted the entire hard drive.

"This should stop them until we can find Skye and fix this. She'll fall in line once we can talk to her," Lenny said on film before Jim reached out and closed the laptop.

Olivia cocked her head at Jim. "Mr. Hexter, would you care to revise the statements you've made under oath or would you prefer I file perjury charges now?"

Skye was so on edge she reached out and grabbed Tandy's hand. She leaned forward, her heart pumping hard and fast as she waited.

Jim's jaw was tight as he thought it through. "Fine. You're right. I forged the power of attorney and thought all you had was a digital copy. With Skye still missing, I wanted to keep control over her empire that I built. *Me*. This doesn't change the fact that the contract is still enforceable."

"Actually," Olivia said, holding up a finger to stop Jim, "section twenty-one, subsection C, paragraph 8 says criminal activity can void the contract at the request of the other party. So, completely ignoring the affirmative defenses my co-counsel has already proven, the contract itself leaves both parties able to void it upon proof of criminal charges."

"That's so I can void the contract if Skye becomes a junkie," Jim sputtered.

"Ah, but your attorney didn't do a good job writing the contract and didn't make that clear. It very clearly states that either party may do so, and I'm putting you on notice that the assistant district attorney is here and ready to charge you with forgery. Further, my client is here and is hereby enacting her right to cancel the contract based on your criminal activity. No further questions, Your Honor."

Henry grabbed the wheelchair and wheeled Olivia over to the desk as Jim stepped down from the witness stand. The judge looked over the evidence and then at the assistant district attorney sitting directly behind Tandy. Skye watched him study the inch thick contract she'd signed and then the evidence Olivia and Tandy had submitted.

"I'm ready to rule," he said after several tense minutes.

A hush fell over the courtroom and Tandy held Skye's hand just as tightly as Skye held hers. Henry reached over and took Skye's other hand and caressed it. Skye smothered a shocked giggle because it tickled. "Always look as if you know you've won," Henry whispered.

"I'm not going to address the criminal charges," the judge began. "I found the contract to be invalid based on its indefinite clause for the period of not only the plaintiff's life but even after her life to control her image. Secondly, I find the contract invalid on the basic ground of it being unconscionable. It seems clear that Mr. Hexter preys on women to induce them to sign these contracts that are grossly unfair. Therefore, I order the contract null and void. Miss Jessamine is free to hire any agent or manager she wishes from this moment forward. I'll write up a more specific order and email it to the parties."

He rapped his gavel and that was it. Skye was free.

Skye walked down the ramp of the courthouse with her friends surrounding her as Henry pushed Olivia's wheelchair down the ramp. The front of the courthouse had been empty when they'd arrived but now it was jam-packed with news vans and reporters.

Gina and Mason each took one of her hands as Morgan and Miles joined her. "You ready?" Morgan asked.

"I am." Skye took a deep breath and stepped before the cameras, and with her friends behind her, she broke free of the Hollywood spotlight and turned them to focus on predatory agents, directors, and unfair pay. Then she stepped away from it all as Gina took over, speaking for the female actors in attendance before handing it off to the next speaker.

Skye was ready to go home to Shadows Landing and begin her time away from the spotlight.

"Skye." She heard Mason say her name and turned to see him join their group. He hugged her tight. "I was so worried about you. Are you okay?"

Skye finally had her answer. "I'm free to do the movies I want and I'm madly in love. I'm wonderful."

"Ah, so that's where you've been. With your woodworker?"

"Yes and all we needed to do was talk it out. Even going through this nightmare, I have had my dreams come true," Skye said before hugging him tightly again. "Thank you for being such a good friend."

"I'm always here for you. Now, get ready to hit the road with me for some press tours. I'll see you soon."

"Skye?"

Skye's jaw dropped in surprise before she schooled herself. Marie Lockend, the director of the drama she wanted the lead role in, stood there with Gina beside her. "Ms. Lockend!"

"Gina told me you'd be here. She also just told me you've been spending time in South Carolina. You know my drama is set in Charleston." The director of Skye's dream movie handed her a business card. "I wrote my personal cell phone number on the back. Send me a clip of your best Southern accent. I've emailed Karri the script. And, Skye, good job in there today."

Skye watched Mason give her a thumbs-up from where he stood among the crowd of supporters as Ms. Lockend walked away.

"Oh my gosh, Gina!" Skye happily cried to her friend.

"Sorry, I know you told me not to tell anyone where you were staying, but I knew that was your dream role, so when she met with me just now to tell me she was going to cast me as the sister, I told her about you. I hope you're not mad."

Skye hugged her friend and smiled, knowing she now had the freedom to pick and choose her parts. "I'm not mad. It would be amazing to be in a movie with you. Thank you for all you did in such a short amount of time to help me."

"Women help women. It's what we do."

Gina headed back to stand with the speakers and Skye joined her Keeneston guardian angels. "Let's get out of here. I'm ready to go home to Shadows Landing."

25

Trent felt as if he could finally take a breath when he saw the media coverage finally show Skye getting into the SUV and leaving the courthouse. She'd won and she'd be in his arms soon. The reporters were showing Gina Toussaint and Mason Hemming speaking, along with other industry leaders. They also commented on the fact that famed director Marie Lockend was seen talking privately to Skye.

It had been tense in the luxurious tower. Goodness knows how much money it was going to cost to repair the wall Granger punched a hole through when Olivia was wheeled into the courtroom.

Trent couldn't sit still. Excitement bubbled up. They could finally move forward. They could finally look to the future. "I'll be right back."

Trent headed out onto the floor and found the assistant. "Where's the back entrance?" As soon as he was told, Trent was off. He wanted Skye in his arms and he wasn't going to wait a second longer than he had to.

Trent shoved open the back door to SA Tech and waited. He didn't have to wait long. The second the first black SUV stopped, the door was open and Skye was flinging herself into his arms. A town car was next, but Trent wasn't paying attention. He had Skye and that was all that mattered.

"Skye."

Aiden and Blythe were already in motion. Aiden had Jim pinned against the car with his hand at Jim's throat and a gun digging into his stomach. Blythe was a little rougher and had flung Lenny to the ground and had one high heel digging into the middle of his back as she stood over him.

"So you like it rough, babe?" Lenny asked crassly.

"You're so not my type," Blythe said with a little dig of her heel.

Trent had shoved Skye behind him and now she was looking around him. "What do you want? It's over and I never want to see you two again," Skye shouted as Karri ran to her side.

"I just wanted to say I'm sorry," Jim called out to her. "I swear, I didn't mean for anyone to get hurt."

"You're sorry? Sorry for trying to pimp me out to your buddy Tony? Sorry you forged my name on who knows how many contracts that you told me I had no choice but to fulfill? Sorry you used me solely as a way to make yourself rich? Then you sent goons after my lawyer and publicist? I could kill you right now!" Skye's voice grew stronger as she stepped out from behind Trent to stand her ground.

"The notes . . ." Lenny began.

"Were torturous. How could you do that to me? You were just using fear to control me. Well, no more. Goodbye, Lenny. Goodbye, Jim. The next time you see me, I'll be getting my award for best actress while you're sitting at home watching it on TV—*if* you're out of jail by then."

Skye spun and marched into the building where four large SA Tech security guards stood on each of the door watching the situation unfold. Aiden released Jim and Blythe followed suit. Blythe headed inside but Aiden stayed as the second SUV arrived carrying the legal team along with Morgan and Miles.

"You're ruining her life!" Lenny yelled at Trent as Jim got into the car.

"You already tried to do that," Trent told him. "I'm letting her live her life the way she wants. Something you weren't brave or smart enough to do."

Trent was about to go inside when Lenny charged forward with his hand cocked back as if he were going to throw a punch. A quick shake of Trent's head had Aiden holding still. Trent waited for the wild swing to come. When it did, Trent ducked.

Trent rose up and threw one very strong cross. His fist connected with Lenny's face and snapped his head back. SA Tech guards and Aiden moved forward.

"You want us to call the cops?" one of the security guards asked as Miles leapt from the SUV with rage in his eyes.

"No. Throw him in the back of his car and make sure they leave," Trent ordered. Jim sat wide-eyed as the large guards shoved a dazed Lenny into the back of the town car and told them they were banned from the property.

"You asshole," Miles snarled and Trent was suddenly very confused. "I wanted to do that."

Aiden shook his head, but a small smile played on his lips before he and Trent hurried to the SUV to help Henry with the wheelchair for Olivia.

"What are you doing here? Shouldn't you be in the hospital?" Trent asked as he reached into the SUV and slid his arms around her. Moving carefully, he lifted her as if she were made of glass and placed her in the wheelchair.

"I want to go home now that the trial is over. Ryker said I

could catch a ride with y'all." Olivia grimaced and then reached into her bag and pulled out a pill container.

"Let's get you home then," Trent said, taking over pushing the wheelchair from Henry.

Trent pushed Olivia to join everyone in the conference room. The assistant had popped some champagne. "What the hell?" The joyous room froze at Granger's outburst. He pushed forward and glared down at Olivia. "What are you doing here? You overdid it today and you need to be back in the hospital."

"Calm down," Ryker ordered. "She has a live-in nurse waiting for her in Charleston. She wants to go home."

"*She* can speak for herself," Olivia scolded with a glare at both Granger and Ryker.

"You're on top of things," Henry said, lifting his glass to her in a salute. "Would you like me to be one of them?"

Olivia snorted, then groaned in pain. Granger cursed and rolled his eyes, Ryker's lips twitched, and all was right in the world once again.

THE TRIP back to Shadows Landing didn't seem as long since the fear of the unknown was gone. Instead, the atmosphere was one of celebration. Karri and Peter were celebrating moving their relationship into one that had them actually dating. They were already making plans to visit Syracuse and Seneca Falls to visit their families as well as arranging for their families to come to Shadows Landing in the future. Karri had already texted Harper and asked her to get a contract ready for their new joint venture.

Granger had taken over as Skye's Southern voice coach to help her prepare for her audition with Marie Lockend as they flew home. Ryker sat back and watched. Olivia had taken pain medication and was sound asleep.

"So, I hear you're looking at the Cramble property. Are we going to be neighbors?" Ryker asked Trent.

"I think we might be. Now that the case is settled and Skye is ready to move forward with her life, I'm going to set up a time to go see the property with her. It's fast, though," Trent admitted.

Ryker shrugged. "No faster than anyone else in the family. Great Aunt Marcy keeps threatening me that we fall hard and fast."

"Our sweet, very old aunt is threatening to Mr. Mysterious Millionaire?" Trent teased.

"Billionaire. And she's scary devious. I was thinking of hiring her for my next business negotiation. She comes in all sweet as apple pie and then you realize the apple pie is drugged and she's the only one with the antidote. You end up doing whatever she tells you to and then you thank her for it." Ryker gave a little shiver and Trent tried not to laugh.

"Why don't you tell us about all this business stuff you're in? Do you think we'd care that you're a billionaire or that you're friends with Sebastian Abel and who knows who else?" Trent asked after a moment.

"I wouldn't say friends. I don't have many of those. I have business acquaintances. I also don't talk about my work because I don't want people to know." Ryker rested his ankle on the opposite knee and leaned back on the cargo plane's old seat.

"We're not *people*, Ryker. We're family and friends. Granger knows better than anyone what you went through. Not counting our cousins in Kentucky—" Trent was about to say more but Ryker went cold.

"I am not talking about it. See, this is why I don't say

anything. Everyone wants to go back to high school. I've moved on. You also need to."

Okay, Trent had tried to be caring, but this tough exterior needed a sledgehammer. "Screw you, Ryker. Yes, you went through what you did, but who was by your side every single day?"

Ryker snorted with faux amusement. "Not my parents."

"That's right. Our parents couldn't leave for Florida soon enough, but not Wade and me. We didn't leave. Tinsley and Ridge didn't leave. Gavin and Harper didn't leave. Granger didn't leave. Gator, Turtle, Skeeter, hell, no one from Shadows Landing left you. We were with you every single day, so cut the bullshit. Who are you and what have you become?" Trent was speaking through a clenched jaw so he could keep his voice down. This was between him and Ryker.

"It's funny. You don't even see it," Trent continued to say. "You were the sweetest, most caring guy until that night. The thing is, you still are. You did all of this for Skye and for me because I care for her. I know you helped the others out too. You help out anyone who needs it. Yet, you keep yourself distant from us. We love you and we want you back. All of you. And if that means no more connections and no more super-expensive speedboats or crashing in your guesthouse, fine. I think I can speak for the others when we say we want you back more than the stuff you bring with you. Let us be happy for you. Let us celebrate your accomplishments, Ryker. Trust us to love you no matter what."

Ryker didn't speak and Trent hadn't realized how badly he'd needed to say all of that. Trent reached over and clasped Ryker's shoulder as he stood up. "I love you, cuz. Don't ever doubt it. I have a feeling I'll be needing a best man in the future."

Trent sidestepped his way out of the row and crossed the aisle to where Granger was rolling his eyes and Skye was laughing so hard her face had turned red.

"I'm sorry, you're one of my best friends, but your girlfriend can't do a Southern accent to save her life." Granger tried to give Skye a disapproving glare but it only made her laugh harder.

"I. Will. Get. It." She managed to gasp between giggles. "Bless my heart!"

Granger's head snapped to look at her. "That wasn't half bad. What did we do differently between you laughing nonstop and my teaching?"

"Not your teaching, your colorful disapproval," Skye said in her best Southern accent.

"Well, you had one shining moment of glory and then it was gone," Granger grumbled.

Trent chuckled and knelt on the seat in front of Skye and looked over the back at them. "We could get her drunk. Every woman I know gets a strong Southern accent when they've been drinking, no matter where they're from," Trent said to Granger.

Granger shrugged. "It's worth a shot. Although, to be fair, you're only around Southern women when they get drunk."

"True, but it could be an experiment."

"Then let's get her drunk as a skunk," Granger agreed.

"Drunk as a skunk," Skye tried to drawl but really only emphasizing the *K* sound. Oh boy. This was going to take a while.

"Stop thinking about it," Ryker's deep voice broke into their conversation. "When you try hard is when it sounds horrible. You have to find the natural music to your voice.

The way it ebbs and flows and rounds out. You drop the harshness and then let it run free."

Trent wanted to lean over and hug his cousin, but Ryker wasn't ready for that. However, it appeared that he was ready to take a step forward.

Skye nodded and tried again. "Ebb and flow. Rounded edges to the words. Okay." Skye began to hum a little and then looked up at Ryker, who was now standing in the aisle. "Druunk as a skuunk," she said, taking off the harsh *K* sound and letting the U roll through her mouth.

Ryker gave her a slight nod of approval and Granger stood up and pretended to bow to Ryker. Skye laughed and soon they were all feeding Skye lines from the movie script to practice. By the time they landed, Trent had felt a change in more than just his and Skye's relationship, but in his and Ryker's as well. It was time to enjoy the present and look forward to the future.

26

Skye didn't look around the house or land as she and Trent toured Mrs. Cramble's property. Instead, she watched Trent the entire time. She wanted to gauge his reaction to see what he really thought about it. They'd been home for two days and Skye had let Morgan handle the PR storm that the trial spawned while she got settled in Shadows Landing.

Agent Shaw had told her while they couldn't close the threatening letters case yet, they were confident that after Jim's and Lenny's upcoming interview with the FBI, they would be able to. Jim and Lenny had both escaped to their houses in the Hamptons to hide from the fallout. Of course, *Skye* owned the house Lenny was hiding in. She'd just never used it. It had been purchased as an investment and, as she was finding out, Lenny used it as his personal estate. Tomorrow morning he'd get a rude awakening courtesy of the private security teams Aiden Creed had arranged for her. They were going to all her properties and removing anyone and anything not belonging to Skye.

Most of Jim's female clients had left the agency. While they were signing with a new female agent on the scene,

Skye was holding off for now. She had the Marie Lockend audition coming up and she was lobbying hard for a part in Gemma Davies's newest film adaptation. Olivia was recuperating and still giving them hell from home. She'd insisted at looking over any contract Skye got between now and the time Skye got a new agent.

But now all of Skye's focus was on Trent and what he thought of the Cramble house.

"This is fantastic. I haven't been back here since I was a teenager and we'd sneak through yards to get home."

Skye felt the excitement bubbling up inside her. "So, it'll work for what you need?"

"It'll more than work. I can open the back of the old detached garage and have a view of the river while I work. There's even enough room to build a state-of-the-art warehouse to store the finished pieces and my wood."

Skye lost her battle to the bubbles and did a happy dance. "Great! I'm going to put down the deposit. Mrs. Cramble said she doesn't have to sell right now, but this way at least I know it's ours while still giving us time to get settled in Shadows Landing."

"*We* will put down the deposit and then *we* are going to make love all night," Trent said, dipping his voice low so it rumbled through her. Trent reached for her and she happily went into his arms. She loved this man so much that every time he touched her, the rest of the world fell away and it was just the two of them.

"That sounds divine, but it'll have to be later tonight."

Trent stopped with the sexy eyes and blinked. "What do you mean, later?"

"I have knitting club tonight!"

Trent chuckled as he looked at her in his arms. "You're very excited about knitting club."

"Mitzy is going to help me make something for you. Do you know Mitzy's daughter-in-law, AKA Karen the She-Devil, told Mitzy that she's worried that Mitzy can't care for herself? Karen wants to move Mitzy into a retirement home that Mitzy would have to pay for so that She-Devil can move into Mitzy's home!"

Trent shook his head. "She's a piece of work. We all tried to warn Mitzy's son. What is Mitzy going to do?"

Skye smiled and felt a smidge naughty. "I took care of it. Mitzy said her son and Satan's bride are coming this weekend. That's when they'll be surprised to find Mitzy has live-in help in the form of a butler who happens to also be a retired registered nurse. I hired him and told Mitzy her insurance covers it. Don't tell her I'm paying for it. But now I need to get to knitting club."

Skye rose up on her toes and kissed his lips. The kiss was supposed to be a quick goodbye kiss, but kissing Trent never went quickly. He elevated kissing to an art form and who was she to interrupt an artist?

"I still can't believe Ryker is opening his gates for knitting club," Trent told her as he took her hand in his and walked out to the car. They'd moved back into Trent's house yesterday, but one didn't mess with the knitting club schedule so Skye pleaded with Ryker to let them hold it in the guesthouse. He'd been surprisingly quick to say yes.

"I think he likes me. And I like him. There's a lot going on underneath, but like Granger, there's goodness in him too."

"They're both good guys. Actually, since you all are knitting, Ryker invited a bunch of us to the main house for some drinks."

Trent opened the car door for her and she got in. Skye loved watching Trent walk around to his door. It was a moment where she could just ogle him and smile to herself that she got to be the one with him.

"That sounds like fun," she told him when he got into the car.

The drive next door from Mrs. Cramble's to Ryker's guesthouse was quick. Edie was already waiting by the guesthouse with Ryker, both holding large baskets as Skye got out to greet them. "You're early!"

"I know. It was my week to bring the food and drinks. Ryker's helping me carry it all inside," Edie told her.

"I still don't know why you bother," Ryker said, pushing the door open. "They'll all bring something even if they're not supposed to."

Edie shrugged as Skye and Trent each picked up a plate from Edie's car. "I know, but I like giving them a little something to take home. This way everyone goes home with a full plate of food for the next day."

Ryker grunted but carried the large basket into the living room. As Skye and Edie worked on setting out the food and drinks, Ryker and Trent moved the furniture. At the first sign of headlights approaching in the dusky night, Ryker and Trent made their escape to the main house.

"They're good guys," Edie said with a shake of her head as they watched the men literally ducking behind a large topiary to hide from arriving knitting club members.

"What about you and Ryker?" Skye gave a little wiggle of her eyebrows at her new friend.

"I'm not ready. Besides, he's like a brother. I haven't been able to think of any man in that special way since I lost my Shane. I don't know if I ever will," Edie admitted and Skye wanted to hug her and do whatever she could to take that pain away. Sometimes it was karma, sometimes it was meeting the right man again, and sometimes it was just learning to love yourself and know you were a badass who could tackle the world head-on without anyone at your side but with love in your heart.

"I understand. My grandmother was a war widow. She never remarried either. Just do you and do it with love, light, and laughter."

Edie turned to Skye as she took a deep, refreshing breath. "Thank you. I like the sound of that."

"You know, I've never been here before," Miss Mitzy said as she came in carrying a plate of brownies and a bag full of yarn.

Skye hugged her and the rest of the women as they joined everyone in the living room.

"It's so strange to have knitting club without Dare," Miss Winnie said as she pulled out her erotic knitting. "I got used to seeing those boobies. Maybe I need to make myself a boobie scarf."

"You'd need extra yarn since they'd be at your knees," Miss Ruby teased.

Miss Winnie responded by making an obscene gesture with the penis potholder. Edie and Skye shared a shocked look and Miss Winnie clucked at them. "You young'uns know so little. You're always so surprised when we don't act like polite old ladies."

Miss Ruby nodded, having chosen to ignore the knitted penis gesture. "Darn tootin', Win. I'm sure we've all done things that y'all could never imagine."

"And I'd love to hear every single story," Skye told them, settling in as she worked with Mitzy on her surprise for Trent.

. . .

THE NEXT TWENTY minutes flew by as they all talked and laughed. Skye was happy.

"Sorry I'm late!" Karri rushed inside and pulled out her knitting. "I was meeting with Suze Bell to discuss the sale of the building next to Harper's bar."

They all listened as Karri gushed over the meeting and her plans for the space. But then the conversation turned to Karri and Peter and Skye and Trent. The knitting club decided they needed to give out relationship advice.

"What's that sound?" Miss Ruby asked out of the blue.

Skye listened but didn't hear anything.

"I swear, I hear something like *thwump, thwump, thwump*," Miss Ruby said to the group who all just shrugged.

"Maybe it's all this sex talk. Like maybe you're hearing phantom sex noises," Miss Winnie told her, causing Skye to bite her lip hard to stop from laughing out loud. But then she heard it too.

"Wait, I think I hear it too. It's coming from out back," Skye said, now curious about the noise.

As one, the group rose and carried their knitting outside to the patio to watch a helicopter began to land.

"I wonder where Ryker is going now?" Skye asked. "I thought they were having guys' night."

"That's not his helicopter. He keeps his at the main house," Edie said slowly as they all watched the doors open. Men in masks vaulted out and ran straight for them. "Inside, now!"

Edie grabbed a shocked Skye and propelled her inside. Doors were slammed shut. Locks were turned and then there was silence except for the sound of the helicopter rotor.

"It's my dream," Karri whispered to herself but Skye

heard it too. It sent shivers down her spine as they tried to see the men from inside the house.

"Where did all those men go?" Miss Mitzy asked as the lights in the backyard went dark.

"We're under attack, ladies. Get your weapons in hand." Miss Ruby sounded like a drill sergeant as knitting was dropped and blades or metal knitting needles were brandished.

27

Trent, Wade, Ryker, Gavin, Ridge, Granger, Kord, and Peter were all enjoying Ryker's very expensive and expansive alcohol collection when Ryker's phone went crazy. They'd been having a great time up until then. Trent had even seen glimmers of the old Ryker until that damn phone went off.

"Shit!" Ryker was up and out of the room in a heartbeat. "We're under attack. Get the ladies safe."

"What?" Ridge asked with a little laugh. "We're right here. Our wives are at Harper's helping Harper visualize what this new venture could be."

"Not them. The knitting club. Skye's tracking unit just sent out an alarm and my backyard sensors also went off." Ryker threw open the French doors and stepped onto the deck where the sound of a helicopter could be heard. Lights around the guesthouse were being taken out as shadowy figures moved around the perimeter of the house. "Let's go."

Trent didn't need to hear more. He was already running for the back door.

. . .

SKYE and the knitting club formed a tight circle in the living room. They had eyes on every door and window they could see. "Don't worry, the doors are steel," Skye told the old ladies who looked more excited than scared.

Skye was about to see if anyone had called 911 when an explosion rocked the house. Skye and the group huddled down, some of them toppling over from the shock of the explosion.

Skye couldn't believe it. Was this a movie set? She'd heard special effects before and this was what it reminded her of, but who would bomb a freaking guesthouse?

Through the smoke, men holding rifles with lights on the end stormed into the house through the shattered sliding doors.

"*En garde,* ladies!" Miss Winnie yelled above the noise.

"Bless your heart," Miss Mitzy said, shoving a knitting needle into Skye's hand. "You need to learn to defend yourself. Here's a ten-inch number eight needle, it'll do just fine. Now, stab anyone you don't know. Neck is always good as bone doesn't get in the way."

Skye felt as if she were having an out of body experience and that this had to be a stunt or a very bad dream. She even looked around for the camera because this couldn't be real life, but the men running toward them were very real.

Skye tried to take a deep breath but the smoke made her cough as someone reached for her. Edie screamed a war cry that shook Skye from disbelief into reality. Edie slashed out at a man. The dagger she had pulled from her purse cut into his arm and Mitzy jabbed a knitting needle into his thigh as he reached for Skye.

Okay, this was real. Very, very real and she was clearly the target.

. . .

Peter took the lead and they were quickly broken up into three groups. One was led by Peter, one by Granger, and one by Kord. Trent stuck close to Granger as they moved through the topiaries toward the guesthouse. They were quickly approaching the front door when men appeared from around the side of the house. They were carrying rifles and were in full tactical gear.

"Sheriff's Department. Drop your weapons!" Granger shouted.

The two men looked at each other but didn't drop their weapons. Instead, they advanced on them. Granger shot one in the thigh and he went down screaming. Granger was on him in a second. He'd flipped him onto his stomach and had grabbed the man's own zip ties from his tactical vest.

The other man looked surprised and Trent made his move. He charged and took the man down with a tackle that would make any professional football player proud. Trent drove the man into the ground and the air whooshed from his lungs as Trent landed hard on top of him. Trent didn't stop, though. Two punches to the man's chin and he was out.

"Take his weapons and tie him up," Granger ordered as he picked up the rifle and slung it over his shoulder. Trent was doing just that when he heard the screams from inside.

Skye clenched her hand on the narrow, smooth metal knitting needle as four more men charged inside. They shared a look and then charged the group of women. One went to push Mitzy out of the way to get to Skye. The women had formed a tight circle around her to protect her, but she felt as if she, Karri, and Edie should be the ones protecting these sweet old grandmothers.

Skye held the knitting needle like a knife and raised it up high. She leaned around Mitzy and closed her eyes briefly as she slammed it down on the base of man's neck who was trying to shove Mitzy to the ground. She felt the resistance as the needle went through the shirt, but then she felt it sink into the muscle. Skye groaned in an effort to stave off vomiting as she pulled the needle back out.

But it was too much. The men were attacking at once and Edie's dagger had been knocked out of her hand. Karri was swinging a decorative boat paddle that had been hanging on the wall. The grandmas were lashing out with various old-looking knives or their knitting needles. Men were reaching for her and Edie was kicking and punching. She wasn't going down without a fight.

"No!" Skye screamed when the fist connected to Edie's face. Tears sprang to Edie's eyes, but she didn't go down.

Mitzy was grabbed by the arm and yanked to the ground. Miss Ruby and Miss Winnie were facing off against another man. They were going to be hurt or killed all because of Skye. She couldn't let that happen.

Skye slid her knitting needle up the long sleeve of her shirt to hold it and then screamed so loudly she knew everyone would hear her over the chaos. The second she had their attention, she moved. She leapt over Mitzy and shouldered past the man who had taken Mitzy to the ground.

Then she ran. She powered through the throng, straight to the blown-out door with all her strength. It wasn't much of a plan, but she had to draw the men away from her friends. She had to protect them. If she could make it outside, it was a straight shot down to the dock and then she'd jump into the river. She could lose them in the shadows of the river grass and that would give her friends time to escape.

Trent and Granger tied the men to each other and then made the move to get inside the front door. Trent had just entered the code to unlock it when the sports car raced down the drive straight toward them.

"Who the hell is that?" Granger asked.

"Don't know, don't care." Trent shoved the door open into utter destruction.

"Skye, no!" Edie yelled as she leapt on the back of a man trying to run out the back door.

Trent saw the older knitting club members helping Mitzy up from the ground among the rubble and smoke of what had been the living room. Edie was hanging on the back of the man and had locked her arms around his neck into a perfect headlock.

"Skye!" Trent yelled into the chaos.

"She ran out the back and they're all following her!" Miss Winnie yelled.

"Save our baby girl!" Miss Ruby ordered and Trent took off with Granger on his heels.

Edie had taken her man down and was leveling a hard kick to the balls when Trent raced by her and into the yard. Ryker, Wade, and Kord were coming in from the left. Peter, Gavin, and Ridge were converging from the right. Trent, Granger, and the knitting club were coming at them from straight down the middle.

Trent saw Skye running. She was trying to go wide around the helicopter, but the men were faster than she was. She wasn't going to make it.

The lights from the sports car appeared as it drove

through a hedgerow and slid to a stop near the group of men grabbing hold of Skye.

"Is that Mason Hemming?" Edie yelled out as they ran toward the fight. "Damn, that man is hot."

Sure enough, Mason was out of the car and yanking men away from Skye, but it was too little too late. One man had her from behind and was carrying her into the helicopter as the others took on Mason and Peter's group as they reached them first.

Trent didn't think. He had to get to Skye and nothing was going to get in his way, even the men who were falling back from Mason's attack on them. He might be an action star, but he wasn't taking the men down like Peter, Gavin, and Ridge were. Their men weren't standing back up and running away.

"I got these guys! Trent, get Skye!" Ryker yelled from the left. Trent cast a quick glance and saw Ryker, Kord, and Wade slamming their fists and the butts of their guns into men's heads. The whole backyard seemed to be swarming with men. Where had they all come from?

"Skye, I'm coming! I won't let them take you!" Mason yelled as he and Trent merged together on their race to get to the helicopter.

Skye was screaming, kicking, and cursing. Two men tried to block his and Mason's path. Trent took one down with a haymaker. Mason tossed his to the ground. The man was probably up and chasing them, but at least they were through.

They were going to make it. Trent saw them all converging on the helicopter from every angle, but the pilot began pulling up. Two men leaned over and grabbed for Skye. They had her and were dragging her into the helicopter as it lifted into the air.

"I'll find you, Skye! Hang on, I'll find you if it's the last thing I do!" Mason yelled as the man he'd tossed to the ground tackled him from behind.

Screw that! Trent was going to save her now or die trying.

28

Skye felt herself being grabbed from behind. Two strong arms locked around her waist and pulled her off the ground. She fought with everything she had. She kicked, she screamed, she almost pulled her needle out from her sleeve, but then she saw Mason appear out nowhere. He wasn't alone either. Peter, Gavin, and Ridge were fighting their way toward her.

Then she heard Edie and Trent. She glanced their way to see them racing toward her. The look in Trent's eyes said everything. He would move heaven and earth to get to her. Hope surged upward and Skye gave the guy holding her hell. She clawed at his hands. She slammed her heel against his legs as hard as she could and felt satisfaction when he grunted in pain.

But she hadn't counted on what was behind her. Two more men grabbed her under each arm and she was being hauled into the helicopter. Mason was tackled from behind and screamed for her, but it was Trent's face she couldn't look away from. His eyes never left hers as he ran full-out to the helicopter. He'd never make it. They were already pulling up. Skye had to do this herself.

She let the knitting needle drop from her sleeve even as she watched Trent race toward her. With her needle in hand, she was ready to take this whole helicopter down. Skye took a deep breath, clutched the needle tightly in her hand, and jabbed it into the man's thigh.

"Shit! She stabbed me!" he cried in surprise. Skye reached over her shoulder with her free hand, grabbed his vest, then yanked forward as she rolled to the metal floor of the helicopter. Her shoulder hit hard, but the move she used to send stuntmen flying over her shoulder in movies worked. The man flew over her body, bounced on the floor, and fell out the door.

Skye cast one last look at Trent as the other man screamed at the pilot to get them out of here. Time seemed to pass in slow motion. Trent ran at full speed, one foot stepped up onto the padded seat of a wrought iron chair, the other foot landing hard on top of the wrought iron outdoor dining table, and then Trent was flying.

His arms were pinwheeling in the air but then Skye lost sight of him. "Trent!"

Arms were around her again. The man was cursing at her to hold still or he'd hurt her. But then the helicopter dipped slightly. The pilot readjusted but her time was over. They were rising to more than twenty feet in the air and her arms were pinned. The knitting needle was useless as she struggled to free herself.

Skye looked out the open door as they began to climb higher in the air. She heard shouts from below, but it was the small slapping sound of a hand on metal that drew her attention. Fingers appeared at the floor by the door. Then another set of fingers. And then there was Trent pulling himself up to standing on the landing rail before stepping into the helicopter.

Rage and relief filled his face and Skye caught her second wind. She'd never stop fighting to get to Trent. Never.

"Trent!" Skye yelled as she used her very limited range of motion to toss the knitting needle toward him.

"What the hell?" the man holding her muttered, but her eyes were on the knitting needle that had dropped about a foot in front of her. She pushed out with her foot and sent it rolling.

Trent bent down and scooped it up.

"Let her go." Trent's words were made of ice as he stalked forward in the small confines of the helicopter. His shoulders were hunched over, just as Skye and her kidnapper were, but it didn't stop his menacing, deadly prowl.

"This isn't how it's supposed to go!" the man shouted as he glanced around.

"Let her go, or I'll kill you with a knitting needle," Trent threatened as the man dragged Skye back against the far wall of the military-like helicopter.

"We're supposed to take her!" the pilot yelled back at them. That seemed to make up his mind that he was going to fight.

Skye felt herself being shoved to the side. Her shoulder slammed into the side of the helicopter as she tripped over the small utility bench. Trent was already moving as he held the knitting needle as if it were a knife. Trent blocked a punch and jabbed the needle into the man's upper arm. The man screamed in pain and Trent followed up with a powerful punch to the man's face. Skye saw the man's head snap back toward her and then his eyes roll back as he dropped to the floor.

"Come on!" Trent yelled, holding out his hand for her.

Skye scrambled to her feet, and the second she placed her hand in his, she knew they'd make it. The pilot was yelling at them to stop, but all Skye could focus on was Trent as he glanced out the door.

Skye followed his gaze and looked down at the river. "Let's jump," she yelled over the sound of the helicopter engine and blades.

"It's a good forty feet. Jump with your legs together and head up high. Before you hit the water, draw your arms to your side like a pencil," Trent instructed.

Skye squeezed his hand. No fear. No hesitation. They looked at each other and jumped from the open door. There was a moment when they were jumping straight out, but then the plummet began. She held on tightly to Trent's hand as her stomach rose to her throat, but the scream she was letting loose stopped it from coming all the way out. Suddenly Trent's hand was pulled from hers and she remembered to pin her hands to her side.

Her feet hit the water, what little air was left in her lungs was pushed out, and the darkness of the water overtook her. She clawed for the surface as her lungs burned. Panic almost took over, but then she felt Trent's hand grabbing her shirt and pulling her upward.

TRENT HIT THE WATER HARD, but he was used to it. With a brother in the Coast Guard, Trent had made these jumps a million times with Wade. Not from a helicopter, but from the cliffs over the rivers along the Appalachian Trail or off the top of boats into the ocean.

The second he stopped the downward plunge, he was using both arms to swim toward the surface. He made sure he entered the water near Skye and felt her almost kick him underwater. He reached out with his right hand and grabbed for her. He got a fistful of shirt and kept swimming with his left arm and kicking hard as he propelled them to the surface.

His nose broke through the surface first and then the rest of his head. He took in a deep breath of air as he yanked Skye up. When she broke the surface, she dragged in a ragged breath as she tried to get her bearings.

"I got you. Take some deep breaths," Trent ordered her. Her arms grabbed him and as she inhaled over and over again, the panic started to fade and she began to tread water.

Voices were yelling for them, lights shone in the distance, and then the light on the deck was turned on and the whole river was lit up.

"Trent! Skye!" he heard Ryker's booming voice and then Edie and Karri's terrified screaming.

"Over here!" Trent yelled back as he raised an arm out of the water and waved. "Look, it's a boat," he said, dropping his voice back down as he talked to Skye. "That must be how the others arrived."

"We're coming!" Ryker yelled and then Trent saw a life ring being flung out downriver from them. Ryker let out the slack and let the river take the life ring farther out into the middle of the river.

Trent wrapped his arm around Skye and used Wade's rescue swimmer technique to begin to swim.

"I can swim. I promise. I'm good now," Skye said as she kicked along with him.

"I've got you. I don't want us to be separated."

"Why aren't we just swimming back to shore?"

"We're going to let the current take us to the ring. Then they'll help pull us back to the shore. It'll save us a lot of energy," Trent explained as they kicked along with the current. "Here it is," Trent said, reaching out and hooking his arm around the ring.

Skye reached forward and kicked hard to climb her way up Trent's body until she could hook her arm over the ring too. "You're right. This was harder than I thought."

"Okay, Ryker!" Trent yelled. "Now kick as they pull and we'll be on the shore in no time."

It took only minutes as they fought the current but with the help of the ring they were finally pulled ashore by Wade, Ryker, and Edie.

His brother, Wade, went straight to Skye and started the standard medical evaluation that he used as a rescue swimmer.

"Where's Gavin?" Trent asked of his doctor cousin.

"Treating the few gunshot wounds," Wade told him. "Granger, Kord, and Peter have formed a chain gang of prisoners. Most are still unconscious, but they're coming around."

"Who did this?" Skye asked what everyone wanted to know as she pushed herself up from the ground.

"You're good, but you're going to be exhausted once the adrenaline wears off," Wade warned her.

"Then let's get to the bottom of this while I'm amped up. I can't believe we just jumped out of a helicopter."

Trent pushed himself up and they trudged their way up the yard. Sure enough, around fifteen men were tied up and being guarded by the knitting club as Gavin and Ridge treated the wounded on the other side of the lawn.

"What the hell is he doing?" Trent asked of Mason. He

was getting in the faces of the men tied up screaming at them.

"Where did he come from?" Skye asked with confusion. "It was like it was right out of an action movie."

Trent shrugged. The man wasn't a good fighter, but at least he had helped. Peter, Kord, and Granger stood off in a tight circle and Trent and his group joined him. "What's going on?" Trent asked.

His friends slapped Trent on the back as they joined the group. They then gave him and Skye a ten for their leap out of the helicopter but only gave Trent an eight for his leap onto the helicopter.

"It would have been cooler if you hadn't almost slipped off the landing rail," Kord said with a shrug.

"Who are these guys?" Ryker asked, bringing them back to the current situation.

"We were hoping Skye could tell us," Granger growled at her in a way that made Trent instantly defensive.

"Me?" Skye asked. "I'd love to know who they are and who is trying to kidnap me."

Suddenly Granger, Kord, and Peter didn't look like her friends anymore. Instead, they looked pissed off and all that anger was directed at her.

Peter shoved a handful of IDs at her. "Please tell me this isn't what it looks like."

"What does it look like?" Skye asked in confusion. What did she do to lose their trust?

"It looks like you hired them to stage your kidnapping," Granger told her as he glared at her. Edie gasped and Trent instantly got in Granger's face defending Skye. As they traded barbs and Granger told Trent to back off, Skye looked down at the IDs in her hands and gasped as she went from one card to the next.

It wasn't the driver's license that drew her attention. It was the other ID card that did. It was a standard union card she knew well. "They're all stuntmen," Skye said in stunned surprise.

"That's right. They say they were hired for a new movie in which you were starring as a kidnap victim," Peter said, his tone deadly serious and accusatory. Gone was the man who had tried to protect her.

"Me? They say I hired them?" Skye was shaking her head. This couldn't be real.

"They think they're in the interrogation part of the movie," Granger said, gesturing to the group tied up, sitting there as Mason talked with the knitting club. "We can't get them to break character. However, the ones who got shot are all too happy to talk. Only they don't know who hired them. It was done through someone who claimed to be a casting assistant. They were sent a script and told to use their talent to stage a mock kidnapping. They were all sent tickets to Charleston and were met by some director's assistant. They were given the supplies they needed to raid a house and get the actress. Then they were to fly you back to Charleston and drop you off—end of scene. When asked about cameras, directors, and movie sets, they said the director's assistant told them the cameras were all hidden to make it appear as real and gritty as possible. They would all be there, but hidden. They wanted one long, continuous take so they wouldn't interrupt unless they had to."

"It's not possible. I didn't hire them. This doesn't make sense. None of this makes any sense. *No one* shoots movies like that. Then there's the big question of why would I stage my own kidnapping?" Skye felt herself flipping out. She had to be dazed after jumping out of the helicopter and dreaming this all up.

"Because you're addicted to the Hollywood spotlight? Because you needed to drum up attention to get that role you wanted so badly?" Granger asked rhetorically.

"Skye!" Mason called out to her when he saw her. He jogged over to her and wrapped her up in a tight hug. "I was so worried about you."

"Hey! Get back here!" Miss Winnie yelled.

Skye glanced back and saw the men who had been tied up were no longer tied up. They were running for the water after having knocked some of the club members down.

"Stop!" Mason yelled and took off after them.

"Go after them!" Skye was so confused. Why weren't Granger, Kord, and Peter going after the men?

"We have their IDs and I have my team waiting for them at the drop off point in Charleston," Peter told her calmly. "Plus Charleston PD and the Coast Guard are boating upriver as we speak."

Ryker crossed his arms over his chest. He looked at Skye and then to the men running. "Why do you want them caught, Jessamine?"

"So they can tell you I didn't hire them." Skye's head was spinning. Her breathing was coming in quick and shallow. This wasn't right. Trent was fighting Granger, the men were getting away, they thought she was behind this . . . "Oh my God."

Skye spun and took off toward the river as the men yelled at her to come back. The answer had been right in front of her the whole time. The sound of the boat engine roared to life and then the boat full of men raced away. They were out of sight in no time.

29

"I won't forget this," Trent threatened his friends and family as he shoved Granger before taking off after Skye. He knew the others were running behind him. Even the knitting club was teetering as fast as they could down to the river.

Trent pushed himself into a full-out sprint as he kept his eyes on Skye racing toward the riverbank.

"Mason!" Skye yelled and Trent would never forgive Granger or the others if Skye left him for Mason. She had to know Trent loved her and didn't believe she was behind this.

Skye opened her arms as if she were running to leap into Mason's arms. The actor turned from the riverbank and smiled at her. He opened his arms wide and Skye bounded into the air to fling herself into his arms.

Wait, no. That wasn't what she was doing at all. Her right hand fisted, her arm came back, and when she flew toward him, she let loose with a beauty of a punch to Mason's face. The punch had the full weight of her body behind it as she slammed into him and the two of them careened onto the ground in a heap of rolling bodies.

Skye seemed to roll twice as long as Mason. Mason was already on his knees when Trent reached them, shaking his head as if to clear it. It wasn't Mason who Trent was concerned about, though. Trent didn't stop running until Skye was in his arms and he was looking into her eyes to make sure she wasn't hurt.

"What is going on? Are you okay?" Trent asked as he put himself between Skye and Mason, who was on his feet already.

"Skye? Why would you do that to me? I'm your best friend. I was trying to protect you and you hit me." Mason had a little whine to his voice that seemed to make Skye very pissed off. Trent could hear her almost growling behind him.

"*You* did this. You set this whole thing up, didn't you?" Skye shouted furiously as Trent fought to keep her back and away from Mason.

"I helped set up the demonstration at your trial. Is that what you mean?" Mason looked thoroughly confused.

"No, you *rat*. I mean tonight and possibly even before tonight. You set this whole kidnapping fiasco up, didn't you? Did you send the threatening notes too?" Skye shouted at him. Her face was red and Trent worried he'd see steam begin to come out of her ears soon.

"How could you say that?" Mason looked hurt. Like, really hurt and Trent was wondering if Skye had hit her head during all the mayhem.

Kord had been the first to reach them, but Granger and Peter were only steps behind, followed by everyone else in his family and the knitting club.

Skye shoved Trent's arm away and stalked around him to get into Mason's face. She poked him in the chest with her finger and he backed up a step closer to the riverbank, trying to prevent another jab.

"Those men were all professional stuntmen, Mason. We have their union cards. The whole thing even reminded me of a movie stunt. That got me thinking," Skye said, poking Mason again as he took another step back. "Who in Hollywood would want me kidnapped? I thought it was Jim and Lenny, but it wasn't. I thought they were just blowing smoke up my ass when they said they'd been worried about me, but they weren't. They were worried because they really did receive those threats. Tell them, Mason."

"Tell them what? I'm sorry, Skye. I know this has been very traumatic for you, but I don't know what you're talking about. Karri, talk some sense into her." Mason held up his hands in supplication and looked sympathetically at her.

"Tell them who your agent is."

Mason finally took in everyone around them. "Jim. Well, it was. I'm firing him over his abuse of you, though. You know that."

"And tell them who your manager was before I arrived in town?"

The first worried look appeared across his face. "That doesn't matter. That was years ago."

"Then it shouldn't matter who it was, so you can tell us without worry," Granger said, his voice a monotone as he stared at Skye and Mason, giving nothing away of his thoughts.

"Lenny was, but he hasn't been my manager in almost seven years."

"You had access to Jim's office and Lenny's home address, so you knew when, where, and how to get those threats against me delivered to them." Trent watched as Skye jabbed Mason in the chest again. She was leading up to something and that role as a defense attorney three movies ago seemed to have rubbed off on her as she began laying out her evidence.

"You live in the same gated community as I do. Granted, you're not super close, but you could pin the threats on my gate without being seen. Another question, Mason." Skye put her hands on her hips and glared. "Which private security firm do you use for bodyguards?"

"Now come on, Skye. Everyone who is anyone uses Star Power. What does that have to do with anything? I really think you need to go to the hospital. Something's wrong with you, Skye."

Skye had begun to raise some questions, but there wasn't any evidence. It didn't make sense. There was no reason for him to stage Skye's kidnapping or send threatening notes.

"The only thing wrong with me is *you*," Skye screamed as she raised her hands and shoved hard against his chest. Mason staggered back a step. The ball of his foot slipped back and he fell onto his stomach in the mud and wet grass. His feet were wet as they lay in the river and his face was first etched in disbelief and then into a rage so great Trent heard the loud hiss coming from him.

No, wait. That hiss wasn't coming from Mason. It was coming from the alligator behind him.

Chirp.

Chirp.

Hiss.

Skye froze along with everyone else as the baby alligator wiggled free from under Mason's armpit. When Mason went down, he landed on the baby gator that had been hiding in the mud and now Big Bertha was mad.

"Shit! Is that an alligator?" Mason tried to scramble up,

but Trent knew Skye was onto something. He jumped forward and placed his foot on Mason's back. "What are you doing? Let me up!"

"Did you try to kidnap Skye?" Trent demanded as the baby gator chirped and stood snout to nose with Mason. "I wouldn't take too long in answering. That baby's momma, Big Bertha, is right behind you and swimming in hot and fast."

"No! I would never hurt Skye," Mason yelled.

"I didn't say hurt, you did. I asked if you hired these stuntmen tonight? Did you try to stage a kidnapping? Did you send those threats to her?" Trent demanded.

"Let me up!"

"Did you stage Skye's kidnapping? Yes or no. Give me the truth and I'll let you up." Trent kept his calm, but it was hard as Big Bertha bore down on them.

"Screw you!" Mason shrieked. The baby gator didn't like that at all and bit Mason's nose. Mason's scream soared like a mezzo-soprano as Big Bertha's hiss turned into a prehistoric, guttural rumble.

"You better hurry. The truth, now." Trent may have said it calmly, but he wasn't feeling calm as the knitting club ladies all started backing up as quickly as possible.

"Yes! Okay? Yes. I planned the whole thing once I saw that Skye was getting all the publicity for our movie. It was all about Skye. *I'm* the action hero, damn it, not her. But all they could talk about was Skye this, Skye that, America's Sweetheart this, America's Sweetheart that. Not a single headline had my name on it. I needed to show them I was the hero. I wanted them to talk about me, not some woman who is just in the movie to look pretty. Now let me up!"

"Not yet," Trent said, keeping one eye on Bertha, who was getting dangerously close. "How did you pay them?

Who did you pay? Prove to me you did this and I'll let you up."

"My assistant tipped off the media about Skye being missing because I wanted to find her. I sent the kidnapping note to Lenny and Jim because I tried to have her kidnapped from her house, but didn't know it was a bust until after I'd mailed the ransom. *I* wanted to be the one who found Skye and rescued her, but freaking Jim and Lenny hijacked my search. It was my Star Power bodyguard that broke into Skye's house. I sent him to Kentucky to try to find Skye from that PR lady, but I haven't heard from him since. My assistant hired everyone for tonight after I found out Skye was shacked up with you. They were all paid with digital currency because my assistant claimed it would help the stuntmen tax-wise and union-wise by hiding the money. The digital account they were paid under is a made-up name, but you can trace it back to my production company, HRO Productions. I wanted to deduct the expenses from my taxes. Now let me up!"

"That's good. Now, *run!*" Granger ordered as he yanked the baby gator from Mason's nose and placed him in the water right as Bertha surged forward.

Trent clasped Skye's hand tightly and took off. Ryker and Wade yanked Mason up by the armpits and ran with him locked between them. Bertha hissed and rumbled as she charged them from the water. Trent shoved Skye forward and up onto the metal table. Ryker, Wade, Mason, Granger, Kord, Karri, and Peter leapt up too. They weren't going to make it back to the house with Big Bertha hot on their tail.

The group crammed together as Bertha stopped underneath the table and tried to bite at them through the decorative iron swirls. Trent slammed his boot down on the table, the vibration surprising Bertha for a moment before she hissed again.

Edie came out of the house with a large picnic basket in hand.

"Edie, no!" Ryker snapped. Edie rolled her eyes at him as she gave Bertha a wide berth and stepped onto the dock. She walked down it until she was near the riverbank. She pulled out a cookie and sent it flying to the grass near the lapping water. Then she tossed out a cookie every four feet or so until she ran out of them.

"Use the chess pie next," Miss Winnie yelled out.

Edie reached into the basket as pulled out a pie dish. She dug in and then sent a hunk of pie flying to the ground until she got closer to Bertha.

"Now the apple pie!" Miss Ruby yelled.

Bertha didn't like the noise and rammed her snarling snout into the bottom of the table, causing Skye to jump and Mason to scream. Trent wrapped his arms around Skye and lifted her up and off the table. If Bertha was going to bite, she was going to bite him, not Skye.

"Here, gator, gator, gator," Edie sang out sweetly and sent a chunk of apple pie flying right at Bertha. It smacked against her tail and Bertha swung around to attack.

"Good gator." Edie tossed another piece, this time a little to the side of the table.

Bertha stepped cautiously from under the table and snapped up the pie. Edie threw another piece a couple of feet from Bertha, but in order for her to get it, she had to turn away from the table and head toward the water. Slowly Edie tossed apple pie pieces until the apple pie met the chess pie and Bertha snorted and snapped up the pieces like a pig with truffles.

"Told you everyone loved my apple pie," Miss Ruby said

as the knitting club stepped outside. "You can get off the table now."

Trent helped Skye down and noticed that she grimaced when he reached for her hand. The hand she'd punched Mason with was swollen and already starting to look red and bruised.

"You're hurt," Trent said into the stunned, gator-induced silence. That one statement caused the world to go upside down. Gavin rushed forward and police helicopters were heard downriver. Peter and Granger had a jurisdictional spat over who got to arrest Mason. In the end, he was escorted to Charleston by both of them.

All Trent wanted to do was take Skye far away from it all and hold her so he could tell her how much he loved her. That wasn't in the cards, though. Karri had glued herself to Skye's side as Gavin wrapped her hand and wrist. Morgan was on speakerphone and Ryker was walking around his property peering up at trees and the high fences.

"What are you doing?" Trent asked his cousin.

"I'm looking for the cameras. Mason has one in his car. It filmed his monologue as he claims he and Skye had agreed to meet here in Shadows Landing after the trial. Then he said he got a text from her as he drove into town telling him that people were after her and asked him to save her," Ryker explained as they watched the FBI place the mounted cell phone into an evidence bag.

"Did he get a text?" Trent asked.

"From an unknown number. I'm guessing his assistant sent it to him," Ryker told him. "But the injured stuntmen said there were cameras set up to capture it. Instead, all I have found was Mason's camera. The way he parked had him in frame the entire time. Almost like he'd staged it," Ryker said dryly. "However, I pulled the footage from my security cameras and have the whole thing—video and audio—from start to finish. I also have the audio from Skye's GPS trackers. I've sent it all to both Peter and Granger. By the way, I never thought it was Skye."

"You were the only one," Trent said, letting his hurt reflect in his voice.

"It wasn't personal. They were trying to figure out what was going on. Sometimes you have to shrug things off."

Trent felt his eyebrow rise in surprise. "Do you shrug things off?"

"Hell no. I systematically dismantle anyone who crosses me, but that's in business, not with my friends and family."

Trent surprised Ryker by hugging him tightly. "Thank you for everything you've done for me, for Skye, and for all of us."

Ryker was tense but didn't fight the hug. At least until Tinsley came running over to them and wrapped her arms around them both. "Family hug!"

"Dammit," Ryker muttered as Harper practically threw herself into the hug. Tinsley and Harper weren't the only ones. Every Faulkner piled onto Ryker.

"Who pinched my ass?" Ryker growled into the huddle.

In the distance, an old lady laughed, but now it was anyone's bet as to who did it.

"Am I allowed in on this?" Trent heard Skye ask from somewhere outside the Faulkner huddle hug.

"Of course you are!" Tinsley said as she reached an arm backward and latched onto Skye.

She yanked her forward and there in the middle of the Faulkner storm was the woman he loved. Trent leaned forward and kissed her with all the love he had. This night might have shaved years off his life, but one thing was crystal clear—Skye Jessamine was the only woman he wanted to share those years he had left with.

"Would whoever is pinching my ass just stop?" Ryker roared.

Trent tried to look over Ryker's shoulder as the whole knitting club hurried off with their hands covering their mouths, laughing the entire way.

30

Two months later...

Skye set the wrapped box on the kitchen table overlooking her new backyard. A lot had happened in the past couple of months. Mason had insisted on a trial and acted his way through the entire thing. Even Skye had to admit it was some of his best work. And he would have gotten off except for his very detailed, videotaped confession and the mysterious appearance of his bodyguard showing up in court to testify against him. Well, that and Mason's assistant flipped faster than a pancake when the FBI swarmed him in Charleston. But Mason got what he wanted. He was *the* headline on every newspaper and gossip show for weeks.

Meanwhile, the movie Skye made with him was released with no press junket. At least the royalties from it would pay for Mason's lawyers and appeals as he sat in prison for the next twenty-five years.

However, Mason couldn't lay claim to all the wrongdoing. Jim and Lenny were found guilty of forging

Skye's signature on a power-of-attorney and several contracts. They were also discovered to be the source of both the fake and real photos. They'd done it to force Skye's hand to take the role in Tony's movie. They'd also hired the men to talk to her parents, but that truly was just in order to find her after getting Mason's notes. Jim and Lenny had turned themselves in to a minimum security prison two weeks ago. They were sentenced to serve four months and were now essentially banished from Hollywood.

Skye testified at Mason's trial with the entire towns of Shadows Landing and Hollywood behind her. Marie Lockend took advantage of the press and announced that Skye would be the lead in her next movie, and just last week, Morgan Davies put out a press release that Skye Jessamine was excited to partner with Hollywood's newest leading man for the film adaptation of Gemma Davies's latest book.

To celebrate, Skye talked with Mrs. Cramble about the house. She'd paid the woman more than she was asking and offered to pay all her moving expenses if she could be in by Thanksgiving. Mrs. Cramble had been thrilled and handed her new address to Skye before leaving to spend a couple of days with Mitzy as all her belongings were moved into her new house.

Today was the first day Skye had woken up to her new life in her new house in Shadows Landing. She smiled at the memory of how she'd woken Trent and the way he'd thanked her. Trent still owned his house and they hadn't talked about moving in together yet, but they were essentially living together anyway. They hadn't spent a night apart since she'd shown up in Shadows Landing.

Shadows Landing was home to her now. Karri, too. Karri was renting Trent's house and, after extensive renovations, was almost ready to open her restaurant. She and Peter were very much in love. A few weeks ago, both families had come to Shadows Landing for the big meeting. Karri and Peter had been nervous as this was the first his grandmother was meeting Karri as well as her family.

It turned out they hadn't needed to worry. Peter's grandmother and Mrs. Hill had glanced over at each other as the group was getting together and pushed passed the couple to get to each other.

"Sister Hill! You're Karri's mother?" Mrs. Castle had gasped as everyone looked around as if they were missing something as the women hugged.

"We are both on the committee for missing and murdered indigenous women," Mrs. Hill had explained to the rest of them. "The issue of unsolved, and many times under investigated, crimes against our sisters crosses all tribes and will only be fixed when all sisters stand together to demand accountability and equality."

By the time their weeklong visit was over, they'd met everyone who was important to Karri and Peter. They'd watched Gator wrestle, had adopted Harper, gushed over the Faulkner family, had Kord's undying love, and even Granger had been nice.

Then, after hearing about the committee Mrs. Hill and Mrs. Castle were on, Olivia had offered pro bono legal services to their cause. Miles and Morgan, who had been visiting one of the nights on their way to the beach, ended their visit with Miles telling them he had contacts in the government who would listen when he told them to. But what Skye would always remember was when Miles dropped his voice and leaned over to Mrs. Hill and Mrs. Castle and had said, "If you need a team of former elite military men to go in and rescue someone the not-so-legal way, I'm also happy to assist."

Now the Hills and the Castles would be arriving for a visit before setting off on a cruise together. The women had planned to compare family trees. When they got back they'd celebrate the opening of Karri's restaurant along with the entire town.

A FLASH of sun off Trent's pickup caught her attention. Karri wasn't the only one celebrating. Trent parked by the sunroom in the back and waved when he saw Skye watching. He reached into his car and pulled out what looked to be a shoebox wrapped in brown print gift paper and tied with a twine bow.

Trent walked toward the door and Skye basked in the feeling of complete happiness. She had found her special someone. Her One. She loved him more and more every day and thankfully, the press had afforded them a moderate amount of privacy.

Trent opened the door and walked in with a little shiver. "It's getting cold out. I'm glad we have the heaters set up outside."

Trent walked over and leaned down to kiss her. Skye tilted her head up and sighed with pleasure when his lips covered hers. "How was your day?"

"Busy but good." Trent took a seat next to her at the table and pushed his box toward her.

"I have a gift for you too."

Trent looked at the tie-shaped box Skye handed him and then smiled up at her. "This is a surprise. But, ladies first."

Skye tore into the wrapping paper and pried the lid off

the cardboard box. Inside sat a stuffed cartoon alligator with a smile on its face and— "Oh my gosh," Skye gasped at the same time she burst out laughing at the engagement ring hanging off a stuffed tooth.

When Skye looked over at Trent with surprise and pure joy, she found him on one knee. He reached for the ring and held it between his fingers as his eyes met hers. "I knew you were special from the first conversation we had. I love how you fought for yourself, how you fought for us, and how you fought for our love. I can't tell you the happiness you've brought into my life since you ran into town with Big Bertha hot on your heels. You're compassionate, you're brilliant, and you're so courageous it's inspiring. Nothing would make me prouder than to be your husband. Skye, will you marry me?"

Skye sniffed as the stupid happy tears made her perfect image of Trent on his knee before her blur. "Yes!" she cried as she used her right hand to swipe at the tears. She held out a shaking left hand and was bursting with happiness when Trent slid the ring home. Then she threw herself into his arms and they whispered how much they loved each other. Take that, Hollywood rom-coms! Nothing could compete with her real life happily ever after—alligators and all.

Trent felt as if he could finally breathe. She'd said yes! He pulled back from the hug to capture her face between his hands and kiss her with all the love and hope he had for their future together..

Skye kissed him back with her whole heart before pulling back with a laugh. "Now my gift won't compare," she said with a giggle as she wiped the happy tears from her eyes. She wasn't the only one misty-eyed. Trent could admit having her agree to be his wife would have brought him to his knees if he weren't already there.

Skye shoved the long flat box forward. Trent tore off the wrapping paper and opened it up expecting to find a turkey tie. Instead, he blinked in confusion as he looked down at the knitted thing in the box. It had a peach-colored pouch on one end and a red knitted handle attached to it. The tip of the handle was topped off with a black triangle knitted thingy.

"It's great. Um, what is it?" Trent asked as he held it up. He could put some nuts and bolts in the pouch and he guessed he'd close it with that little tie on it that seemed to cinch it up. Or maybe the handle somehow closed it. Oh, wait, the handle was hollow. "Oh, I know what this is. It's a hammer warmer."

Laughter snuck out of Skye's mouth as she struggled to keep it together. Trent was sure he was missing something. "It *is* a hammer warmer, but a different kind of hammer. It's called a willie warmer."

Willie? He didn't have a hammer by that brand.

"Let me show you," Skye said and her voice suddenly wasn't laughing as she reached for his pants. Willie warm—ah! Now he got it. Skye kissed him hard as she slipped her gift on.

"Oh, that's really warm," Trent said, looking down at his snuggly erect hammer. "Wait, is that Santa Claus?"

"Ho-ho-ho," Skye said as she yanked him forward to her, leaning back onto the tabletop and sending the stuffed Bertha toy flying.

"Well, Miss Jessamine, have you been naughty or nice this year?" Trent asked as he began undressing her.

"I think you'd better get used to calling me Mrs. Faulkner."

His lips were on hers, her hands were on him, and when she pulled off his willie warmer, he kind of missed it. Good thing he wasn't cold for long.

~

"Are you all ready for this?" Skye asked.

"Do I take your purse now or later?" Trent asked with a wink as the limousine pulled up to the red carpet.

Skye laughed and then felt bad for doing so. It was Trent's first awards show and this was not his thing. However, she was going to take him to every black-tie function imaginable from now on based solely on how sexy he looked in his tuxedo.

"Don't worry. I'll hand it to you if it's necessary. Just smile and have fun. Talk to whoever you want and get as many pictures as possible." Skye gestured for Trent to get ready.

The door opened and Trent's wide shoulders blocked part of the camera flashes. He got out and turned around to offer his hand. Skye took his hand in hers and got out of the limo as gracefully as she could in the long gown. It was an ice-blue silk dress with a plunging back that hugged her curves before flaring out at the hem. If she weren't in Hollywood, she'd be freezing, but January in L.A. was barely chilly and the lights would quickly warm her.

"Skye! Skye!" the reporters shouted as she posed with her group and then posed separately and finally with just Trent. She didn't answer any questions here. Instead, there was a gauntlet of different media outlets, to stop at. At some she posed only for photo ops, while at others she gave interviews to select television and print outlets.

The carpet seemed to go on forever as she smiled, posed, and made her way to the main interviewer. She stepped up onto the little podium and waved at the fans before turning to her interviewer.

"This is so exciting. I'm here with Hollywood's hottest actress, Skye Jessamine," the interviewer named Orchid said. "You are presenting this year, but if all the rumors are true, you'll be up for multiple nominations next year and the year after."

Skye gave her a twenty million dollar smile and nodded. "That's right. Tonight I'm presenting best picture, but after my wedding, I'll start shooting Marie Lockend's film. As soon as that wraps, I'll begin on the Gemma Davies adaptation."

Orchid looked excited as she practically sparkled with gold bronzer. "And I hear you have a family relationship with Gemma Davies."

Skye gave a little laugh and turned to hold out her hand for Trent. Trent paused for a moment, but then stepped up next to her on the small podium. "I'm not related to Gemma, but my fiancé is her nephew. It'll make next Thanksgiving dinner very interesting if she doesn't like my performance."

Orchid laughed and Skye worried she would get attacked by a bronzer cloud. "And this is your soon-to-be husband, Trent Faulkner?"

"Yes. He's the renowned furniture designer and owner of TAF Designs. We couldn't be more excited for our wedding."

"Any details you're willing to share about your big day?" Orchid asked.

"Sydney Davies McKnight, owner of Syd, Inc., designed

not only the gorgeous gown I'm wearing tonight but also designed my wedding dress. The rest is a secret for our wedding day."

"Your dress is stunning!" Orchid announced as she asked the cameraman to get a full 360 view of it. "Now, that clutch is adorable! Tell me about it."

Skye raised the little clutch covered in lace for the camera to see. "It's a Syd, Inc., clutch in the same material as my dress. However, my dear friend Mitzy Coburn handmade this lace alligator appliqué for me. Come on up here, Mitzy."

Trent stepped down and held out his arm for Miss Mitzy who beamed up at him as she slipped her hand onto his arm. Trent turned and held out his other hand for Mitzy's grandson to take and together they all squeezed onto the podium. Mitzy's grandson moved to stand in front of Skye and Mitzy. Skye put a hand on his shoulder and looked down at the boy. "Can you tell my friend here who you are and what your name is?"

J.R stood up straight in his little tuxedo and beamed a big smile at Orchid. "My name is J.R. Coburn and I'm turning five next week. Miss Skye is my friend and she even had a cupcake on the plane for me," he said in his adorable Southern accent.

Orchid laughed as she bent down to interview J.R. "Is there anything else you'd like to say?" Orchid wasn't stupid. Kids were ratings gold.

J.R. beamed up at his grandmother and then back at Orchid. "Only that I have the bestest Mimi in the entire world."

Skye thought her smile might explode across her face as Mitzy teared up. Skye put her arm around Mitzy. "She's not only the *bestest* Mimi but is also the *bestest* knitter. In fact, she's my mentor at knitting club." Skye might have been telling Orchid that, but she was really telling Mitzy's family who were back in South Carolina, watching.

"Knitting club? Skye Jessamine *knits?*" Orchid's fake smile dropped as plain old shock made her blurt that out.

"That's right. I'd like to give a shout-out to Miss Winnie, Miss Ruby, Edie, Dare, and all my dear friends in knitting club."

"What does she knit?" Orchid asked Trent, who suddenly looked a lot less shy.

His lips twitched and Skye prepared to put her hands over J.R.'s ears if necessary. "She's gotten really good at it. Skye made her whole family scarves for Christmas. Let's see, she's also made some potholders, a couple of hats, and of course my favorite, the hammer warmer."

Orchid blinked and wanted to ask more but the producer was moving them along. Marie Lockend was up next to interview; she was up for best director this year and that took precedent over hammer warmers.

Trent helped Mitzy and J.R. off the podium while Skye lifted her dress and stepped down. When she looked up, Marie winked at her. "Hammer warmer? I need more details." Marie kissed her cheek, then stepped up to begin her interview.

Trent held out his arm for her and Skye laced her hand through his elbow to rest on his arm. She looked past Trent at Mitzy who'd dropped Trent's arm and made a beeline for one of Hollywood's hunkiest men.

"Hi, Blaze." Skye waved to the hunk as she pulled out her cell phone and joined them. "This is my good friend, Miss Mitzy."

"It's good to meet you, Miss Mitzy," the six-foot-six muscled action star said with a grin.

"Can I get a picture of you two?" Skye asked.

Blaze nodded and Mitzy flushed pink. "Do you have a heart condition?" Blaze asked.

"No, why?" Mitzy answered.

"Good." Blaze grabbed Mitzy, bent her over his arm, and kissed her smack on the lips. Skye videoed it but by the explosion of flashes that went off, it hadn't been necessary. That photo would be everywhere in minutes.

"Oh my," Mitzy said, patting her hair once she was upright again. "Well, young man, I'll knit you something for being so nice and have Skye send it to you."

"Nice." Blaze grinned and then looked over at the young actor who played a vampire in last year's blockbuster and had been voted as having the sexiest eyes by the media. "Miss Mitzy's knitting me something. Suck it up, vamp."

Mr. Sexy Eyes, whose real name was Patrick and who would be her co-star in Gemma's adaptation, joined them to say hello to everyone. Of course, he played it up when he turned to Miss Mitzy. Video cameras closed in on them as they quickly became the red carpet centerpiece. "Miss Mitzy, it's a pleasure to meet you. Can you help Blaze and me with something?"

"Of course, young man," Miss Mitzy said seriously.

Patrick pulled Mitzy close and she actually giggled right before he planted a kiss on her lips.

"So, tell the world who the better kisser is," Patrick said with a wink after pulling back.

Mitzy smacked him playfully on the arm, but the smile on her face was something Skye would never forget. "I'd say it's too close to call so we better try it again."

Skye leaned over to Trent and whispered in his ear. "And just like that, America has a new Sweetheart."

EPILOGUE

Spring, Shadows Landing...

TRENT STOOD in front of the riverbank behind his house. An arch of pastel flowers was directly behind him as he watched Skye walk down the aisle between the rows of white chairs filled with friends and family. The assembly was a mix of Hollywood, Shadows Landing, and Keeneston. Trent couldn't imagine anything better.

Skye met him by the arch. He didn't even notice when her father put Skye's hand in his. Trent's eyes were only on his bride. Reverend Winston began the service, and before he knew it, Trent was kissing his bride. A camera flashed, but there were no paparazzi here tonight. They all thought Skye and Trent were off in Italy to get married, thanks to a body double seen boarding a private jet in Charleston and the reservation they'd made under a not-so-fake name at an Italian vineyard.

However, he and Skye had agreed to publish one photo. They put it up for auction. The site that bought the rights to the exclusive photo made the check out to the Daughters of Elizabeth charity and agreed to write about the charity Sydney Davies McKnight chaired in the column about the wedding when it ran.

Trent linked his hand with his wife's as Reverend Winston announced them. People stood and cheered as they walked by all their friends and family. Trent had never been prouder nor had he ever been happier than he was in that moment.

TINSLEY WATCHED as the couples filled the dance floor behind Skye and Trent's house. Karri and Peter took to the floor followed by Gavin and a very pregnant, due-at-any-moment Ellery. Then Wade and Darcy, Harper and Dare, and Ridge and Savannah. Kord and Maggie Bell were followed by Gage Bell and Cassidy Davies, one of Tinsley's cousins from Kentucky, then they made their way to the dance floor.

"And then there were two." Tinsley nodded as Ryker joined her. "Here."

"Thank you," Tinsley said as she took the glass of champagne. "Looks like Mitzy's having a blast."

"So, she and the butler?" Ryker silently saluted her and then took a drink.

"They look happy. They all look happy."

"You'll be happy too, Tins."

"Aw, Ryker. You're nothing but a big sweetie pie."

Ryker growled at her.

"Goodness, is that you or the cake?" her cousin Greer Parker from Keeneston asked.

Tinsley laughed as they all looked at the groomsmen's cake in the shape of a large alligator.

After talking with Greer for a bit, Ryker headed for the group of men. Tinsley had always liked Greer. She was the complete opposite of Tinsley, but she had a good heart and that was what mattered most.

"I hear there's going to be a new FBI agent in Charleston and his transfer is controversial," Greer told her after Ryker left.

"I think I'm the wrong person to tell," Tinsley said. "I know your whole family is FBI, but I don't think painting has anything to do with them."

"Oh, but it does. Peter told me all about it. Agent Kendry was big in the violent gang task force down in Atlanta. He was shot three times and managed to survive. He wanted to take over the task force, but politics came into play and he was transferred to Charleston under Peter to run the new art crimes division."

Tinsley did a double take. "He went from violent gangs to art crimes? Do they understand the complexity of art crimes?"

"That's why it's controversial. See, he's the most experienced to take over the task force, but the higher ups claim he's injured and on desk duty until he's cleared. They moved him here because I guess art crime is on the rise with the tourists and such. He happens to have an art degree along with a criminal justice degree. Don't think it's a big team or anything, apparently Agent Kendry is the *entire* art crimes division."

"Poor guy. I guess he won't be around long."

Greer shrugged. "I don't know, but I know he's not happy here and Peter doesn't know what to do with him. He was hoping to foist him off on Ellery to show him around the art world here, but much to my Grandma Marcy's delight, Ellery looks like she could deliver any second."

Tinsley looked as Great Aunt Marcy plied Ellery with pie. "She'll be a great-great-aunt. Right?"

Greer shrugged her shoulders. "I lose count. Heck, I lose count of my own cousins. Hey, is Gator here? I was hoping he'd take me out gator wrestling tomorrow. I think I'm getting the hang of it. I tried on a pig, but it's not the same."

"You're an adrenaline junkie. No wonder you're in the FBI, Miss Sharpshooter." Greer smiled at that but it wasn't a full smile, and Tinsley began to wonder if something was going on with her cousin. "There's Gator. And you know you can talk to me about anything, right?"

Greer smiled at her. "Of course I know that. That's what cousins are for."

Greer walked off to join Gator and Tinsley knew she wouldn't be asking for help any time soon. It wasn't her style.

"Come on, cuz! Let's show them how to do this dance."

Tinsley laughed as her cousin Porter took her hand as the music turned into one of the trendy pop songs that had its own dance. One she couldn't imagine her rough rodeo cousin Porter knowing.

Tinsley was proven wrong moments later when he put his hands on his hips and made a slow circle with them before doing a version of hip gyrations that had Miss Ruby and Miss Winnie fanning themselves.

Tinsley laughed out loud and soon found herself in a dance-off with Porter and his twin, Parker, and several A-list celebrities.

"So, what exactly is your involvement with Sebastian Abel?" Uncle Miles asked Ryker. Ryker tossed back his drink and motioned for the bartender to pour him another. Skye had just leap-frogged her way up to his favorite cousin-in-law by stocking his obscenely expensive but favorite cognac for the reception.

"Why does it matter?" Ryker asked instead of answering. Most of the time he could get away with it, but not with his family from Keeneston.

"The arrogant jerk was involved with my daughter-in-law at one point," Uncle Pierce, the nicest and only non-military uncle said. Sebastian had dated Abby? That was news to Ryker.

"Dad, he wasn't a jerk to Abby and we're actually friends now." Pierce's son, Dylan, said as if he'd said it a million times before. Although Ryker would need to learn more about Sebastian and Abby. Ryker looked for any weakness a business adversary had and he would exploit it mercilessly.

"Whatever. He's cold and arrogant. I don't like him," Uncle Pierce said.

Uncle Cole agreed, but then everyone turned to stare at Uncle Miles as if he fit that bill too.

"I'm not cold anymore. Morgan changed that," Miles said, a bit defensively.

"And what happened to Mason's bodyguard who went after Aunt Morgan?" Dylan asked his uncle.

Miles took a deep sip of bourbon before answering. "Old habits and all. He showed up when and where he needed to with no visible bruising."

Ryker felt his lips twitch. He liked his family from Kentucky. They were entertaining and they teased each other the way he and his Shadows Landing cousins did.

Wade walked over with his happy-go-lucky smile and slapped Ryker on the shoulder. "Cuz, Great Aunt Marcy has it in her head it's time for you to settle down. I'd start running now. She looks old and frail, but she'll take you down with that cane without missing a beat."

Ryker looked over to where Marcy was now holding court with Ellery, Miss Winnie, Miss Ruby, and Savannah. They all stared at him. Ellery looked as if she were envious of his drink. Savannah looked as if she were trying not to laugh, but the other three . . . well they were trouble and he knew better than to walk into trouble. Ryker turned around and slipped into the shadows.

Trent spun his wife under the soft glow of the lights they'd hung across the backyard. He'd never been happier as he was in that moment. He had his bride in his arms, and all his friends and family were celebrating with him.

"How does it feel to be out of the spotlight?" he asked Skye.

"I've never been happier. The bright lights hid the best parts of the world in shadows. Now I'm free to experience it all—the glitz and glamour of Hollywood, the friendship of Shadows Landing, and the love of my life. I don't know how I got so lucky."

Trent bent down and kissed his bride in the middle of the dance floor. People cheered around them. Gator danced by with Gina Toussaint on his arm. Blaze was leading Miss Winnie out onto the dance floor as they joked about what the media would make of their dance. Patrick had Miss Ruby on his arm and was already challenging Blaze and Miss Winnie to a dance-off. Blythe and her girlfriend, Veronica, danced by next, followed by Olivia and Henry Rooney and all their friends and family.

Trent took a deep breath and it was like the air filled him with warmth as his heart expanded. People were people.

They wanted to be treated nicely and loved. It was the same if you were a gator-removal expert, a Hollywood action hero, a dark, mysterious businessman, an attorney with a weakness for bad pick-up lines, a sheriff, or a furniture maker.

"What do you think of doing this every year or two?" Trent asked, looking around.

"What? Getting married?" Skye asked as she looked around. As she did, her smiled widened. "Oh, *this*."

"All our friends and family in one place and having fun."

"I love that idea. It's almost magical here out of the glare of the spotlight where we can all be who we are."

"No matter what, you'll always be in the center of my spotlight. I love you, Skye."

"I love you more than words can ever describe. Now let's go show your cousins Porter and Parker how to really dance to those 90s boy bands."

Trent loved the way Skye laughed as she spun around and then held out her hand for him. He tossed his tuxedo jacket onto the back of a chair, rolled up his sleeves, took hold of his wife's hand, and jumped into his future with Skye by his side.

THE END

Bluegrass Series

Bluegrass State of Mind

Risky Shot

Dead Heat

Bluegrass Brothers

Bluegrass Undercover

Rising Storm

Secret Santa: A Bluegrass Series Novella

Acquiring Trouble

Relentless Pursuit

Secrets Collide

Final Vow

Bluegrass Singles

All Hung Up

Bluegrass Dawn

The Perfect Gift

The Keeneston Roses

Forever Bluegrass Series

Forever Entangled

Forever Hidden

Forever Betrayed

Forever Driven

Forever Secret

Forever Surprised

Forever Concealed

Forever Devoted

Forever Hunted

Forever Guarded

Forever Notorious

Forever Ventured

Forever Freed

Forever Saved

Forever Bold (coming Jan/Feb 2021)

Shadows Landing Series

Saving Shadows

Sunken Shadows

Lasting Shadows

Fierce Shadows

Broken Shadows

Framed Shadows (coming Apr/May 2021)

Women of Power Series

Chosen for Power

Built for Power

Fashioned for Power

Destined for Power

Web of Lies Series

Whispered Lies

Rogue Lies

Shattered Lies

Moonshine Hollow Series

Moonshine & Murder
Moonshine & Malice
Moonshine & Mayhem
Moonshine & Mischief

ABOUT THE AUTHOR

Kathleen Brooks is a New York Times, Wall Street Journal, and USA Today bestselling author. Kathleen's stories are romantic suspense featuring strong female heroines, humor, and happily-ever-afters. Her Bluegrass Series and follow-up Bluegrass Brothers Series feature small town charm with quirky characters that have captured the hearts of readers around the world.

Kathleen is an animal lover who supports rescue organizations and other non-profit organizations such as Friends and Vets Helping Pets whose goals are to protect and save our four-legged family members.

Email Notice of New Releases

https://kathleen-brooks.com/new-release-notifications

Kathleen's Website
www.kathleen-brooks.com
Facebook Page
www.facebook.com/KathleenBrooksAuthor
Twitter
www.twitter.com/BluegrassBrooks
Goodreads
www.goodreads.com